The Two Terrors of
TULELAKE

WM GUNN

Cover by Sadia Shahid
© 2024 by WM Gunn
Print ISBN: 979-8-9914932-1-5
E-Book ISBN: 979-8-9914932-0-8

Contents

Foreword

No state shall make or enforce any law which shall abridge the privileges or immunities of citizens of the United States; nor shall any state deprive any person of life, liberty, or property, without due process of law; nor deny to any person within its jurisdiction the equal protection of the laws.

— 14th Amendment, U.S. Constitution

I became the enemy because of my face –
   not because of what I thought, or what I did.

— Author unknown

Chapter 1
8:35 a.m., May 28, 2017
Tulelake High School, CA

"Hey, Fatso!" echoed down the hallway of the high school's first floor. Fred Wallace flinched, and his gut immediately twisted in a knot. He knew who was calling him, just like almost every morning at school. It never seemed to stop, no one stopped it, and he was afraid to stop it. Today, like every day after school he would run to the bus, hunker down in a seat, and hope he was not discovered. When he got home, he would throw up.

Fred softly said to no one, "Why does he do this to me? What did I ever do to him? What did I do wrong? I feel so alone, and my grades are bad. Maybe I can get my parents to move. Maybe I just end it. I am so tired of all this."

Fred stopped talking when he felt a slap on his shoulder. He turned to see a six-foot, two-inch boy built larger than other classmates, replete with intimidation and harassment skills. "Oh, hello, Bobby," Fred said as he tried to swallow hard. Instead, the lump stuck in his throat. Bobby King was a sixteen-year-old underachieving sophomore at Tulelake High School, one of the 223 students in seventh grade through twelfth grade. He enjoyed two things in school – playing baseball, and bullying students, and even some teachers. He thought of himself as an equal-opportunity bully. He was mean to anyone and everyone, no matter their race, sex, religion, or how much or how little they pissed him off.

"No, No, No. You know the drill, Fatso," said Bobby, the school's bully.

"M-m-my apologies, Mr. King. Good morning, Mr. King." Fred looked as if he would bolt and run for the nearest exit.

"Much better, Fatso. I know you would not like a visit from my three associates or a personal educational session with me. Right, Fatso? Say, when was the last time you saw your feet? It must be difficult to put your shoes on in the morning when you can't see your feet."

"No, sir, Mr. King. I mean yes, Mr. King, I mean …" was all Fred could say.

"Oh, get out of my sight!" Fred left in haste for the bathroom next to the cafeteria. He could not wait until he got home to throw up.

As Bobby rounded a corner just before lunch he saw Sandra Rodriguez, a junior, helping her brother, an eighth grader, navigate his wheelchair into the cafeteria. Sandra's brother Miguel had muscular dystrophy, which was steadily worsening. Last year he experienced muscle pain and involuntary spasms. Now he had difficulty standing, walking, and sitting, so he was in a wheelchair full time and struggled with learning, concentrating, and socializing with classmates. This might be the last year Miguel could attend school, and it would be extremely hard on the Rodriguez family to home-school him with the many medical expenses piling up against what would certainly become an even more limited income if someone had to stay at home with him.

"You know I could help you with that if you would go on a date with me," came an all too familiar sinister voice behind Sandra. She stopped pushing Miguel's wheelchair and laid a hand on his shoulder to calm his tremors. She turned to face her nemesis.

Sandra always defied Bobby's insults, intimidations, and innuendos. Once she had tried to get Bobby to understand what was happening. She had told him Miguel was not only struggling with his muscular dystrophy but was also experiencing mounting anxiety about his disease, its impact on his family, and the resulting lack of sleep for everyone. She tried to explain his slurred speech, tremors, and tingling pain that coursed through his arms and legs. She explained that sometimes the school nurse had to help her change Miguel's catheter or diaper. Sandra's statement had been a mistake. When she finished, Bobby had just smiled and laughed. He snickered as he said, "Thanks for sharing. I will remember that. All of it."

"What do you want today, Bobby?"

The girl had guts, Bobby thought to himself. He ignored her and walked to squat down and face Miguel. "Hey, Spazz, what's shakin'?" Bobby chuckled as he stood to face Sandra. He flayed his arms and legs, imitating a convulsion, then straightened up and smiled. He knew what was coming.

Sandra's right arm swung a good slap toward Bobby's face,

but he caught her hand before contact. Sandra softly said, "Someday I will complete that slap!"

"Someday I might let you," Bobby said as softly as Sandra had spoken, but he added an evil, sarcastic grin to end the conversation. He patted Miguel on the shoulder as he walked off and said over his shoulder, "Hang in there Spazz!"

Sandra was determined to get even with Bobby for the meanness of his words and intent, and for the additional problems Bobby took pleasure in creating. She repeated her comment aloud, "Someday I will complete that slap … and maybe someday you will get what you deserve."

Bobby's lunchtime was usually the same experience: no lunch. His father never made him a lunch and he usually got up late and only had time to get to school. He often thought to himself, *I don't know why I even bother to come here. The teachers ain't teachin' me nothin' so I ain't learnin' nothin'. I could be workin' somewhere, makin' some money, and makin' plans to escape this one-horse hick town disguised as a prison. Maybe I will go search for that slut of a mother I called Mom.*

He never had enough money to buy lunch at school. *All they serve is crap anyway.* Sometimes he would grab a soda from a machine or steal a sandwich from an underclassman's lunch bag.

The cafeteria was a study in chaos. Conversations grew louder over other conversations, all struggling to be heard. Teachers hated 'Lunch Duty'; they would rather have had a few moments of quiet in the Teachers' Lounge. *This place reminds me of watching ants swarm over fried chicken at a picnic*, Bobby said to himself. His stomach growled in agreement. Some students plugged in earphones to tune in some music and tune out the surrounding pandemonium. Wave after wave of unusual different ethnic food smells of meals brought from home by so many students floated across the tables.

Bobby took one look and one breath inside the cafeteria and turned around. Besides, there was no one inside the cafeteria he wanted to sit with, so he sat alone outside on the baseball bleachers. It was a warm, sunny day with light breezes. He enjoyed the quiet and the time to think about who he would attack next. He flipped through all the social media on his cell phone and attacked many classmates, those he knew and those he didn't. Some comments he made online were funny, but most were hateful, antagonistic, and harmful. He made fun of their looks, their names, their friends, and their pictures. The school principal, Mr. Stevens, had called him to the office many times after parents complained about the nasty things he posted about their children. After Stevens read him the riot act, Bobby would leave and blow it off. He never knew he was misquoting Harry Truman by always saying, "If you can't stand the heat, stay off the internet." Stevens called Bobby's father several times to complain, but never connected with him so was forced to leave a message. The messages were never returned. Ed King did not appear to be concerned with, or interested, in his own son.

Bobby stared at the baseball diamond and tried to imagine how things would have turned out differently if he were on the team. Peter Bauch and Bobby King had grown up together, gone to school together, and played baseball together. Opposing pitchers did not like to face them as back-to-back hitters in Little League – that's where they got nicknamed "Pete" and "Re-Pete". Something happened last year though, and the best friends became bitter enemies. Many people never knew what caused it, but Peter and Bobby did. When the two freshmen tried out for the high school baseball team, Peter became a starting second baseman and Bobby sat on the bench. Bobby didn't like that, not one bit. Their friendship became a rivalry and then became resentment, followed by warfare.

The team's starters got more time and tips in the batting cages than the lowly subs. The starters also got more time, attention, and pointers with infield practice than the guys sitting on the bench, gathering splinters in their backsides. Peter waved at Bobby a couple of times from second base, but Bobby flipped him the bird. After the day's ball practice, Bobby split before Peter got out of the shower. Bobby watched through the field house window as Peter dried off and walked through the foot powder box as their coach always ordered. Bobby could barely contain his laughter when Peter got to his locker and his clothes were gone. All of them. The only sounds in the field house were the sounds from the semi-steamy showers until, "Bobby, one of these days, it will be your turn!" he yelled, standing in front of an empty locker as teammates broke the silence and began to laugh. Bobby scampered off toward downtown Tulelake.

Bobby was still laughing at that prank as he walked down to the intersection of Ontario Street and Sacramento Street where his father worked at Glass Service Station. Then he remembered he had found no money in Peter's wallet when he pitched all the clothes into a storm sewer about two blocks from the high school. *I have a hankerin' for an ice cream soda at the Corner Drug Store, but I need some cash*, he said to himself as he walked. *I'll bet the old man has some, unless he spent it all on booze.*

The twenty-foot-tall signpost at the street corner announced Glass Service Station to every driver. Junie Glass, Ed King's boss at the station, put that one up three years ago. The station's wall still had the fading sign Junie's father, Pat, put up. The time-worn sign said, "Gas by Glass." Junie's grandfather, Mitch, opened the original station but was killed in the big riot out at the Internment Camp in 1944. No one knew how he died or what he was even doing there, but nevertheless, his body turned up beside the railroad tracks outside the camp. Junie's Uncle Herbert kept the station going until Pat returned to Tulelake when he got back from Vietnam.

Bobby quietly slipped into the service bay where his father hung his jacket each day beside the toolbox, retread tires, and lube guns. Bobby hoped to find some folding money. But just as he walked into that service bay, Ed King came in from the station office. Ed stared at his son and asked with a hint of accusation, "What the hell do you want?"

"I wanted to find out if you need me to start dinner, and when you are coming home." So much for a pleasant greeting shared between father and son.

"Junie and me, we got some business to discuss. I won't be home until late. Fend for yourself."

Bobby said to himself, *That means he's going drinking and will be totally shitfaced when he gets home. If he gets home.* "OK, we can play it by ear."

"Yeah, well I gotta get back to work. See you later," and Ed turned away.

Bobby turned as well and said, "Bye." *That means no ice cream soda. And that means I fix dinner for myself, as usual.* His stomach growled and his anger built as he trudged down an almost empty Ontario Street, hands deep in his pockets. Shadows deepened on storefronts as a handful of cars and pickups passed each other. He strolled by the appliance repair shop owned by Mr. Martin Hodges. Bobby never could remember seeing any customers go into or come out of the smelly place. Ed King always warned Bobby to stay clear of the shop and especially of that man.

The American flag flew in front of the store 24/7, but it was frayed and faded. Bobby once noticed it only had 48 stars on the flag, but he never asked Mr. Hodges why or asked him anything else, come to think of it. Ole Man Hodges was pushing 90 but looked more like 110 or older. An old high-back cane chair was nested on a soda box for balance because one leg of the chair was missing. Ole Man Hodges sat in that same chair every day, almost every hour. He wore the same faded flannel shirt under the same dirty bib overalls that were accessorized by steel-toed work boots covered in tobacco juice. In fact, the chair sat within a six-foot radius of years and years of tobacco juice spit. He could hit a roach, cat, or a dog within that radius with great accuracy by spitting tobacco juice through his missing two front teeth in a mouth with brown, orange, and yellow jagged fangs.

Ole Man Hodges walked out the door and sat in his chair. Bobby watched him spit on a beetle that scampered from the curb into his line of fire. "Got 'im!" Hodges said and let out a donkey snort, followed by a wheezy laugh while tobacco juice dripped from an unkempt, lopsided mustache. Bobby stared at the mustache touched with gray, brown, and yellow streaks. His stare was broken when he heard, "What are you lookin' at, kid? Git out of here or I might jist aim fer you!" Bobby walked away as he heard another donkey snort and a wheezy laugh.

Two doors down, Bobby saw Sara Mohammad walk from the pharmacy. "Hey, 'Say-Ray'! How's everything in the Wonderful World of Jihadist Terrorists?"

"Are you always so evil, or is today an exceptional day for you?"

She stands her ground, thought Bobby, *And I don't like that.*

He looked the twenty-year-old woman up and down. She was dressed plainly in a dark-colored sweater over brown slacks. "Sara, let me ask you a question. Do you have to shave your head so that towel fits better over it?"

Over his shoulder, Bobby heard, "A Muslim woman shelters her head with a hijab, which means cover. It leaves only her face showing as part of an overall dress code when around men besides her father and brothers, and eventually one day around her husband. It is prescribed by Islam in the Qu'ran and is therefore part of our social system of Islam, you infidel dog."

Bobby turned slowly to see a man coming from the pharmacy where Sara was standing. Abdul Mohammad, Sara's brother, was twenty-eight years old, six foot, three inches tall, with dark hair, brown eyes that could shoot lasers to melt steel, and no smile. Ever. Bobby had never seen him smile, but after all, Bobby never seemed to bring out any joy in any people. Abdul had been an interpreter and intelligence analyst for the U.S. Army and was now a civilian.

"Hi, Abdul. I was just visiting with your sister. I was asking her …"

Abdul cut him off in mid-sentence with a response that even Bobby could not challenge. Abdul raised a hand and then pointed a finger at Bobby. "If you ever disrespect my sister again, your body will be scattered across several counties, and you will be alive as we remove your body parts. This I swear to Allah and his Prophet Muhammad; peace and blessings be upon him." Bobby's eyes went wide without his knowledge. Abdul recognized this and continued, "Never speak again to her. Never approach her. Never even look in her direction. Do you understand me?"

"Ah, well, I was just …" Again, Abdul cut him off, and this time patted his pocket. *What's he got in there?* Bobby was a whole head shorter and probably twenty pounds lighter than Abdul.

"No, no, no. I want to hear you say, 'I understand' and mean it!"

"OK, I understand, I understand. Geez."

Abdul fixed Bobby with a glare that lasted ten seconds or twenty minutes, depending upon your perspective. "You see. You insult even your prophet, Jesus. That word you just said, which I will not repeat, profanes your church's prophet. You are truly disgusting." Abdul finally turned to his sister and whispered, "Come, Sara, it is time to leave."

Bobby finally swallowed and thought, *Yeah, there are many more slobs to choose from, that need my special attention and talents. I will cross her off my list.* His stomach started rumbling louder as he stuffed his hands into his pockets and trudged down the street, talking to himself. "I don't like somebody trying to intimidate me. We need to put all those people in a cage or a prison. They are all terrorists." He kicked a box on the sidewalk. "And I ain't got a clue what I'm gonna eat for dinner."

The front of Pauley's Produce was always open this time of year, and there were always fresh vegetables from local farmers on display. Inside the store, Taylor Pauley sold goods like any convenience store, but in spring and fall, customers found eye-catching vegetables and fruit out front. Bobby bit his lip and walked in. "Hi, Mr. Pauley," he said just as his stomach growled loud enough for Mr. Pauley to hear it. "Have you got some chores around here that I could do? I need to buy some potatoes, but I ain't got any money."

Taylor Pauley knew the situation must be grim if Bobby King would ask like this, so he took a chance. "Sure do. I was just about to sweep out the store and wash the veggies out front. Think you can handle that?"

"Yes, sir."

Mr. Pauley gave him a broom and got him a hose to connect to the faucet outside. Pauley noticed that Bobby swept slowly to prevent kicking up dust onto everything on the shelves. "Thanks for being so careful, Bobby."

As he pushed the broom, he thought, *I hate this hick town and I hate school. Yeah, the Honkers? Whoever came up with that stupid name for a mascot?* He used his hand to get the dirt that had built up in the corner. Without thinking about it, he carefully swept it into a pan and continued. *Stupid town of 1,000 miserable people. And I'm stuck here with a sorry excuse for a father! My mother is probably lying in a ditch somewhere from a drug overdose, or a bullet to the head, or an empty bottle of tequila.* He turned the water on and began to softly spray the boxes of tomatoes and apples. *And I don't care where she is. And why is this hick town called Tulelake, but the lake is called Tule Lake? That's just dumb!*

When Bobby finished washing the vegetables and fruits, he washed down the sidewalk and the street in front of the store. "No sense in having dust from the street get on these, Mr. Pauley," he said absentmindedly.

"Excellent job, Bobby!" He grabbed some potatoes and put them in a bag. "You know I could use you around the store after school and on Saturdays if you are looking for some work. Interested?"

"I'll think about it. Thanks for the potatoes!" After he had walked about a block, he sensed the bag was too heavy. He looked inside and saw four potatoes, two cans of soup, and a five-dollar bill. He thought, *Why did he do that?*

Chapter 2
1:05 p.m., May 29, 2017
Tulelake High School

"You got my lunch money today, or are you and I gonna dance without the music again?" Bobby threatened Larry O'Shaughnessy like this once a week. "Hey, bullies gotta eat too, you know." Larry's back was jammed into his open locker at Tulelake High School. If Bobby backed him any further into that locker, Bobby could just close the door and be done with Larry. He did that last year to David Matthewson. As he closed David into his locker, Bobby jammed a pencil into the latch so it would not open. He laughed as he turned to face other students in the hallway, and they laughed nervously out of fear of the self-proclaimed Terror of Tulelake. Other students walked by with total indifference and acted as if nothing was happening. Teachers were busy preparing their classrooms for the next class, and there were no campus police. This allowed Bobby to get away with anything he wanted to do.

Larry said, "I ain't got no allowance for over a month 'cuz

the potato crop is so bad. Dad told Mom we may even lose the farm! I ain't got no money to give you!"

Bobby leaned six inches from Larry's ear and whispered, "That's too bad. I still don't care, but that's too bad." He leaned closer and hissed, "Get me my money."

"How?" pleaded Larry.

"Steal it. I bet your mom has a cookie jar with emergency money in it." Bobby leaned even closer and said, "And this is an emergency, you twerp."

"I'll try," uttered Larry in resignation.

"You better do more than try. Hey, I bet I can get that money from your little sister. That might be entertaining now that I think of it."

Fear entered Larry's voice, "Please, I'm begging you, leave her alone. I'll find a way."

"You better, 'cuz you know what I can do. Remember? Do you remember a black eye and a bloody nose I delivered by special delivery just months ago? Now, you don't want that again, do ya?" Bobby could tell from Larry's reaction that he remembered because Larry had grabbed his tightening gut and peed in his pants. Bobby stepped back and remarked, "Yes, I see you remember. Get me my money."

He saw Darrell and Wayne standing in front of their friend Arthur's open locker. Arthur was visibly shaking and crying. Bobby whined, "Gee, Arthur, I could hear you wailing down the hall. Did you lose your teddy bear or something?" He glanced at the pictures of a Marine in combat gear that Arthur had taped up everywhere. "Who's the killer in the pictures with the fancy gun?"

Darrell watched as Arthur turned and ran down the hall for the exit that led to the fields and the creek behind the school. Darrell said, "You know, Bobby, sometimes you can be as insensitive as a brick wall, but right now you are an A-1 prime asshole." He walked quickly so he could catch up with Arthur.

Bobby said, "Arthur is such a little goody two-shoes. He and his father, the do-gooder preacher. They're both losers!"

Wayne said, "Yeah, great timing, jerk. Arthur just found out his big brother, Taylor, was killed in Afghanistan two days ago. Someday Bobby, someday, you're gonna get yours. Someday something like this might happen to you or someone in your family."

Bobby laughed with no sign of regret. He said, "Right, and will it be from you?" He mocked a boxing stance and said, "How about now, clown? No?" As Bobby turned away, he softly said, "Not on your best day with a lot of help. Be careful what you ask for, Wayne. You may get it. Besides, there ain't nobody else in my family 'cept me and my loser father."

Wayne responded, "Gee that ain't much of a surprise. Your family is batting 1.000 . . . all losers!"

Bobby thought about starting a fight right there in the hall by the lockers but decided to just walk farther down the hall to his last class of the day. *Boring. Stupid. History. What do I care about what happened in the past? What a waste of my time,* he thought and sighed deeply as he plopped down hard onto the chair at his desk near the back of the classroom. *At least I can catch a nap before heading home.* He looked up and smiled as he saw Ned and Nancy, the Simmons twins, walk in. Ned always had on overalls and today, Friday, those overalls were filthy from a week in the barley fields. Ned was carrying Nancy's books as well as his, so as Ned passed by Bobby's desk, Bobby had an idea. Bobby shot out his foot, and Ned and the books went sprawling. Bobby jumped up and shouted, "Oh my gosh, Ned, are you OK? How did this happen?" He was laughing as he asked, "Are you hurt?"

Ned Simmons quickly jumped to his feet. Fists clenched and ready to fight a bully at least four or five inches taller. Ned worked on the family farm when he was not in class which meant he was solid muscle. He was ready to match Bobby when a voice shouted, "Bobby, that is enough! Come with me to the principal's office immediately." Mrs. Carson, the history teacher, was usually soft-spoken, but right now her voice commanded attention and obedience. "Now, I said!" She regained some composure and announced to the class, "When I return, we will begin our discussion of how the start of World War II impacted California. Please excuse me for a few minutes."

As he passed Ned, Bobby whispered, "I will get you for this."

Ned said just loud enough that most could hear, "I'll be waiting."

Bobby stopped and turned to Ned. As his eyes squinted, an evil sardonic smile appeared, and he whispered to himself, *You won't have to wait long, you grubby loser. The Terror of Tulelake will deal with you.*

The principal, Mr. Patrick Stevens, grimaced as he listened to Mrs. Carson explain all that she witnessed. He popped aspirin-like jellybeans every day. She finished by reporting the final exchanges between Ned and Bobby. She turned and fixed Bobby first with a stare of condemnation and then one of pity. Then without saying a word, she left the room and closed the door. Mr. Stevens stared at Bobby and eventually began to slowly shake his head. "Bobby, I just don't understand what is happening in your life that causes this, but I will get to the bottom of it. This is not your first encounter with classmates. I know you have bullied people, beaten people, and extorted money from some. Yes, that is the proper term when taking money from someone by threatening harm, 'extortion.' Another term is 'robbery,' young man. I am even aware of threats you have made against two teachers. We all remember your caper in the teachers' parking lot."

Bobby put on his shocked-and-surprised face. "Why I have no idea about whatever you are referring to, Mr. Stevens. If you will remember, I was home sick that day."

Mr. Stevens said, "You were home because you were suspended for that day after you caused a catastrophe at the afternoon pep rally the day before. Coach Crandall sent you home." Mr. Stevens remembered that twelve cars had tire damage when 'an unknown person' spread nails over the parking lot wet with rain. At least an inch of water had made the nails almost invisible. "So, here is what I must do. Effective immediately, you are expelled from Tulelake High School. You are to leave this campus when I am done with you. Second, I will call your father and have him meet me here today."

Bobby tried to make light of this when he snickered and said, "You gonna call my old man and have him come down here? Well, good luck with that! Maybe he will be sober. Or maybe Arthur's father can pray over him."

"I'm disappointed that you fail to see just how serious this situation is, Bobby. If you don't turn your life around, you may find yourself in jail, or worse." As Mr. Stevens reached for his telephone after flipping open Bobby's file to get Ed King's number, he announced, "Now leave this office, the school, and these school grounds!"

Bobby walked stiffly yet defiantly down the hall between classrooms. The few classmates that were in the hallways avoided any eye contact with The Terror of Tulelake. He smiled as he looked ahead at the approaching fire alarm on the wall. He said to himself, *I'll show them.* He looked around to make sure no one would see him as he activated the alarm. The area was immediately engulfed by the loud sound. After several seconds, students began to pour out of the classrooms and head to their designated fire drill exits, most in an orderly fashion, all talking and enjoying their newly found freedom from class. One girl stumbled near the last classroom before the eastside exit doors, and Bobby stopped to help her. She was screaming and holding her arm which was at a crooked angle. Bobby thought, *That's probably a confound fraction, or whatever they call them.* Some teacher farther down the hall was yelling Bobby's name, but he did not turn around. He ran through the exit doors, down the steps, and across the parking lot.

He stuffed his hands into his pockets and slowed to a trudge as he walked off the school campus. He half-turned and looked at the first-floor windows. Briefly, a sardonic smile crept across his face as he contemplated breaking every one of them with an old baseball bat he had in his closet. *My old Louisville Slugger signed by Hank Kitchens could make a big mess with all that glass!*

He shoved his hands deeper into his pockets and kept walking. He said to himself, *Naw, that's too obvious – they will know who done it.* He changed the subject and said, *I wish Mom had never left. Maybe I will leave town and go find her.*

Later that afternoon, Ed King sat and listened to Mr. Stevens explain why Bobby was kicked out of school. He heard about extortion, physical and mental threats, and every manner of bullying possible. All the while, Ed was wringing his hands on a rag, trying to wipe oil and gasoline off. Maybe he was also trying to rub off his own failure as a father. Mr. Stevens noted the smell of gasoline did not hide the smell of gin on Ed's breath, his skin, and his clothes. Ed had not shaved or bathed in a week. Ed, first and foremost, blamed the bitch whose name he had not repeated since she snuck out of town. She left with that dope head who made meth in a trailer near the lake who split town because he got word the sheriff was coming to bust him. *Good riddance to both of 'em,* Ed said to himself.

"Are you listening to me, Ed?" said Mr. Stevens.

"I'm sorry. This is so much to soak into my brain all at once."

"And last, but certainly not least, Bobby intentionally pulled the fire alarm today after I sent him home. Students and staff had to stand outside for over twenty minutes while the fire department checked the entire building. You might not know this, but the school is fined for false alarms. Who's going to pay for that? You? Yes, you will be paying for this incident, and your son may do jail time. I hope to buy security cameras in the future to guard against these situations."

"One student was injured and required medical attention, so you may be hearing from that parent or his attorney. Bobby is an angry young man, who was expelled today for his own bad choices, and sought retaliation. So, I'd like to know what you intend to do about all this?"

"What do you mean 'me,' Kemo Sabe?" Ed responded with a startled look on his face.

Mr. Stevens shot back, "I am not the Lone Ranger, and you are definitely not Tonto. So, I repeat the question – what do you intend to do?"

"As far as I can tell from what you've said, the problem is here at school. That means it's your problem, Kemo Sabe," responded Ed with a bit of edge to his voice.

Mr. Stevens sat quietly for a moment, tapping a pencil on Bobby's file. "Now I realize where he gets this behavior."

"Gets what?"

"In Bobby's mind, someone else is always at fault, he never assumes any blame. He is never responsible for any of his actions."

"Are you saying this is all my fault, Mr. Stevens?"

"Ed, while we sit here and haggle over who is at fault, the problem is not being addressed nor corrected. So, I ask again. What do you intend to do about it?"

"I'm not sure, but I will whip up something," Ed softly said with the same evil sardonic smile that Bobby had displayed in Mrs. Carson's classroom earlier. *My belt makes a very, very convincing whip*, he said to himself as he walked out to his truck.

Mr. Stevens stood at the window and watched Ed cross the parking lot to his old truck. *I think Ed may do something he might later regret. I think Bobby may not survive the night.* He turned and stared at the phone on his desk for several seconds. *Do I call or not? If I call, then I may be accused of meddling in their home life. If I don't call, then Bobby may be severely beaten or even killed.* Finally, he slowly picked up the phone and dialed. "This is Mr. Stevens at the high school. I need to speak with Sheriff Coulter. Thanks." He turned back to the window and watched Ed's truck being followed by a plume of blue smoke as he left the parking lot. He turned back to face the door of his office and make sure no one came in. "Howard? Pat Stevens here. I just expelled Bobby King and sent him home. The talk I just had here in my office with his father, Ed King, did not go well. Maybe I said something I should not have said. Maybe I was too harsh with both of them." He listened to the sheriff, then said, "Yes, I know you were just here an hour ago with the fire department. Yes, I know the mayor, city council, fire chief, and you will have to deal with the false alarm and the injured students."

Stevens felt the sheriff was about to crawl through the phone and strangle him. He let the sheriff vent for several minutes and calmly said, "Yes, Howard. Yes, I realize I'm in charge of Tulelake High School students and have counselors who can help with mental health issues." There were blistering words coming through the phone. Yes, I want to keep my job!" More blistering words, then Stevens interrupted, "Yes, I know so much gets shoveled onto your too-small a plate in a big hurry, Howard." Stevens popped another pair of aspirins and continued, "Howard, please listen to me. I called you for two reasons, mainly out of concern for this troubled boy – in case something happens to him away from school where we cannot help him."

"First, what can I do to help you with this mess?" He listened to a lengthy but softly spoken lamentation from the sheriff. "Uh-huh. Uh-huh. Yes. Oh, I completely agree with you, Howard. Howard, please call me and tell me what I can do to help. Listen, we are in this together, my friend." Before he could hang up, the sheriff asked a question. Mr. Stevens responded, "Hmm? Oh, the second reason I called. My skin started to crawl when Ed King left here. No, no, he did not threaten me. On the contrary, I think he may harm Bobby tonight." The sheriff raised his voice and Mr. Stevens could feel the heat. Stevens loudly said, "No, I'm not joking. Of course not, I am very serious! What do you mean 'He may have it coming?' My God, Howard, he is just a teenage boy! Look, all I am asking is that somebody drive over there this evening and check on them! I think you call that a wellness check. Maybe under the pretense of making sure Bobby does not skip town, or that Ed brings him to court when ordered by the mayor. Yes, Howard, I am serious." There was silence on the phone then a dial tone. "Howard? Howard?"

Mr. Stevens slowly lowered the phone back onto its cradle. He ran his fingers across his balding head and thought, *He hung up on me! Now what do I do?*

Chapter 3
5:00 p.m., May 29, 2017
Simmons Farm

Carl, Jason, and Andy ran across the field that led up to the old barn on the Simmons Farm. Well, Carl ran, while Jason and Andy struggled to carry a five-gallon can of gasoline they stole from the feed store where Carl's father worked. Carl's job on this mission was to make sure the coast was clear and that the boys weren't seen. The trio finally reached their target, the two big mounds of hay about one hundred yards from the old barn next to an even older smokehouse. It looked like one of the hay mounds was holding up what was left of the doorless, roofless shack. And that was where they met up with Bobby, their leader.

Bobby King, the sixteen-year-old, self-appointed Terror of Tulelake wanted revenge. He was a great kid if you agreed with him and did as he ordered. Otherwise, you were a marked boy or girl, man or woman, and you had better stay out of his way or leave town. Bobby was now out for retribution for what happened at school. "That jerk, Ned, got me thrown out of school. I'm gonna fix him real good."

Bobby's father, Ed, worked at the only gas station in town when he was sober, which was now only about seventy-five percent of the time. But Ed spent one hundred percent of his time, drunk or sober, making Bobby's life hard and too often painful. Bobby's mother ran off with a meth head ten years ago, and Ed had been miserable since, which meant Bobby bore the brunt of Ed's frustration, anger, and pain. A coat rack in the mudroom next to the back door of Ed's small two-bedroom house was where Bobby's mother hung her apron. She no longer lived there, and that apron had been replaced by Ed's leather belt that Bobby's butt and back knew all too well.

Bobby looked up at the approaching trio, the ones he called 'The Three Stooges,' because he could always find a way to get them in trouble and shield himself from blame. He smiled when he remembered the Great Toilet Paper Prank. Bobby talked Andy, Carl, and Jason into rolling the front of the high school with thirty-six rolls of toilet paper. Bobby walked behind them with a Hudson pump sprayer he stole from the feed store. He had filled the sprayer with water and red food coloring so he could soak the TP in the colors of Tulelake's big rival high school.

After the deed was done, the sheriff gathered all four boys and took them to the jail for questioning after he called their parents. But Sheriff Colter had to release the boys because there was no evidence. Carl, Jason, and Andy had used all their TP, so there was nothing in their getaway pickup. Bobby had looped the straps of the Hudson sprayer through the holes in a concrete paving block and tossed it into the stock tank on Old Man

Henshaw's farm. As Bobby left the jail with a big smirk on his face, Sheriff Colter said, 'You talked Carl, Andy, and Jason into helping you with that little caper. I know you did it; one day I will prove it, and I will arrest you."

The Terror of Tulelake needed to come up with some new terror scenarios, like today at Ned's home, the Simmons Farm. Bobby announced to the three boys walking up, "What the hell took you so long?"

"This can's heavy, Bobby! And we didn't want to slosh any out," Andy quickly responded. Andy Pickering found out two years ago that it was easier to do what Bobby ordered than to question it. Safer too. Once Bobby pushed Andy into Tule Lake, the town's namesake, and almost let him drown before he helped him out. Bobby often reminded Andy of that day and how the results of Bobby's magnanimous act of kindness could have been different.

Jason said, "Yeah, and it's hard to carry with just one good arm." Jason's left arm looked slightly deformed, but the reason was shocking. Five years ago, many of the boys were playing baseball on a freshly planted barley field. Jason was pitching and hit Bobby on his left arm. Bobby carried his bat out to Jason and pummeled him with the bat until the other boys pulled them apart. Bobby's bat broke Jason's arm in several places. Jason was afraid of retribution if he told on Bobby, so he told his parents he had fallen off their plow horse when it was spooked by a rat in their barn. Jason's family was poor and had no money to spend on doctors. They wrapped it and left it to heal on its own. "How bad a break could a fall from a plow horse be?" they reasoned aloud. None of the players or spectators ever spoke the truth about that day because everyone was afraid that Bobby would come after them next.

Bobby snarled and said, "Stop whining, Zit Face, and let's get started. Carl, you did remember to bring the matches, didn't you?"

Carl stammered, "Sssure, Bbbobby. I gggot 'em. Hhhere." Carl's speech impediment was discovered when he finally began talking around four years of age. Carl, Sr. sacked and delivered feed for farms around a smaller town of 1,102 people, which meant there was never enough money to get Carl proper medical treatment. Bobby was always making fun of Carl and referred to him as Weirdo, C-c-c-arl, or Dummy, but Carl still looked up to Bobby as a role model since no one else befriended him.

Bobby started dictating orders, and as the boss, he never dirtied his hands unless he had to or wanted to. "Jason and Andy, pour a little trail of gas from about there, all the way into the shack, and leave the can in the shack." He turned and in his best mocking voice said, "C-c-carl, give me the matches and then spread a little hay over the trail of gas into the shack."

All did as they were ordered and joined Bobby about fifty feet from the shack. They all looked around to make sure they saw no one and no one saw them. Bobby said, "Here goes," as he struck a match. Carl, Jason, and Andy were already running away, but Bobby waited to watch the punishment of one of the peasants in his kingdom. He watched as the line of fire followed the straw path into the shack and to the can of gasoline.

There must have been something else in the shack that was flammable because the entire shed exploded. Embers, metal, and wood splinters flew in every direction. The hay was engulfed in flames, but Bobby did not see it. Siding around the doorframe hit him on the forehead and knocked him out as the concussion from the blast hurtled him twenty feet further away.

Everything seemed fuzzy when he came to about thirty minutes later. At first, he thought a fog had settled in, but then realized it was heavy smoke. The world seemed to be moving one way and then another. *Maybe this is what my old man feels like when he sobers up from a two-day binge,* he speculated. He tasted blood on his lip and traced it upward to a bleeding knot the size of an egg on his temple. He winced in pain as he felt it and immediately thought he was going to puke. His head started to clear after a few more minutes, and he focused on a large man standing over him with hands on his hips. Sheriff Colter said, "I'll have Doc Wilson take a look at that when I get you in a cell downtown at the jail. Then I will call your father and hope he is sober. Boy, you are in a heap of trouble this time and you ain't gonna wiggle your way out of it." Bobby tried to sit up but passed out instead. Sheriff Colter grimaced and hit the switch on his radio. "Dispatch. This is Sheriff Colter."

"This is Betty Sue, Sheriff. Go ahead."

"Betty Sue? Please call Doc Wilson and have him meet me at the jail. I'm bringing in Bobby King, and he is going to need medical attention after I lock him up."

"Is he hurt bad?"

"Right now, he is lying in the backseat of my squad car unconscious with a real beauty of a reddish-purple knot on his forehead. I should be there in fifteen minutes."

"10-4. Will that boy ever grow up?"

"At this rate, the answer is definitely 'No'."

* * *

Bobby woke up just before he threw up all over the lumpy bunk he was on. Doc Wilson moved out of the line of fire just before the first hurl. He stuck Bobby's head in a bucket, in case there was more coming, and put a cool compress on his forehead without putting pressure on the nasty goose egg he had. Bobby offered, "I don't feel so good" and let loose with another volley.

Doc Wilson softly explained, "Actually, you are lucky to be alive. Sheriff Colter told me the half of the board that missed you had a large nail in it that could have been pushed into your head or eyes."

"Where . . . am . . . I?" came between gasps and groans.

"You are in Sheriff Howard Colter's Bed and Breakfast," he said and then added, "also known as the Tulelake Jail in the fair county of Siskiyou in the state of California."

"What happened?"

Doc Wilson watched Bobby's eyes and asked, "First tell me what you remember."

Bobby knew exactly what happened and how he was going to weasel out of it. "I don't know. I was walking by the Simmons Farm and smelled smoke. While I was trying to find the source of the smoke . . . I don't remember after that."

Sheriff Colter stood at the door of the cell. "Sorry, Bobby, but thanks for playing Truth or Consequences." He walked into the cell, stood before Bobby, and put his big hand on Bobby's shoulder. "Bobby, there was Exhibit A, a charred gasoline can in what was left of Mr. Simmons's smokehouse. Exhibit B was matches found in your pants pocket. Exhibit C was gasoline on your pants. There is no Exhibit D because the smokehouse and hay were destroyed, but we have a couple of pictures of how they looked. Son, that hay and shack might be valued at $700 to $800. You are just lucky as hell that the barn didn't go up. You'd be looking at a much stiffer penalty including a longer jail time. Bobby, I can charge you with destruction of private property, malicious mischief, and felony arson. Some of your buddies were seen running across the field, but they could not be identified. Officially, I will have to track down clues to determine their names, that is unless you want to tell me. I know who they are, and you know who they are. Hell, boy, you and your buddies could be looking at a minimum of one year in jail and $5000 in fines."

"You gotta be kiddin'!"

Sheriff Colter spun around to see Ed King with his hand over his mouth, standing in the cell doorway. Colter's eyes narrowed as he sighed, "Ed, you need to get a lawyer. The Simmons may force me into locking Bobby up until his trial."

Ed was staring at his son sitting on a jail cell bunk with his head in and out of a bucket when he said, "Until that happens, Sheriff, let me take him home so he can get some rest and heal." Ed looked up at the sheriff with eyes that only pretended pleading but displayed anger. "He ain't goin' nowhere. Right, boy?"

The two stared at each other for a few tense moments until Sheriff Colter said, "Well, they haven't forced me yet and the judge is on the other side of Tule Lake fishing."

"Thanks."

"But I will come get him if it comes to that. I strongly recommend you get a lawyer, Ed."

The ride home in Ed's 20-year-old truck with fading paint was silent until Bobby asked, "Have you started building it?"

Ed's mind had been miles away. "Huh? What?"

"You know. The battleship you were gonna build from all them beer cans in the garage and half of the kitchen. So, have you started?"

Ed's backhand caught Bobby across the face, fast and hard. "You're really a smartass know-it-all. I could say, 'Wait 'til you grow up,' but I don't think you will live that long, Sport."

As they walked into the house, Bobby instinctively flinched, expecting a blow to the back of his head. Nothing came. Instead, Ed went to the refrigerator and took out two beers. While he handed one to Bobby, he said, "When you feel better and this is all finished, you and I and that belt hangin' on the wall are gonna have an extensive conversation that you will not enjoy. The end result of that conversation will be when my boot makes contact with your ass, and you bounce across the yard and onto the road. Then we are done."

Bobby left the beer unopened on the counter and dejectedly walked into his own Fortress of Solitude, his ten-foot by ten-foot bedroom with a window that never seemed to hold back the rain or wind. The Terror of Tulelake was used to this, the threats and the estrangements, but he'd always felt vindicated for his misdeeds – at least he'd convinced himself he was. His favorite spot in the room was on the floor, against the wall, opposite the window. Usually, he sat there to plan attacks on classmates, plot revenge, or scheme. Sometimes he let the world in, but most of the time the world did not exist after he closed and locked the bedroom door. He had stolen a chain lock from the feed store last year and installed it himself. This evening he just sat and looked at the distant clouds as they passed. The sky was being colored by streaks of purple, red, and gold as the sun sank. It dropped almost as much and almost as fast as Bobby's spirits.

He threw a schoolbook in the direction of his closet. *I ain't gonna need these anymore,* he said to himself. He did not speak aloud so his father could hear him. *I wonder where those clouds are going? Maybe I will follow them when I leave this dump.* His hands shot up to his head as he muttered just above a whisper, "Damn, this hurts, and I know there ain't no aspirin in the bathroom cabinet." He rubbed his neck and eyes and said as he yawned, "I'll sleep it off."

He took off his shoes but left the rest of his clothes on and lay on top of the bed. They still smelled of gasoline. As he put his forearm over his eyes, he thought, *I wish I had never been born.* After a moment, he amended that thought and imagined, *Maybe I should have been born in another time. Yeah, another time.*

He was asleep, but his world was about to change forever.

Chapter 4
5:00 a.m., May 30, 1942
Tulelake, California

"Open up! Open up, immediately!" someone screamed as the front door was almost kicked in. Bobby groggily struggled to his feet and then fell back on the bed. His head was throbbing like a drum. He heard whistles screeching, which didn't help his headache. Then he noticed that flashing lights reflected on his ceiling and walls were like those on a police car, and then he noticed flashlights outside the house searching for something or someone. That's when he heard women screaming inside the house. The deep voice repeated itself, "Open this door right now or we will break it in and drag you out! Open it! Now!" Dogs growled and barked.

Bobby slipped on his shoes and noticed his clothes looked and felt different in the flashing lights. *Those are searchlights. What's going on? Has the sheriff come to arrest me?* He slowly opened his bedroom door and thought, *Hey, where did the chain lock go? It's disappeared. Who's screaming?*

He was met by a soldier with a rifle pointed at Bobby's gut. "You have two minutes to gather clothing into one or two suitcases or in two pillowcases. I don't care which, but in two minutes you will either be out that door or lying dead in here in your own blood. Your choice, you filthy Jap!"

For the first time in his life, Bobby felt terror. The Terror of Tulelake felt terror. How ironic. His headache was instantly gone, and he moved quickly to cram clothes in a pillowcase. As he walked to the door, he realized he had never seen these clothes before. *They must be mine 'cuz they were in my dresser. What's going on? Why did that soldier call me a Jap?* He turned to go down the hall, except there was no hall in the usual direction. He did not know where he was in his own house. *Or is this my house?*

The soldier shoved him roughly toward the front door. His nose caught strange smells from the kitchen that he had never smelled before. Bobby's father, Ed, only cooked when he was sober, which was not too often, and the pans and plates he used stayed in the sink until green and brown stuff grew on them.

There was more screaming to his left and as he looked, he saw an older woman and a girl about fourteen years old. And they were Japanese! More yelling behind him made him turn around. There was a mirror hanging on the wall, one that had never been there before. He stared and the reflection of a sixteen-year-old Japanese boy, with a look of horror and surprise, stared back. Bobby's pale blue round-shaped eyes had been replaced by dark almond-shaped eyes. Bobby's shoulder-length strawberry blonde hair, which Mr. Stevens always said was too long for school, was gone. Instead, he saw short-cropped dark brown or black hair. Bobby always had a good tan from playing baseball, but what he now saw was a bit more of a yellow tan. He stared and thought, *That's me, but that's not me! Who is that? Where am I? What is happening?*

Crashing dishes and pans in the kitchen broke him out of his stupor. Soldiers were ransacking everything in the kitchen looking for something in particular, or just trying to destroy everything in their path. He shot a glance into his father's bedroom and got another surprise. An Army sergeant pointed a pistol at a Japanese man as he yelled, "Who is hiding in that shed outside? If you don't tell me, I will order it burned to the ground along with any saboteurs inside. Who are you hiding, you stinkin' Jap spy?"

Blood trickled from the corner of the mouth of the forty-five-year-old Japanese man. A bruise on the side of his face was beginning to turn blue and red when he exclaimed, "We hide no one. We raise chickens and sell eggs at the market. We hide no one!"

"What is happening, Otōsan?" Even after Bobby said it, he thought the words came from someone else. *That's not my voice; whose is it? Why did I just call him 'father?' Wait, how did I know that Otōsan meant 'father?' Have we been invaded?*

The sergeant shoved the mother, father, girl, and boy out the front door. Bobby saw trucks being loaded with people with their few belongings like cattle when shipped to a slaughterhouse. *Hey, something like this was discussed in my history class about World War II. Jews were shipped on trains to concentration camps or death camps. But I ain't Jewish. This is a terrible dream!* He saw through eyes not his own the mother on the ground crying and the father trying to get her up and into the truck.

Gunshots rang out from farther down the street. A neighbor was running away, wearing only her nightgown. More gunfire. The woman stopped running as a red stain spread across her shoulder. She turned and just before another round was fired at her, an officer shoved the shooter's rifle into the air. "I said no firing, you idiot! Your orders are to round them up onto the trucks and haul them out of here. That's all!"

"But sir, these Japs may be spies sent to prepare Jap landing troops to invade California! Don't you understand?"

"One more word from your mouth and I will have you arrested for insubordination and firing at civilians!"

"They ain't civilians. They are Japs!"

The officer did his best to control the anger boiling in his gut. Finally, he ordered, "Corporal Westerman! Front and center!" Westerman arrived and snapped to attention. "Corporal, I have two orders for you. First, get this woman some medical attention. Then, disarm this soldier and put him in my staff car. He is under arrest. Understood?"

Mrs. Izanami Donaldson collapsed on the pavement with growing shrieks from Mr. Donaldson as he fell to his knees beside her.

Mr. Tsutomu, another neighbor Bobby somehow knew lived next door, was unconscious, his glasses shattered and dangling from one ear as two soldiers each had an arm and dragged the bloodied man to a truck half-filled with other people from the neighborhood. Tsutomu was thrown into the truck as if the soldiers were loading sacks of feed. His wife stood and watched as if in a trance.

A sergeant screamed in Bobby's face, "Do you need a printed invitation, Jap?"

The father politely bowed and stated, "Sir, with respect, we are not Japanese. We are Americans. I was born in Los Angeles, my wife was born in Anaheim, and our children were both born here in Tulelake."

Through squinted eyes and with a voice dripping acid, the sergeant shouted, "You're still Japs!"

Bobby stepped between the sergeant and his new 'father' and pleaded, "No, sir, we just don't understand what is happening. Please tell us."

"We're gonna put all you murderin' Japs in one place and guard you like you were in prison. It's not what you deserve. You deserve to be dead!"

"Deserve for what?" Bobby challenged. "We do not understand, sir."

"Are you serious? Are you touched in the head, boy? The surprise attack you murderin' Jap scum launched on Pearl Harbor less than three months ago killed a lot of people, including three friends of mine!" He pulled a service revolver from his holster and cocked it. "Shall I explain it further with a bullet from my gun?"

Bobby's eyes went wide, and his jaw dropped as he turned to his new father and asked, "Otōsan, what is he talking about?"

Otōsan took his son by the shoulders and looked into his eyes. "Ichiro, he speaks of the aggression and shame of the military leaders of Japan. They ordered a secret attack on the United

States Armed Forces in Hawaii on December 7, just months ago, and now we will pay for that evil shame. It all happened while you were away at the dry lakebeds at Tule Lake on your school trip." Otōsan saw something in Bobby's/Ichiro's eyes – a strangeness, an uncertainty, an unknown.

A captain came forward and got nose to nose with the sergeant and yelled, "Is there a problem here, Sergeant Weston? Must I relieve you of your responsibility and your rank to find someone who can complete this job? Perhaps your talents would better fit scrubbing outhouse toilets! Well?"

Someone standing next to Sergeant Weston could have almost heard the crunch as Weston clenched his fists tightly. Bobby/Ichiro swallowed hard enough to swallow his tongue. His eyes went wide open again in amazement and he thought to himself, *What is happening? Where am I? Who are these people?*

Sergeant Richard Weston stood rigidly, seethed in controlled anger. He would rather respond with his fists, but instead stiffly said, "Yes, Captain Shackleford. I am ready and willing to complete my task, sir! These Japs, though, are too damn stupid to obey orders, sir. I will complete the assignment, sir." A sly smile snuck onto his face as he thought, *And then I would like to insert my rifle butt deep into your face.*

Captain Shackleford softened some and quietly said, "Sergeant, none of us want to do this, but these are our orders. 'Tag 'em, bag 'em, haul 'em, and deposit 'em'." He half-heartedly saluted Sergeant Weston but turned before Weston could return the salute. Shackleford thought, *I don't like this, not one bit. These are American citizens, but we are about to treat them like POWs. Our troops are not herding German Americans on the*

East Coast, so why are we doing this to Japanese Americans here?

"Corporal Williams. Corporal Arnett. Front and center," yelled Sergeant Weston.

A scrawny, brand new, nineteen-year-old soldier, in a uniform a little large for him, ran up. "Yes, Sergeant!" Corporal Arnett looked and sounded younger than his age. Twenty-four months in the future, this scrawny kid would become a hardened hero by throwing himself onto a grenade during the Battle of Anzio, when he and other soldiers of the U.S. Fifth Army would be surrounded by Germans in February of 1944. He will save four fellow soldiers, trading his life for theirs. But today is a different day.

Corporal Williams, a farm boy, got saddled with guard duty at the new internment camp. He asked to volunteer for more active duty but was turned down by Captain Shackleford. The captain had said, "I need men that can think and act, not overreact. You will be very valuable at the camp."

"Corporal Williams, start logging them in. Corporal Arnett, let's clear the next house. We may need to torch it if any subversives are hiding in the attic or walls."

"Yes, Sergeant." Williams took his clipboard loaded with registration sheets and walked up to Bobby/Ichiro. "Do you speak English?"

Ichiro looked at the corporal with disbelief and said, "Of course, but we do not understand what is happening. What is going on?"

Corporal Williams nervously looked around, especially to see if Sergeant Weston had heard that. He quietly said, "I would keep my voice down if I were you. I have my orders and now you have yours. Do as you are told."

"Alright, but can you tell us where we are going?"

"You and all people of Japanese ancestry are to be transported from this area to the new camp up at Tule Lake. Now move it! Get your family together right here so we can start!"

Ichiro struggled to process this information. He walked over to his father and said, "Otōsan, we must listen to this corporal and do as he ordered us to do. We have no choice."

His father was trying to understand all this, and at the same time, he was trying to calm his wife of twenty years. Ichiro and his father then gathered the two suitcases and the two pillowcases that contained their entire world of clothes, pictures, and important papers. They walked to the corporal who said, "I need the name, age, and place of birth for every member of the family, please."

"I am Saburo Hisakawa, age forty-five, and born in Los Angeles. This is my thirty-nine-year-old wife, Etsuko, born in Anaheim. Both her parents and mine came to the United States from Japan long before we were born. Our oldest son, Taro, is a student at the University of California at Berkley, studying architecture. He is not here. My fourteen-year-old daughter, Masako, and my sixteen-year-old son, Ichiro, were both born right here in Tulelake." Saburo heard more screaming, crying, and yelling down the street. As he turned, he saw his neighbor Yoshio Oshiro being dragged from his house and over to a truck. Yoshio's wife Kiku was screaming and begging as she ran. She was followed by their four frightened and crying young children.

Corporal Williams ignored that distraction and captured the

family's information. Then he asked, "What is this address and what is your occupation, Mr. 'Hist-A-cow-ah'?"

"Hisakawa, sir. This is 11981 Scotland Road. We raise chickens and sell eggs at the market in town. My children go to school here in Tulelake."

Corporal Williams turned and said, "Private Escobar. Front and center. I have completed the initial registration. Use this form to complete their temporary identification coat tags and get them on the truck. Any questions?"

"Ok, ok, ok!" with little enthusiasm. As Williams walked down the street to the next house, Escobar did as he was told without saying a word. When he was done, he tagged each family member on their coat and said, "Do not remove this until you are instructed to at final registration at the camp. If you do, you could be severely punished or shot. I need to hear from each of you that you understand you will get on the truck and stay on that truck until you are instructed otherwise. Understood?"

Each affirmed. Saburo asked, "What will happen to us? What will happen to our home and our business?"

Private Escobar said, "I honestly don't know, and I don't even care. What I do know is that all this has taken the pressure off me being a Mexican, and right now you Japanese are lower on the totem pole than even Negroes. Get in the truck."

They heard Sergeant Weston barking more orders. "Hey, there are chickens back here! Round them up and we will have fried chicken tomorrow!"

* * *

The truck rocked Ichiro and his sister Masako to sleep, but it was no lullaby. The truck seemed to find every pothole in the road. The blast from the truck's horn woke them from a fitful sleep as they turned from State Highway 139 into the camp entrance. Bobby/Ichiro said, "I had the strangest dream we were arrested. There were a bunch of soldiers and gunfire. I thought..."

"And that's what you get for thinking, Jap. It will be worse than that in sixty seconds if you don't get out of that truck and line up right here! I will promise you a nightmare!" yelled Sergeant Weston.

The Hisakawa family struggled down from the truck and lined up with the other detainees from their neighborhood. They were marched one hundred yards, then across the Central Pacific Railroad tracks near a watchtower, and were led into a large wooden building with a sign stating it was the 'Reception Center.' The outside fencing was six feet high, topped with barbed wire, and stretched around the camp measuring 1.5 miles by just over one mile. Ichiro realized it was all new – the fencing, the gate, the buildings, and the grounds within. It was not quite dawn, but the sound of saws and hammers could be heard coming from several directions. As they stood there, another guard tower was raised up. Even the building they were in was still being slapped together. "They must be in a hurry to get us locked up," Ichiro pointed out. He doubled over almost instantly when the sergeant's rifle smashed into his stomach.

"Umph," came from Ichiro's mouth, but he thought he heard it come from somewhere else as well. He thought, *Maybe that was just an echo.*

"Keep talking, smart boy, and the next words will be your

last. I have no problem leaving your dead body out here by the gate as an example to the other Japs coming here. Got anything else to say?" Sergeant Weston teased. Saburo helped his son to his feet without looking directly into Sergeant Weston's eyes. "You're smart too. Maybe you can help teach your son, but not until after processing."

A private on duty was bored as he said, "Keep moving. Stay in line. Keep your family in line. The head of the family must be the first in his group. Take off your identification tag, put it in your luggage, and leave your luggage on these tables for inspection. Keep moving. Stay in line. Keep your family in line. The head of the family must be the first in his group. Take off your identification tag, put it in your luggage, and leave your luggage on these tables for inspection." Over and over he repeated that monotonous wording all day long.

The Hisakawa family carefully placed their belongings on the tables which had been quickly built by placing two 2" x 12" x 12' boards on barrels. They had written their names on the pillowcases and suitcases to make sure they would get their few belongings back. As they walked into the Reception Center, soldiers were taking their belongings and dumping them on the ground as they looked for any contraband – knives, guns, maps, compasses, straight-edge razors, short-wave radios, money, liquor, etc. The soldiers roughly stuffed contents back into the cases, along with the dirt and weeds around the belongings on the ground.

The inside of the Reception Center was divided into an initial processing room, six cubicles, two offices, a jail cell, and a departure room that allowed access into the camp. Armed guards were everywhere. The Hisakawa family was crammed into a cubicle where a seated soldier asked, "Who are you, and who are these people? What papers do you have?"

Saburo, Etsuko, and Ichiro were still wiping the ink off their fingers from being fingerprinted. Masako stood in a trance with fingerprint ink on her clothes. Saburo completed the registration for the family, picked up their new ID badges, and moved to the next room. A soldier dressed like a doctor examined their eyes and throats, then checked their heads for lice. The family was forced to strip to make sure they did not have hidden contraband. Next, they moved into the departure room. Ichiro saw a bloodied man on the floor of the jail cell as he passed by. *He might be alive, or he might be dead. This is terrible,* Ichiro thought to himself. *Or, was that his own thought?*

As they stepped out of the Reception Center door, they saw piles of personal belongings of so many people. They found their own after rooting around and shaking out as much dirt as they could.

Masako picked up her pack and said, "It is wet. Something broke inside." She opened the bag and stuck her face in to find the damage. She recoiled immediately and dropped the bag. Fighting back the vomit, she softly said, "Someone used my bag for a bathroom!" She left the bag and walked away, but Ichiro drug it on.

The first time Saburo could speak was when they left the Reception Center. "We are assigned to Block 4, Barracks 4-8, Apartment C. This soldier will take us there." As they moved forward, Saburo softly said to Ichiro, "Start learning where everything is so we can find our way around."

As they walked, they saw long buildings being rapidly thrown together. Some had wooden walls with knot holes through which you could see inside, but most just had tar paper walls that flapped and fluttered in the dusty wind even after the paper was nailed to the walls. After walking fifty yards, Ichiro looked over his shoulder at the building they had just left. He could not see it. The dust was so thick that visibility was greatly reduced.

They stopped in front of a wooden barracks with a sign by the door proclaiming to the world that this was Block 4, Barracks 4-8. "Welcome to your new home, Jap scum, and I don't care if you enjoy it or not." He pointed to a pile on the ground and said, "There is your bedding and linens for each family member. Maybe you can pick out the bedbugs and make a soup. Sorry, there ain't no mattresses. Each of you gets one spoon, one fork, one plate, one bowl, and one cup. There ain't no replacements, and there ain't no knives. You can eat cafeteria-style in the mess hall, or you can starve. The chow times are posted on the inside of the door. There may be more clothes coming tomorrow, or next week, or next month, or never. Enjoy!"

They stood looking at a wood and tar paper building, 40 feet by 120 feet, that they would eventually share with ten other families. They gathered their supplies and quietly walked into their barrack. They froze when they realized their new living quarters measured 20 feet by 20 feet, with a plywood partition eight feet high that left an open space between each partitioned room. Their apartment had a big black stove and a heavy-duty bucket beside it. Saburo said flatly, "That soldier said the bucket will be used for laundry, water, coal, and as a chamber pot."

Etsuko had remained mute since she got off the truck at Reception, but now she asked, "What is a chamber pot?"

Ichiro said out loud before he realized he had said anything, "It's a toilet, Okāsan."

Masako put her hand over her mouth and began to moan, rocking back and forth. Etsuko embraced her and tried to comfort her. "Everything will be alright. You will see."

Ichiro thought, *What have we done to deserve this kind of treatment? Why is this happening?*

Ichiro heard another voice quietly exclaim, *Holy Guacamole! This is an upholstered dump without the upholstery!* Ichiro turned completely around looking for the source of that statement but found none.

"We are in Hell," Ichiro said dejectedly.

Maybe, and maybe not, but you can sure see Hell from here. Geez!

"Who said that? Where are you?" He spun around until he collapsed in the dirt when no one answered. He sat there angry, confused, and forlorn.

Chapter 5
1:00 a.m., June 1, 1942
The White House, Washington, DC

The 60-year-old man in the wheelchair looked more like 90 years old, haggard and sickly with sunken, sad eyes. Those bloodshot eyes emphasized his serious lack of sleep. Polio had left him permanently paralyzed from the waist down and continued to ravage his body. His constant battle with sinus infections also inflicted constant pain. On top of all that, the stress and daily tension of the war ate away at the limited stamina of President Franklin Delano Roosevelt.

His day started 18 hours before and had never stopped. A one-hour, fitful nap did more harm than good. Every time he thought he had reached one solution to a problem, then three more problems arose. In January, after the horrible tragedy of the December 7 Pearl Harbor attack, he had one positive event: when he had the opportunity to meet one of the few American heroes of that day, a Captain Allen Maxwell, U.S. Army Air Corps. Then he had another in April: when the Doolittle Raid on Tokyo succeeded in making the Japanese realize their homeland was vulnerable to attack. Newspapers and radio broadcasts about the daring raid bolstered the sagging spirits of the American people. Only key authorities knew the raid's bombs had minimal actual destruction and that many of the crews had had to crash-land their planes.

Earlier in the year, German U-boats were discovered operating successfully off the East Coast of the United States, the first American forces had landed in Great Britain, the German Luftwaffe was destroying London with their blitzkrieg bombing, the German Army (the Heer) was dashing across Russia, Rommel's Afrika Corps was sweeping across Africa, Dunkirk was lost, and the United Kingdom was alone in facing the German onslaught when most of her allies were conquered and occupied. The Japanese met little resistance as they rolled across the Pacific Ocean and China. The United States would be fighting a truly global war at the same time with the same limited resources after entering the war just six months before.

Ups and downs, like his blood pressure. FDR's sinus infections got worse as did his headaches and body pain. An aide in the last meeting of the day pointed out that it was "forward-thinking to have signed Executive Order 9066. Can you imagine how many Japanese spies are on the West Coast?" The President had no complete answer to the question, and the weight of the world felt heavier and heavier each day.

The Munson Report, submitted to the White House on October 17, 1941, reported that "loyal Japanese are loyal to the United States." A Naval Intelligence report in January 1942 suggested they could find no 5th column, subversive actions by

Japanese Americans, and strongly urged against internment. Both reports were ignored when President Roosevelt signed Executive Order 9066 on 19 February 1942. Over 120,000 men, women, and children of Japanese ancestry were to be arrested and locked up. The President's tired eyes grew heavy, and he fell asleep in his wheelchair as papers fluttered to the ground. Carl Masters, Roosevelt's personal attendant, rushed to his side and checked for a pulse. He relaxed when he found one and announced to the other aide, "He's asleep for the first time in almost 24 hours. Let him rest here."

Breakfast the next morning was silent as President Roosevelt reread some reports from the previous night and some fresh reports just brought to him. Sketchy, unconfirmed reports were being analyzed that said Jews were being mass murdered by means of hydrogen cyanide gas at Auschwitz. Reports were just coming in about the 1000 British bombers launched for a 90-minute attack on Cologne, Germany. The United States Navy was about to enter a massive sea battle against the Imperial Japanese Navy's attempt to surround and invade Midway Island. Ups and downs.

Eleanor Roosevelt sat next to her husband at the table and Carl Masters sat within earshot. Mrs. Roosevelt stirred and stirred her morning tea until the clickety-clickety-clickety sound of the spoon hitting the inside of the cup made President Roosevelt stop reading. "Babs, is there a train station now open in this dining room?" The only response he got was the continued clickety-clickety-clickety sound of the spoon hitting the inside of the cup. "What time is the next train?" He set the papers down as he exhaled loudly. Removing the gold antique rimless Pince-nez eyeglasses, he said, "I know you always seem to stir your tea that way when you want my attention. What is it?"

She continued the clickety-clickety-clickety until she realized that Franklin was staring at the cup. She thought, *He looks so old and so overwhelmed. Perhaps I should say nothing.*

"I'm waiting, but not for long."

She stopped and took a sip to garner some extra courage. "I am concerned about Executive Order 9066 that you signed a few months ago. Information has come to me that made me gasp. Shall I share it with you, Franklin?"

Their relationship had become icy in the last two years and the two-front war was not helping. She had known of his affair with Lucy Mercer Rutherford, Eleanor's social secretary, for over 25 years. She knew that FBI Director, J. Edgar Hoover, despised her and her views on race relations and the fledgling civil rights movement. She had privately urged the president not to sign Executive Order 9066 and was horrified when he did. Before this moment, she had avoided challenging him face-to-face on the subject, but now it was time.

He knew he needed to at least listen to her now. She made public appearances for him when he was unable to stand the rigors of office, and in some areas of politics, they were in sync. Publicly, they were husband and wife, the parents of six children. Privately, they barely co-existed. He knew she was now, and had been for some time, an outspoken champion on racial issues. He suspected where this conversation was going but resigned himself to the discussion that would evolve into an argument. He said, "Please, go ahead, Babs."

"I have learned that two-thirds of all American citizens of Japanese ancestry have been unceremoniously forced at gunpoint to surrender their homes, their businesses, and their way of life. Some have even lost their lives, Franklin. Some spent days and nights sleeping on hay mixed with manure in horse barns at race-tracks and fairgrounds while others endured being placed in concentration camps, shamefully called American Relocation Centers. Are you aware of this?"

"Yes, yes, I am, Eleanor, I did sign Executive Order 9066. The concern is many of them are guilty of espionage or sabotage or will be in the near future."

"So, the American Bill of Rights concept of 'innocent until proven guilty' does not exist for these people? Is that what you are saying?" She pulled a stack of papers from the small table beside her and flipped through the papers to find a certain page. "Ah, here it is. I realize you have so much to read and study to make critical decisions, but have you ever read the Tolan Committee Report from March of this year?" Franklin was silent, so she continued, "I know you are aware of the report, but did you actually read it?" He remained quiet and she pushed on, "I draw your attention to the testimony of a journalist named James Omura, who asked, 'Has the Gestapo come to America? Have we Americans not risen in righteous anger at Hitler's mistreatment of Jews? Then is it not incongruous that citizen Americans of Japanese descent should be mistreated and persecuted?' Well, have we, Franklin?"

He took the Tolan Committee Report from her and set it beside his plate. He started to place the eyeglasses on his face but instead said, "Eleanor, it's not a simple case of yes or no. In many instances, our soldiers are preventing harm to these Japanese Americans by local hate groups. The West Coast was bursting with racial hatred for them even before Pearl Harbor. Now their protection is essential."

"I see. How many German Americans have been locked up? There may be spies and saboteurs among them."

He thought a moment and then softly said, "Ah, perhaps 10,000 were arrested." She was pushing and he was getting a headache.

She pushed on. "And how many Italian Americans were arrested? Oh, don't forget the Irish-Americans because many of them support the Irish Republican Army and are working with the Nazis. There are rumors that the IRA had asked Hitler to help expunge the English from Ireland. How many of them were arrested, Franklin?"

"Alright, Eleanor, you've made your point."

She shoved her plate away. "Let me ask you a hypothetical question. What do you call the roundup of an entire population based upon ethnicity or religion, transporting them forcefully by trucks and trains to live behind fences topped with barbed wire in sloppy deplorable housing with despicable sanitary conditions?"

He knew he could not win this conversation, but he asked anyway, "I don't know. What would you call it, Eleanor?"

"I'm not sure. Perhaps you can call Adolph Hitler and ask him what the Nazi term is for such activities in imprisoning all the Jews across Europe. Perhaps you can model the American system after the Nazi system." She threw her napkin on the table and walked loudly, briskly away, leaving President Roosevelt to mull over the conversation.

He slowly sighed and said under his breath, "She has a point." He twisted in his chair and yelled, "Carl! Please call Missy LeHand and have her meet me in my private office. If she is not here yet, call her at home." *Have we done this all wrong? Have we allowed war hysteria to force the wrong decisions?*

Just then the phone rang, and Carl answered. "Yes?" His facial expression turned dour. "Yes, sir, I will tell him." As he hung up, Carl said, "Mr. President, that was an aide to Admiral Ernest King."

"And why is my Chief of Naval Operations calling so early this morning?"

Carl paused a moment before answering, "It's Midway, sir."

Chapter 6
8:00 a.m., June 4, 1942
Tule Lake War Relocation Center, California

I chiro and his sister, Masako, sat staring through the barbed wire fence trying to imagine what happened to their home and to their way of life. They gasped at guard towers with machine guns pointed inside the camp.

Masako asked, "Did the soldiers take all our things – our furniture, our clothes, and our private things? Do you think my new Easter dress is gone?"

"Probably. I'll bet the place was busted up and things were stolen."

They stared in silence through the fence. "What is happening out there? Why were we locked in here and treated like criminals?" Masako wondered aloud.

"They are afraid of us," Ichiro explained.

"Why? What did we do?"

"We have the faces of their new enemy," Ichiro sighed.

"Why are we fenced in?"

"To make sure you are guarded from the outside world," Ichiro said. But he wondered, *or to guard the outside world from us?*

A loudspeaker on the guard tower announced, "Step away from the fence or we will shoot to kill!"

Ichiro and Masako stepped back from the fence as if it was electrified. "That's why. After all, every Japanese American is a Jap spy or saboteur," Ichiro said with disgust as they felt the bright morning sun on their faces.

"People don't think that, do they?"

"If they didn't think that way, then why have we been thrown in prison?" Ichiro kicked the dirt and said, "And I'll bet everything in our lockers at school has either been stolen or tossed in the trash." Ichiro gasped, "Jeez, I just remembered my baseball glove was in my locker!"

Masako changed the subject, "Our mother did not sleep well last night. I heard her crying until the early morning hours."

"Hai. I'm sure Father tried to console her, but …" and his voice trailed away. "I wonder what happened to our brother, Taro? Is he still at UC Berkeley? Has he been imprisoned? Is he alive?"

Masako faced Ichiro and cautioned, "Never talk like that in front of our parents. They already have us to worry about. You and I must work hard to protect them." She dusted herself off and said, "Let's get some breakfast, then we can explore this place a little."

"I'm not hungry. I'm going to read a newspaper I found."

Ichiro sat down on the steps of Barrack 4-8 as dry dirt was lifted into swirling dust devils while he read a two-day-old copy of *The Los Angeles Express Telegram*. Large headlines proclaimed, "Roundup of all Japs in California Near Completion!" Smaller headlines said, "Army Searches for Jap Saboteurs" and "Army Prepares for Jap Invasion on West Coast." He read about the "Battle of Los Angeles" on February 24 when machine guns and anti-aircraft guns fired into the air at reported invading Japanese aircraft. An air raid alert began at 7:18 that night and sporadically sounded alarms well into the night until a blackout order was lifted twelve hours later. It turned out the invasion was just a wayward weather balloon. He read that paranoia was rampant.

He turned the page to find a picture of a man pointing to a sign that stated, "We don't want any Japs here." There was a political cartoon of soldiers guarding a chicken house with Japanese inside. An article explained that many Japanese were given a week to gather their belongings, complete all their business, and leave for the relocation centers. Ichiro laughed as he said to himself, *That is not how we were treated!* He stopped when he felt someone looking over his shoulder. He turned but no one was there.

On the next page was a picture of a sign on the Yamachi Grocery the owner had put up as he boarded the front window. The sign proclaimed that he was an American, but someone else had written in red paint over it, "No you are not!"

Ichiro read that President Roosevelt signed Executive Order 9066 on February 19, 1942, which authorized a roundup of all people of Japanese ancestry on the West Coast. Ichiro gritted his teeth as he said, "I thought Roosevelt was president of all Americans, not just the white Americans!" He read about Major Karl

Bendetsen and Lieutenant General John DeWitt, who were ordered to relocate and incarcerate all people of Japanese descent into ten relocation centers. The West Coast would have exclusion zones, in which no people of Japanese descent could live unless interned. *They are treating people like cattle! They are treating my people like cattle!*

There it was again – the sensation that someone was standing behind him and reading over his shoulder. Ichiro turned slowly, but no one was there. He shivered, took a deep breath, and continued reading. An article explained the War Relocation Act Commission's creation of the Tule Lake Relocation Center and how it was almost finished. They were proud of finishing a barrack almost every hour – apartments, latrines, laundry rooms, and kitchens. It would become the new home for many Japanese American families, supposedly where they could be protected from racism. He heard a voice say, *Don't turn the page yet. I'm not through reading that one.*

Ichiro jumped up and turned to find where the voice came from, but there was no one. "Who said that? Why are you hiding?" He sat down again with the newspaper and now he was shaking. He turned the page and froze when he saw the picture of a poster in a hardware store stating they had Jap Hunting Licenses for free.

Two voices at the same time said, "That's just not right!" One voice was Ichiro's, but he did not know where the other voice came from. He was alone as the dust devil covered him. His eyes stung.

Chapter 7
10:00 a.m., June 25, 1942
Tule Lake War Relocation Center, California

Each of the eight blocks consisted of fourteen barracks, a mess hall, one men's latrine, two women's latrines, one laundry room, and one ironing room. Depending upon the size of a family, about 20 people lived in each 40-foot by 120-foot barrack. There were 893 barracks inside the camp, though many were not yet occupied. The camp was designed to hold about 15,000 internees.

The two Ogawa sisters, teachers from Lost River, Oregon, shared Block 4, Barracks 4-8, Apartment A, 16 feet by 20 feet, and the Suzuki family of three shared Apartment B. The Hisakawa family first thought Apartment C was larger, so they chose that one. It wasn't. The Kamida family of five were in Apartment D, which was 25 feet by 20 feet, and the three Takata brothers had been in Apartment E until one of them, Norii, had been killed trying to escape over the fence. The other two Takata brothers were moved to a growing section for dissidents. Three brothers named Ando were now assigned to Apartment E. The other apartments in the barrack were currently empty but would be filled in the next week or so.

Spring seemed to be departing late, along with the occasional downpour that came right through the roof and upper parts of the walls. And yet, the area got less than eleven inches of rain a year. Most of the time there was no breeze, so Ichiro walked slowly through the Relocation Center, or Concentration Camp, or what-ever it was called today. Everyone was locked inside a birdcage of barbed wire fencing. There were guards with machine guns in nineteen watchtowers every 100 yards. There were guards with dogs walking every 50 yards with rifles. A curfew kept people behind their barrack doors from 10:00 pm until 6:00 am. There was a roll call every morning and every evening. Step out of line and there was a vacancy at this fine hotel. Saburo told Ichiro that a guard said they were protecting all these people from the angry citizens of the West Coast that might harm them for what happened at Pearl Harbor. Saburo said, "If they are here for our protection, why are their guns pointed inward instead of outward?" Saburo's lip was still swollen and blue from the roughing up he got when the soldiers forced them from their home last month.

Most of the 'guests' at these types of places were of Japanese ancestry and were born in the United States, like Saburo's entire family. About two-thirds of these were. They were called Nisei, 2nd generation Americans born to 1st generation Japanese Ameri-cans called Issei, who were the children of Japanese-born immi-grants. Most Issei had never returned to Japan, but that did not matter. Technically Ichiro and Masako were second-generation Japanese Americans known as Sansei.

The Hisakawa family ate every meal together in the communal mess hall assigned to them in the middle of fourteen barracks – 75 to 100 people at a time in two shifts. Ichiro's mother and sister had problems with the food, which often found them in the horrible latrines that lacked partitions for privacy. Steamed rice, tsukemono (vegetables pickled in brine), and boiled vegetables seemed to find their way onto every meal plan in the mess hall. And there was fried fish and steamed fish. The menu created a real problem. Nisei preferred a more 'American-style' diet whereas Issei preferred a more 'Japanese-style' diet. The food at Tule Lake War Relocation Center was a compromise – nobody liked it.

The washrooms had ten showers with partitions but no curtains. Hot water for showers and laundries was often in short supply. Etsuko and Masako could not bring themselves to bathe in the showers, so they bathed in the coal bucket in their apartment. Many chose to follow the same routine.

By noon every day, all walked upwind by the latrines because the smell was overpowering downwind. Sometimes the latrines backed up and there was no water. On those days, everyone gave the area an even wider berth of avoidance.

Many in the camp suffered from colds, diarrhea, sores, and digestive problems like malnutrition due to the rapid, unexpected changes in their cultural and social life. The good news was that medical services were free; the bad news was there weren't many medical services available. Incoming parcels were inspected for contraband, but letters were not yet.

Ichiro and Saburo were allowed to rummage through scrap lumber piles left from camp construction. They found wood scraps to make bedframes to keep their bedding off the floor and away from the nightly visits of rats. They also built small storage boxes, for clothes and personal belongings, which fit under the beds. This was hard work, as they had to pull scrap nails from the wood and straighten them before using them. Bobby/Ichiro worked with someone for the first time in his life and he enjoyed it. He learned cooperation and teamwork; but most importantly, he learned some self-worth. He also learned to avoid Sergeant Weston, who often toured the camp to find someone to pick on, intimidate, humiliate, and beat. If Weston went left, Bobby/Ichiro went right. Ichiro kept a low profile.

The Army wanted the camp to become more self-sufficient by growing and managing its own food. The farm areas even had their own warning fence, security fence, and sixteen guard towers. Saburo and Etsuko earned $5 a day to supervise the raising of chickens and the resulting egg production, something they were very good at doing. Ichiro and Masako tried to attend the makeshift school in the compound, but she was often sick, and he was often working to offload coal from coal gondolas. Four carloads a day arrived to provide barrack heat, hot water, and fuel for cooking. Ichiro was surprised the soldiers allowed students to attend a half-day of subjects taught in Japanese, and then switch to a half-day of subjects taught in English. Ichiro told his sister, "I think it is a test. I think they may be trying to trip us up.

Ichiro heard a voice say, *That's probably a good guess. These guys look very sneaky. I don't trust them, do you?* Again, Ichiro spun around looking for the source of the comment but found no one standing there except Masako.

Ichiro said, "Did you say something, Masako? Did you hear someone else?"

She twisted her head slightly, burrowed her eyebrows, and thought, *My brother has been acting strangely. I think he may flip his wig*. Instead, she calmly said, "I heard nothing, Ani."

Then there was the incident in Apartment B in Block 4, Barracks 4-5.

One night around midnight, Nobu Rie and his wife, Maiki, were screaming and yelling, "No! Stop! Get out! Help! Help! Stop! Get out!!" No one dared go out to help because it was long after curfew, but people did look through the many cracks and gaps in the walls. They saw two people, maybe dressed as guards, running from the barrack holding something. It was almost fifteen minutes later that an alarm went off, floodlights shone, and guards with dogs appeared. The next morning the camp rumor mill flew into high speed. It was reported that Mrs. Rie was stabbed, and Mr. Rie was almost beaten to death. The residents in the other apartments in that barrack were loaded onto a truck and taken to another camp. The belongings of Mr. and Mrs. Rie were supposedly scattered around their apartment and blood was everywhere. Everything was removed from the apartment and burned. The walls were washed, but red-brown bloodstains on the walls and floor never left. The guards never said what had happened, and the camp office's official statement was that both Mr. and Mrs. Rie were moved due to a security risk.

One rumor said he failed to do something ordered by the Loyalists, a hate group loyal to Japan and extremely anti-American. Another rumor speculated that drunken soldiers decided to have some special fun with Mrs. Rie and Mr. Rie objected. Still another rumor suggested they were beaten and stabbed for hiding gold coins. The Bobby-conscience thought *That's a load of fake news*.

Ichiro spun around again, then wondered, *Who said that? Where did I learn that phrase about 'fake news'?*

Ichiro was becoming more aware of a change in his mind. Something was there now that was not there before that horrible night when his family was loaded in a truck. It almost seemed as if someone else was in his body — as if he, Ichiro, was listening to radio messages being played in his head that only he could hear. Maybe it was his conscience or maybe the result of that blow to the head from Sergeant Weston or maybe this place was just driving him crazy.

And it don't look like it will be a very long drive to Strait-jacket City, Cowboy.

Ichiro turned in a complete circle looking for the person that said that. There was no one there. *I am delusional*, Ichiro thought.

I'm not sure I know what that means, but you and I are OK, was the reply Ichiro heard in his head. *I can't explain this either, but I guess you and I are now partners. Two minds in one body. Hey, no wonder it is crowded in here. Can we order some pizza to be delivered?* Ichiro turned to run and collided with Sergeant Weston.

"Hey, lil' Jap! Hold up there! Where you goin' in such a hurry?" Weston was holding him by the shoulders but trying to see who or what the boy was running from. Ichiro winced from the tight grip Weston had. Weston was currently running down the growing rumors of gangs being formed to sabotage the camp. The camp's project manager, Elmer Shirrell, and California's Attorney General, Earl Warren, agreed that such gang violence needed to be dealt with firmly but with compassion and with an understanding of what internees were faced with. Sergeant Weston felt differently. *I could use those gangs for bayonet practice, and then we would not have to feed them.*

"Ah, I was running to get away from that robbery scene near our barracks. I am afraid."

Sergeant Weston showed disingenuous surprise. "Robbery? What robbery? Where?" He looked around feigning care.

"You know what I am talking about. Mr. Nobu Rie and his wife, Maiki, in Apartment B in Block 4, Barracks 4-5. They were stabbed and beaten last night."

"Oh, that! No, no. No one was killed. Just a little disagreement," deflected Weston. "You see everybody in that barracks was moved so we could treat the entire barracks." Weston looked around to make sure no one else could hear him when he lied, saying, "Keep this under your hat. They had a rat problem, and that was where the blood came from. So, we are bringing in an exterminator because we were worried about disease. After all, we are supposed to be protecting you," Weston said with a broad grin.

Ichiro said, "There is a rumor that someone broke into their place looking for hidden gold and that Rie-san had his head cut off."

"Of course not. I can't believe you would swallow that kind

of baloney," responded Weston with phony incredulity. "He's over in the hospital. Go see him."

Ichiro thought it best to change subjects. "I heard screams coming from that building over there, behind that fence. Is that a hospital?"

Weston slapped his sides and laughed. "Now that is funny! You're a good comedian, lil' Jap." His face turned from laughter to loathing in a split second. "My lil' Jap friend, that is the jail in the stockade for special prisoners. All we was doin' was asking a guy some questions and he broke my Louisville Slugger signed by Hank Kitchens. Yeah, he broke it right across both of his knees. When I get another bat, he's gonna show me how to break that bat across his hands."

A wide-eyed Ichiro could hear the Bobby-conscience say, *Wow, he is a really good liar! I'm surprised his nose didn't fall off.* Ichiro fought to control the budding smile that was replacing the shocked look on his face.

Weston caught the stymied smile and harshly asked, "Why are you smiling?"

"Oh, no. I'm just glad to hear that there was no murder." Ichiro looked around, mimicking Weston's previous looks, and said, "I'm glad you confided in me. I feel so much better, honorable sergeant-san."

Weston now had the weirdest expression of confusion. "Are you making fun of me, lil Jap?"

"Oh, no sir. I could never be so stupid to do such a dishonorable thing!" He bowed.

Ichiro heard the Bobby-conscience laughing and saying, *Wow, you got him with that one, and now he does not know how to respond. Great job, kid!* Weston just turned and walked away without any reply.

Ichiro knew a quiet spot where he would not be interrupted, but he carefully looked around for any company. Ichiro often came to this spot, most often alone. When the weather cooperated, he could sit and look at the beauty of 14,000 feet of Mount Shasta. *Yeah, if the weather cooperates, and most of the time it don't, Kemo Sabe,* came the other voice in his head. This camp or prison or whatever it was called was situated on a dry lakebed, drained in 1920 to create farmland. There was mostly sagebrush and sparse grass on the treeless, flat, sandy loam plain. Not much to look at. But Ichiro always found something. He absentmindedly turned over some of the tiny white shells of dead freshwater mollusks. He needed time to think and adjust to the realization that he was losing his mind. Satisfied that he was alone, Ichiro softly said with a lowered head, "Who are you? Where are you? Why are you here? What's happening?" He did not have to wait long.

That's a lot of questions, Kemo Sabe. First, my name is Bobby, and I think I am inside your head. I don't know how I got here and believe me, I would rather be at my house. Oh, and I have no idea why I am here or what is going on.

Ichiro mulled that over and then said, "I must be going crazy because I am now hearing voices in my head."

Have you ever heard a song that you just can't get out of your head? Well, I guess I'm kinda like that.

"I must have gotten a concussion when the soldiers threw us out of our house. Yes, that must be it."

Yeah, I know a thing or two about concussions myself. I got one when the old smokehouse blew up on the Simmons farm.

Ichiro quietly muttered, "That's why my head, I mean our head, hurts so much?"

The Bobby-conscience decided it was time to drop the big load on Ichiro. *There is a bit more to this, my new friend, and this will box you up and send you express mail to the looney bin. Like you, my home is in Tulelake, but my home is in 2017!*

Ichiro's feet collapsed under him, and he sat down hard on the dirt. The dust rose up to almost engulf him. He started to jump up and run, but where would he run to? Who would believe him? Who would help him? So, he just sat there in silence, drawing stuff in the dirt with a stick. He doodled for an hour before he ventured saying, "I think the stewed fruit and oats I had for breakfast must have been bad. Or maybe one of Sergeant Weston's rats bit me and I have plague or fever or fleas or something, and now I have become crazy."

I thought the same thing when I woke up, in your head, in 1942! I'm here. You're here. And it's 1942! Now what, Kemo Sabe?

"My name is Ichiro Hisakawa, not Kemo – whatever you said. What is your name?"

Just call me Bobby.

"OK, Bobby. What are we going to do?"

We don't tell nobody, that's for sure! They would lock us up on the funny farm and claim we are a few French fries short of a Happy Meal!

"Where?"

The funny farm, a psycho shack-o, the looney bin! Try this on for size, a hospital for the insane where your coat of arms ties in the back. Got it?

"Oh, okay, then what do we do?"

Then we just play it by ear, Picasso.

"The name is Ichiro, please. And we will do what?"

Play it by ear. You know, deal with things as they come up, adapt. I'd look it up on my cell phone for you, but I, er, we, don't have it.

"What is a cell phone?"

It is a telephone that doesn't need wires and you can carry it around in your pocket. Bobby realized this arrangement would be harder than he thought.

"Oh, Bobby? What is a Happy Meal?"

Yeah, this is gonna be a lot harder! So, Kemo Sabe, let me try to explain what a Happy Meal is. There's this big famous hamburger place in 2017 Tulelake called McDonald's off Highway 139 and . . . well, maybe we should go over all this stuff one step at a time.

They sat in silence for an hour. Just sitting. Lots of sun and wind, no chance of rain, and little shade. Masako came up behind Ichiro and said, "Ah, here you are, ani. What is my brother doing here?"

"Watching clouds and trying to think about our future."

"I will join you."

They sat for some time before Bobby's voice said, *Hey, that one looks like a bear, and that one over there looks like a train. I've never done this!* Ichiro did not respond because he wanted to let his mind rest, hoping the voice would disappear.

A dark shadow outside a nearby barrack hid ... watching

Ichiro talk to himself. "I might be able to use this kid as a diversion," a voice mumbled. "When the time comes."

Chapter 8
7:00 a.m., June 27, 1942
Tule Lake War Relocation Center, California

People learned to eat with a handkerchief over their faces and lift the kerchief when they took a bite. If the dust was blown around this early in the morning, there would be practically zero visibility by mid-afternoon. Freshly washed white shirts hanging on a clothesline to dry would be brown in less than an hour. The dust was in their clothes, hair, eyes, noses, mouths, and other more delicate places of the body. Etsuko spent many days just cleaning the barrack apartment only to turn around and start over and over. No clothes were too clean, and no crack was too small. Someone even found a lightbulb with dirt inside it. Ichiro retold a joke that Bobby had told him. "Well, in one way there is some good news about this wind. We can face the wind and smile. It will polish our teeth." No one ever laughed.

Bobby's voice said, *I can write 'em, but your delivery is horrible. Maybe this is the way Penn and Teller got started.*

Ichiro slowly shook his head at that comment. Masako and he had just eaten a breakfast of stewed prunes, cold cereal, pancakes, and dust. Well, Ichiro ate his cereal and Masako's while she ate his and her pancakes. She loved pancakes, and neither of them liked prunes. They often laughed about the after-effects. They were walking to the barracks converted to school classrooms for elementary and high school classes taught by Caucasian and Nisei, split about 50/50. Ichiro said, "80% of my teachers are 'Buddhaheads' and I could find something better to do than listen to them."

Masako stopped in her tracks and said, "I don't like that word and that's a terrible thing to say."

"Well, it's true. Why would a good teacher give up working elsewhere to work inside this prison? There are few books, fewer pencils, and no desks." Bobby's influence and thinking occasionally crept through in Ichiro's spoken word, all to the chagrin of the Japanese half of this new arrangement. "Somebody drew a red 'X' through Japan and Germany on the map on the wall of our classroom."

Bobby's voice added, *Yeah, they must be pretty bad and can't get a job anywhere else.*

Masako shook her head and said, "To the contrary, I think they are very dedicated to teaching and are doing so under a difficult situation. I may become a teacher when I grow up. Mrs. Waters said that more books and desks are being donated by local churches to help us out." She smiled and said, "Mrs. Hooper brings her chalk from home, and when she is finished with it, she puts it back in her purse. Every time she needs it, she has to go back to her purse."

They could both laugh over that, but their laughter was frozen by the sudden blast of air raid sirens. Soldiers were running up and down the alleyways between barracks looking for someone. And then Sergeant Weston strode up.

"Ah, my little Jap friends. Built any bombs today? Killed any Americans today?"

"We are Americans, too," Masako said with emphasis.

"Hey, I was born here," Sergeant Weston responded.

"So were our parents and so were we."

"No one cares, Jap."

The sirens were still sounding. Ichiro looked around at everyone running in every direction. No one seemed to know where they would be safe. "Well, is there a plan to protect everyone in case there is a real air raid?"

"Yeah. We will put you in clusters and have you hold up sheets that read, 'Drop bombs here.' Sounds good to me."

Corporal Williams ran to Sergeant Weston and announced, "The captain is coming this way! We should get these people out of here, so the captain doesn't have something to holler about."

Williams looked at Ichiro, and Bobby thought, *Did the corporal just wink at us, Kemo Sabe? We might be able to trust this guy.*

Ichiro blurted, "Sergeant, if you will tell me where these people need to go, I will move them in that direction."

Sergeant Weston just stared at Ichiro for a few moments and then asked, "Why would you help us? What are you after?"

Ichiro immediately responded, "Survival. I now realize we must accept our fate here and make the best of the situation. If I have questions, maybe you would let me ask you first." A dangerous step was just made, but it seemed to soften the sergeant. At least temporarily.

Nice job, but only if he buys it. Let's see how the big lug reacts, came a voice in Ichiro's head.

Weston thought about that for even longer. Williams softly said, "Sergeant. The captain is almost here."

"Corporal, are you still here? I thought you had orders to ship out?"

"Yes, Sergeant, I think I do. Not sure yet. I hope I am headed to the Pacific."

Weston paused and softly said, "I wish I were going too. You will have an opportunity to kill Japs. I have to stay here and babysit Japs. It's not right. It just ain't right."

"I'll bet they have bigger plans for you, Sergeant. You're too valuable to just be stuck here."

"Yeah, sure." Weston turned and stared a hole through Ichiro and snarled, "OK, Corporal. Get them to the mess hall. But remember one very important thing, Jap. Don't mess with me – ever." Weston moved within inches of Ichiro's face and hissed, "You won't like the results."

Ichiro did not ask for any clarification. He just took off and started telling people where to seek shelter.

Bobby's voice was laughing, and the sound reverberated through Ichiro's head. *Oh, that's all we need! First, it is imprisonment, and now intimidation! What's next? Executions? Hello? Is there a guillotine in the house?*

Ichiro softly said, "Will you just shut up?"

Weston spun around saying, "What did you say?"

"I said that I will shut up and get to work, Sergeant."

"And be sure to get the windows closed!" came the second order over his shoulder. Ichiro turned, nodded understanding to the sergeant, and took off.

Williams did not dare smile, but he did inwardly as he said, "Finally. Maybe we are getting some civility out of Sergeant Weston."

Bobby's voice in Ichiro's head said, *I ain't holding my breath for that to happen.*

Dinner that night was fresh fried fish, stewed corn, tsukemono, steamed rice, pickled fresh beets, spice tea, and butterscotch cookies. The camp was beginning to resemble a small town with a police department, fire department, and a quasi-government. The soldiers spent less and less time inside the wire and began to turn law enforcement over to the camp police led by Sergeant Weston and six section corporals, including Corporal Williams. A judicial tribunal handled misdemeanor offenses, but more serious criminal cases were handled by Tulelake courts.

Internees could work in or around the camp for 44 hours per week and earn a whopping $12 to $20 per month. There were jobs available in barrack construction, hospital construction, the hog farm, the chicken farm, warehousing, transportation, cooking, janitorial services, and garbage disposal. There were even doctors, pharmacists, dentists, orderlies, and nurses inside the wire. After some internees unsuccessfully tried to escape while unloading food and coal provisions from trains, Sergeant Weston brought in more soldiers to guard that particularly soft spot.

After each mess that night, a town hall meeting took place. The first speaker stood and tapped a glass to get everyone's attention. In a big, booming voice he announced, "My name is Jamison, and I am with the WRA."

Someone yelled, "What more can the War Relocation Authority do to us?"

Jamison ignored the taunt and continued, "I am here looking for recruits to work five days a week for $18 a month. You will also receive food and board, plus transportation to and from the job so you can get back here every other week."

A different voice from the middle of the room asked, "Why? What is this about?"

"That is a very fair question, sir. With me today are Mr. Dauer and Mr. Hubbard. They both farm in Malheur County, Oregon, about 200 miles from here. They have a problem, and the federal government thinks you can solve their problem. There is a labor shortage in Oregon and the sugar beet harvest is in jeopardy. We are here recruiting to solve that labor shortage." Jamison took a drink of water because he was thirsty, but also to allow people to mull this information over. He inquired, "What questions might you have?"

"How long would this be?"

"At least until mid-summer."

"Doing what?"

"The first recruits would be thinning the beet crop, but I believe this work could lead to harvesting onions, potatoes, haying, threshing grains, etc. Tractors will need to be driven and serviced. Oh, and irrigation work as well."

"Will there be guards?"

"Yes. They will watch you, but they will also be there to make sure any of the locals harboring anti-Japanese feelings do you no harm. I promise."

"To what end is all this?"

Jamison started walking up and down between the tables and made sure there were no guards in earshot. "You and I both know what was done was wrong. Yes, I said it and I may get in trouble, but it was still wrong. I hope this program can demonstrate to you that not every American thinks you are evil. I hope it can demonstrate to you that we can do something about this by working together. And, I hope this demonstrates to Americans that you have been, are, and will be productive Americans. So, what do you say?"

"Can we think about it?"

"Of course, and if I were in your position, I would do the very same thing. For those interested now, I can sign you up right now. But if you want to talk to your family and friends first, I will be at the Reception Office in the morning. Thank you for your time tonight." Jamison walked to the back of the room and set up a table to register people. A few slowly made their way to sign up.

The next speaker was an internee named Walter Tsukamoto, a prominent Nisei lawyer. In fact, he was appointed to the Judge Advocate General's Office of the United States Army in 1937. Yet here he was with his family, marooned like other Nisei and Issei. Tsukamoto was trying to encourage involvement in the community affairs inside the camp, but the younger Nisei were increasingly apathetic. Many were leaving the mess hall after listening to the first speaker.

Bobby said, *Come on, Kemo Sabe. Let's get out of here before this place becomes a boxing ring.*

Ichiro said louder than he intended, "No, let's stay and hear him. We might learn something."

Masako looked at her brother and asked, "What did you say?"

Saburo sternly silenced both of the children. "Shh! I want to hear this. You will hear more and learn more with your ears open and your mouths closed."

Bobby said in Ichiro's head, *Wow! That is exactly what my history teacher, Mrs. Carson, always said ... right after she grabbed and twisted my ear.*

Tsukamoto looked at what was left of the crowd before him and said, "Look at this! We are not here to talk about our daily bread, but to discuss the vital questions affecting the very life of the Nisei world. And only this many of you are interested. I sometimes wonder if the Nisei themselves desire to have their rights protected." More left as he spoke for a few more minutes, and he finally gave up for the day.

* * *

After curfew, the Hisakawa family gathered to discuss the day, especially the job offers made by Jamison. Saburo said, "But I am the head of this family, and that means this is my decision."

Masako countered, "Otōsan, in a traditional Japanese family the father works, and the mother tends the family and home. But we are Americans and should be open to new ways of living; even *Okāsan* works with you to take care of the chickens and eggs. Americans think for themselves, and I want to work and help."

Saburo sternly looked at his daughter, but inwardly he felt pride in her resilience in such a difficult situation and in her determination to contribute to the family's well-being. Finally, he said, "These are different times, and they call for different actions. However, I will only permit it after we discuss whatever job you consider. Agreed?"

"Thank you, Otōsan."

"I, too, will find work," Ichiro declared.

Saburo quickly said, "But not in the sugar beet fields. It sounds like a good job but if something went wrong here or there, we might never see you again. Please consider a job here in this community, Ichiro."

"Hai," Ichiro said with some hesitancy.

He heard Bobby's conscience whisper, *Yeah, well maybe. We'll see.*

Etsuko still maintained the quiet style of the Japanese women of generations before her. She never contradicted her *saiai no otto* (beloved husband) in front of others and especially not in front of the children. But she suddenly said, "I am glad Taro is not here to see this and live through this."

Silence. Masako softly said, "I wonder where he is and if he is well."

Silence. Saburo then said, "Your ani is now a man and will survive. We will see him again. Of that I am convinced."

Masako said, "I will get a job as a teacher's aide for little children." She realized she had spoken that instead of just thinking it. She looked at her father and pleaded, "Oh, with your permission, Otōsan."

His daughter was truly growing up. With a small smile, he said, "Hai." He looked at his younger son and knew something was changing within this young man. A sense of duty? A sense of responsibility? He turned slightly and watched Etsuko, who was also thinking that Ichiro was no longer a boy, but almost a man. Saburo announced, "Then we are done. We must sleep now."

Ichiro tossed and turned on his mat until he finally came to a decision. *I must find Corporal Williams in the morning,* he thought.

Bobby's voice added, *And you must be very careful when you find him.*

A voice came from outside. "Hisakawa-san. Are you there?"

"Who is that?" Saburo called.

"Haruki Sato. I must speak with you."

Saburo wrapped a kimono tightly around himself and stepped outside. "What is it? We were about to go to bed."

"Yuusei is dead!" was the whispered response.

Saburo gasped. "That cannot be! I saw him sitting at lunch. He only stared at me with a most somber expression, but he was alive!"

"Yuusei Kimura committed *harakiri*!" came another whisper.

"How is that possible? They would have confiscated his *tantō* blade when he was brought to this camp!"

"He used a kitchen knife he stole today. After he disemboweled himself, he stabbed himself in the throat! He bled all over his Death Poem!"

"Yuusei Kimura was of a samurai dynasty," Saburo said as he shook his head. "He must have felt he dishonored his ancestors."

"What do we do?" Sato asked.

"We must explain this to Captain Shackleford," Saburo said as he placed an arm on Haruki's shoulder. "Tell him everything! Explain it is in the best interest of everyone that we perform a traditional *otsuya* (a wake) and a *kasou* (a cremation) for Yuusei Kimura immediately." Sato bowed and scurried off.

But someone watched and listened from the shadows of the next barracks.

Chapter 9
7:00 a.m., July 1, 1942
Tule Lake War Relocation Center, California

The turmoil had receded some, but not the anger. Government officials forbid the cremation of Yuusei Kimura. They barely tolerated allowing the internees to gather for a wake. Kimura had no family to offer incense during the closely guarded and minimized the *ososhiki* (the funeral service) presided by a Buddhist priest who chanted sutras. Kimura's body was taken by soldiers to the hospital after the service and buried in the middle of the night in secrecy. "This is all new to us," Captain Shackleford told a small delegation in his office. "This is what my superiors will allow at this time. Good day, gentlemen," he added as he rushed them out the door.

He sat down hard in his chair, then glanced up at Private Lawson. "Now where the hell is that damn supply train?"

"We're on it right now, sir," Lawson said as he saluted and ran for the warehouse.

The supply train arrived eight hours late to be exact. It was due in at 7:00 pm the night before but did not roll into the camp until 3:00 am which meant it would not be unloaded until 6:00 am. The camp's food supply warehouses were never completely full and often threadbare. Each food supply train usually delivered enough rations for four days. These food supplies were in great demand to keep internees and soldiers alike fed. The daily demand for food rations was approaching five tons of rice, four tons of beef, three tons of chicken, one ton of sugar, 750 pounds of salt, 120 cases of eggs, 2,500 loaves of bread, and 2,500 gallons of milk.

Men had waited until 9:00 pm last night to unload, and since that was after curfew more guards were on duty to watch the internees milling around and waiting near the rail line. Breakfast would be late today for everyone, including children headed to school which would upset the whole camp's routine. Teams frantically attacked the boxcars like ants at a picnic to unload as quickly as possible. Each boxcar had ten men unloading and one man with a clipboard who watched and recorded the count. Then the boxcar counters met with the Camp Supply Manager to complete the entire inventory tally. The Supply Manager, an internee worker himself, totaled everything and shook his head, "It does not add up right."

"Add it up again."

"I have now added it up three times and it still isn't right."

"Again?"

"Yes, we are short on food rations again."

"Damn those suppliers! They are skimming stuff off our trains and selling it themselves on the black market."

"They don't care. We are just Japs to them, and they don't care if we live or starve."

"Oh, make no mistake. They would prefer we just die in here. Starved or executed makes no difference to them."

"All they are interested in is protecting their own families."

"Yeah, and the money they make on our food helps them too."

"Okay, enough. Let's see what we do have so we can get people fed something. What do we have and what are we missing?"

"Let's see. We have all four tons of beef, one ton of chicken, 250 pounds of salt, a half-ton of sugar, all 120 cases of eggs, 500 loaves of bread, and 2,400 gallons of milk. Oh, and three, no make that two, tons of rice."

The Supply Manager looked up and said, "This is strange. What is missing is more of an Asian diet than an American diet. We are missing chicken, rice, and salt. I will speak with the Camp Director, Mr. Shirrell."

Twenty internee men were crammed into a barrack apartment shortly after sunrise. They were dirty, sweaty, and exhausted, but cared less and less about tiredness as they passed around some jugs of homemade alcohol appropriately named 'Tule Lake Sake.' They were getting drunk or already were drunk.

"This is not good sake, but it is because it is here and it is what we have, but it is not very good, but it is here," rambled

Shige as he tried to stand. After several attempts, he gave up and fell asleep under the window.

Isi passed a jug to Yasuo and said, "I never thought we would have been able to do all that without the guards catching us."

"Hai. Isao-san and Kaede-san created a great plan."

Kaede said, "The plan was created by Juan Tu."

Yasuo said, "Building a doorway at the end of the car and trap doors in the bottom was worth the extra effort it cost us in the beginning. It has allowed our 'shopping' time to be shorter and safer. We just open the doors and then close them back when we are done for the next supply train."

Isi added, "The secret rooms we built under two barracks can hold even more supplies if we need them."

Naoko staggered to his feet and yelled, "It is not right! We just stole food from the mouths of our children and our parents! It is not right!" He swung a jug of the sake around as he pointed at people, spilling some. "You, you, and even you have children that will now be hungry!"

"Quiet, Naoko, you drunken fool!"

"Stop shouting."

Naoko would not be silenced. "Why are we doing this? This is exactly what the Americans want us to do – starve! Why do we do this?"

A man sat away from the rest of the group and deep in the morning shadows in a corner of the small apartment. He drank no sake, in fact, he almost appeared to be asleep since he had not moved or spoken since they had finished their work. His voice from those shadows now spoke, "Because we need something more valuable than food."

Naoko spun quickly to the sound and said, "What?"

The voice said, "We need weapons. We steal the food, sell it on the black market, and buy guns, rifles, ammunition, mortars, and knives so that one day we can leave this place. Is that understood?"

"Naoko was splashing sake again on people when he shouted, "And who are you to give me orders?"

After several moments, the voice from the morning shadows said, "I am Juan Tu."

Naoko started to back up to the nearest door to escape, but he fell over his own feet. He sat on the floor and only said, "Oh. I did not know who you were."

The feet disappeared into the shadow as Juan Tu stood up. He dusted himself off and stepped into the light so he could be seen. "Your name is Naoko, correct?"

"Yes, sir."

"Naoko, if you do not agree with my plan, you can join Mr. Rie or at least his head. It's buried under one of the barracks. You remember Mr. Rie, don't you? He objected to our midnight raids on the hospital and medical clinic for bandages, alcohol, and other supplies. Naoko, you are holding a jug of sake made from some of the alcohol we borrowed from the hospital. I'll bet Isao and Kaede can find a larger container for that sake and your head. Would you like for them to find one, Naoko?"

Naoko swallowed hard and bowed as he uttered, "Īe. Ah, no, sir."

Juan Tu strode to the center of the room and slowly turned to stare into the eyes of every man. "I am glad we had this little discussion so there can be no doubt as to our plans, our actions, and our resolve. The white dogs will pay for how they have humiliated us and locked us up like dangerous, wild animals."

The silence was broken by the loud snoring coming from beneath the window. Isao said, "Shige says he agrees. Loudly."

* * *

The camp was almost 5,000 acres, of which almost 4,000 acres were farmlands. That meant 15,000 to 20,000 people, plus soldiers, warehouses, a school, a hospital, train yards, a stockade, mess halls, laundries, latrines, offices, and a reception center were tightly packed into about 1,000 fenced acres, encircled by over 100 miles of barbed wire. The town of Tulelake, California, just seven miles away only had a population of 785 in 1940. The camp dwarfed the town and continued to grow. The Hisakawas had been in the camp for just over a month and still got lost when exploring. Ichiro found Corporal Williams getting coffee in the mess hall. Occasionally a guard would stop by for a cup, and casually listen to chatter for information. Williams did it so he could be accessible to people needing to talk. Today was different though. Williams distractedly said, "Now is not a good time, Ichiro. Trouble may be brewing. Big trouble."

"I need a small favor. It is important."

"OK, what?" said Williams, half-listening. His eyes darted around the room looking for the three people he was ordered to spot watch.

"Actually, I can help you with your problem if you help me with my problem. Please."

Williams' focus turned to the 16-year-old in front of him. *I'm not sure this kid has ever asked many people for help before. What is different now?* "Let's hear it."

Ichiro confided, "I think you are one of the few people I can trust. I guess it is really not a small favor, but a very large one." Ichiro fidgeted as he stood rubbing his hands and looking at his feet.

Bobby thought, *Geez, kid. You are more nervous than a pig at the bacon factory. Get a grip!*

Williams was losing interest quickly. "Please get on with it. I have a load on my plate today." He was now more interested in finding Kaede Matsumuro, Isao Hun, and Juan Tu.

"Sorry. I need your help with some deception. I need you to help me lie to my parents."

Williams's eyes immediately snapped to Ichiro and thought, *This kid is devoted to his family and would never disobey his father.* "So, what do you want and why do you want it?"

"My father has forbidden me from working in the sugar beet fields, but that is the only way I can earn money to help support my family," confessed Ichiro almost to the point of tears. "I have never disobeyed my father. Until now."

"I don't know what I can do. I am shipping out tomorrow night," said Williams.

Ichiro's shoulders sagged as if he had been carrying a heavy load all day. His eyes pleaded with the corporal without any words passing his lips.

After several tense moments, Corporal Williams capitulated. "OK, OK. I'll see what I can do. Maybe Private Lawson can help."

"Thank you. Thank you."

"Hey, no promises. I said I will see."

"Thank you," said Ichiro as Williams walked away.

Bobby's voice said, *Ichiro, I don't know what to say. I don't have the kind of relationship with my father as you do with yours, so I would not think twice about disobeying him. Now I understand why you are so upset.*

"You do not listen and obey your father, Bobby-san?"

Sure, I do. I listen, then he hits me, and I obey. Well, some of the time I obey. Okay, I rarely obey.

"Have you ever thought he has gone through some of the same situations as you have? Maybe his life path has been like yours. You could learn from both his successes and his failures, Bobby. Ask him."

Interesting idea, but I'm not sure I will ever get that chance. Remember, Kemo Sabe, as of this moment, he ain't yet been born! And I don't think I'm ever going home again!

The next morning Ichiro and Masako had breakfast and were headed to class. The school was attached to the canteen in part of a barrack. The Bobby voice laughed and said, *Some canteen. They don't serve any alcohol, it's only open on Fridays, Saturdays, and Sundays, and it closes on those nights at 10. Big deal. Hey, is that Private Lawson up ahead?*

Ichiro stopped and turned to Masako. "I must speak with that soldier. You go ahead and I will see you at lunchtime."

Masako said, "Oh? Private Lawson? I like him; he treats us

with more respect than most of the other soldiers. Corporal Williams does too. I'll wait for you."

"No. You go ahead," Ichiro said more firmly than he intended.

Bobby's voice in Ichiro's head said, *Yeah, she cannot know what you are planning. She will blab to your folks.*

Ichiro walked up to Private Lawson and nervously looked around to see if anyone might hear their conversation. "Sir, may I please speak with you for a few minutes?"

Lawson's face had a sour look, and he seemed to be grinding his teeth. After a few moments, he said, "Huh? What? I'm sorry, my mind was somewhere else. What did you say?"

"I asked if I might speak with you, please?"

"Not right now. Sergeant Weston just ate my as. . . ah, chewed me up and down, and I'm still looking for bandages. Later?"

Ichiro shook his head, "Thank you. I look forward to it." He looked around and did not see Weston. "Is the sergeant here?"

"Oh, no. He read me the riot act an hour ago and it still hurts. I swear that man is not right in the head."

"He does not like me, I am sure," Ichiro shared.

"As my old granddaddy in East Texas would say, 'His cornbread ain't completely done in the middle.'" He quickly looked at Ichiro and said, "I shouldn't say that. He is my immediate superior and what I just said was disrespectful."

Bobby's voice offered, *You could have just said he is a well-rounded individual. He is a perfect asshole!*

Now both Ichiro and Private Lawson were embarrassed. Ichiro could not help but laugh at Bobby's comment. He slightly smiled, which was then replaced by a cough to hide a soft laugh. Private Lawson did not know why Ichiro was laughing but soon joined him. "I am Private John Lawson," he said as he extended a hand.

"I am Ichiro Hisakawa. Where's your home?"

"A small cattle ranch on the Double Mountain Fork of the Brazos River in Yellow House Canyon, east of Lubbock, Texas. And you?"

I'll bet you he couldn't say that again if he had to!

"I was born in Tulelake, but now I guess I may live and die right here."

"Things will change. You wait and see."

Chapter 10
2:15 p.m., March 11, 1943
Tule Lake War Relocation Center, California

Things did change … but not for the better.

Tensions were already high, but then the pressure shot straight through the roof in February. The U.S. War Department, in conjunction with the War Relocation Authority, created a 'Loyalty Questionnaire' for primarily two reasons. Question 27 was, "Are you willing to serve in the Armed Forces of the United States on combat duty, wherever ordered?" Many in the camp read that question to mean 'fight against Japan,' and quickly answered "NO."

Question 28 was not much better. It asked, "Will you swear unqualified allegiance to the United States of America and faithfully defend the United States from any and all attack by foreign or domestic forces, and forswear any form of allegiance to the Japanese Emperor or any other foreign government, power, or organization?" Many in the camp read that as an insult. The internees never had a voice in their treatment, never had compensation for their lost homes and businesses, nor had they the freedom to leave their prison. Many answered "NO." Another question even asked if the internees wished to renounce their American citizenship and return to Japan. Many of the 5,589 that answered "YES" were later found to have been pressured to answer that way by pro-Japan factions in the camp, like the *Loyalists*. That number made the *Sokuji Kikoku Hoshi Dan*, a pro-Japan society within the camp, very happy. Their name translated meant "Organization to Return Immediately to the Homeland to Serve." No one was returned to Japan during the war and not all of those that finally departed the U.S. after the war were accepted in Japan. Still, only 42 percent of the camp population answered "NO" to both Question 27 and Question 28. Most of the young men in Barrack 42 answered "NO" to both questions and so were labeled dissidents, and were jailed pending shipment to other, more punitive and heavily guarded, camps.

Thefts of food or anything that could be bartered happened almost daily from incoming freight trains or from the warehouses. That was a given of daily life. But now, riots of epidemic proportions were breaking out, some internees were shot by the guards, and many were arrested and thrown into the crowded stockade. People complained that the U.S. government asked them to fight for the very rights others enjoyed, but which were denied to the internees. The questionnaire set off a firestorm that could not be contained. Any Japanese Americans who cooperated, actively or even passively, with camp management, the WRA, or the FBI were dragged out onto the dirt streets and were beaten by the *Loyalists*, who marched down the streets shouting slogans, banging drums, and threatening anyone and everyone, and occasionally breaking into barrack apartments. Military Police responded aggressively to these demonstrations and cracked down by a daily show of force with increased foot and jeep patrols down the dirt streets, and with a more active presence in mess halls, canteens, laundries, and even latrines. One hundred men were rounded up and thrown into the quickly-built jails in the deserted CCC Camp next door.

One day, Saburo was forced from the apartment and into the street. But before he was beaten, Ichiro, Gordon, and Ken were beside him. Ichiro stood tall and yelled, "Which of you cowards would rather fight someone more your age than this old man? Come and face me."

A laugh came from the middle of the crowd, and Isao Hun stepped up. "He is just a little fish that we can cook for our dinner!"

"Oh? You are not able to land this little fish by yourself? You need all these men to help you? I think it is because you are a coward." Ichiro kept his arms at his side, his feet at shoulder width in a karate stance his father and older brother called a modified hachiji-dachi. The stance showed no aggression but awaited an attack with a defensive position of power. The goading had worked. Isao Hun laughed nervously, but he felt humiliated by this kid, and let his anger control his actions. He charged Ichiro.

Nail him, Kemo Sabe!

Ichiro hit Isao so hard and so fast that some people standing there missed the movement completely. Gordon's chin almost fell off and Ken's eyes bugged out. They had no idea their friend knew karate, nor had they seen anyone move that fast ever. That is until someone from the left side charged and Saburo entered the fray. Saburo yelled, "Ah-yee!" and leaped into the air, performing a double aerial kick called a Wushu Butterfly. The assailant went down in a heap, unconscious before landing face down in the dirt.

Isao hasn't fallen yet. What is keeping him up?

Isao Hun seemed asleep on his feet, simply frozen to the ground with his eyes wide open. Finally, gravity took over and he fell backward with a big thud.

Timber! yelled the Bobby-voice.

Ichiro formally bowed to his father and remarked, "Otōsan, I believe you never instructed me on that move."

Saburo returned the bow with a sly smile. "Old man? You called me an 'old man?'"

"Sorry, I apologize, Otōsan."

"And I apologize for never completing your training, including manners." His smile faded as he turned and looked at the small mob around them that was getting smaller by the moment. "Ah, we are rude to our guests. Perhaps someone else would like to play?"

Corporal Williams stood behind them with a rifle and said, "I think you should break this up before Mr. Hisakawa breaks you up." The remaining crowd departed quickly as Williams added, "Say, don't forget these two punching bags on the ground here. Take them with you – they may need to visit the hospital."

Gordon and Ken ran up to Saburo and began pestering him with questions.

"How did you do that? Did you see how fast Ichiro was?'

"I didn't know you knew how to fight!"

Bobby's voice said, *Neither did I, come to think of it.*

"Mr. Hisakawa, I've never seen anyone leap that high before! Can you teach me to fight like that?"

"He taught both my brother, Taro, and me to defend ourselves."

Saburo finished the thought, "But not be the aggressor. The Christians say 'turn the other cheek,' but you do that only once, then put the aggressor down so he cannot rise again to harm you."

Corporal Williams strolled up and said, "Mr. Hisakawa, I promise never to make you mad." He winked, smiled, and walked away. He turned by the next barracks and found Sergeant Weston leaning against the wall, waiting for him.

"Why didn't you stop that fight?"

"It started before I got there, Sergeant, but I broke it up after I arrived. I was just now going to the MP Office to write up the incident while it is still fresh in my mind. I know you want me to be accurate on such things." A little sarcasm ended the sentence, but Williams' face betrayed nothing.

"Yeah, you do that." Weston stared at Williams for some time. "The fuse has been lit on this keg of dynamite, and there is no doubt it will explode. The first question is 'when,' not 'if.' And the second question will be if you survive, corporal."

"Or you, my sergeant."

"There will be internees and soldiers injured or killed. There ain't no getting around that." *And maybe some outsiders will take a seat at this card table,* as Weston believed would happen.

"I will follow my orders as you give them."

Weston turned as he walked away and said, "Make sure you do, or I can guarantee results you will not like."

Williams watched Weston walk away and softly said, "I wonder who has his back? Somebody else is involved. Who?"

* * *

By mid-May some of the tension had eased, but not completely. Though Saburo still had his 'day job' herding chickens, he offered karate classes three evenings a week in an exemplary example of internees' attempts to reach new levels of mind-calming normalcy in an ocean of insanity.

Karate became a way for some internees to protect themselves and their families, so several karate schools opened. The growing number of camp internees meant a growing need for medical professionals. Pharmacists, dentists, doctors, nurses, and orderlies found work in the hospital that offered limited but expanding services. Four hundred men worked in camp maintenance collecting garbage, delivering coal needed for boilers and stoves, and offering janitorial services in the mess halls, laundries, and latrines. Eight hundred workers met transportation and warehouse needs. Three hundred and fifty people worked in the mess halls so everyone could have three meals a day. Captain Shackleford ordered Sergeant Weston to hire internees as patrol police and as firemen. More internal camp security was being turned over to a civil internee police force so external security could be dealt with by Army personnel. This also allowed the Army to slowly rotate soldiers out of the camps and onto the war fronts in Europe and the Pacific without coming under scrutiny from inside or outside the camp. These rotations were designed to prevent soldiers from becoming overly sympathetic to, or overly friendly with, the inmates they were guarding.

Barber shops and funeral homes opened. Garden clubs worked feverishly to turn the hard, rocky, dry soil into stretches of green with flowers and grass. Their successes led to the growth of flower shops. Ken worked as a reporter for the *Daily Tulean Update*, the camp newspaper. The newspaper articles were written by the staff in English because FBI and WRA agents in the camp offices censored everything, including mail. Once the censors released the approved copy, Ken and Gordon cranked out the copies on a mimeograph machine by hand. Ken spent much of his time on music and education since these were two important subjects to Masako Hisakawa, and she was now the focus of his interest. Masako did get a volunteer job as a teacher's aide for small children, and Ken would often bring her old, discarded copies of the paper so Masako and he could help the children make hats to shield them from the sun.

The junior and senior high school was between Central and Main Streets to the east and west, and 5th and 6th Streets to the north and south. Empty barracks in Block 6 across 5th Street from the school were used for elementary grades. Children sat in learning circles by grade on the floor. No desks, chairs, and too few books were available. Masako taught first graders with pictures of birds, trees, animals, people, and anything that would help children learn numbers, colors, and animals. The pictures were drawn by other camp internees since teaching materials were not always at hand. Mrs. Takahashi told Etsuko one evening in the mess hall that Masako was well on her way to becoming an exceptional teacher. "When this war is over and we all return to a new normal, I will do whatever I can to help Masako get into a college where she can continue to grow her education skills. You are raising an extraordinary young woman and a future teaching star."

Many internees tried to move forward finding meaning and growth in their lives and their relationships, but there were those young men, absorbed in self-pity, had all the time in the world yet found nothing to do and accomplished less. The already existing pre-war racist wounds now festered in self-exile and misery. Discontent grew into riots and the Army continued to clamp down.

Ichiro sat on the steps of an empty barrack in Block 3. He watched tall, rolling clouds turn from white to red and gold and the sky turn from blue to yellow. A stick in his hand absentmindedly drew shapes in the dirt that mimicked the clouds he saw.

Talk to me, Kemo Sabe. Something is eating you from the inside out.

'I must find a way to help provide for my family. Masako is doing something worthwhile, but there is nothing in this camp that offers me what I need, what I want."

And what do you want?

"That's the problem. I don't know! I want to help. I want to make things a little easier on my parents, but I don't know how."

Maybe it's time now for that conversation with Corporal Williams about sugar beets.

Chapter 11
11:15 a.m., April 19, 1943
Terrace Hotel, San Francisco

"**W**hat do you mean 'things have gotten worse'? That is not possible! They have already been deplorable and now you say they are worse? What do these people want?" Thomas Hennessey screamed into a telephone. He slammed the phone down and turned. "Will someone please explain to me why this is happening?"

"Boy, they sure ask for a lot, don't they? They probably want their freedom and their lives and businesses back. Something like that." Carter DuBois said to no one in particular. DuBois was another of the Assistant Under-Secretaries to the Director of the War Relocation Authority, Dillon Myer. DuBois poured himself another cup of coffee and picked over the remaining Danish on a tray. He looked up at the picture on the wall of Milton Eisenhower, the original director of the WRA and brother of General Dwight Eisenhower, Supreme Commander of Allied Expeditionary Force, North African Theater of Operations. He pointed at the picture and said, "Eisenhower never did like this idea of internment. He had an idea to relocate them as family units to areas needing help with farming and its support industries. He said that after the war, this would come back and haunt every politician. But governors fought him at that meeting … where was it?"

"It was in Salt Lake City – ah, last year."

"Yes, that's right. The governors of those states were afraid of the security risks to the general public."

"They were more afraid of losing votes than of losing crops."

"Maybe. Eisenhower only lasted 90 days in that job, and the pushback on his ideas was rough. Can you imagine how frustrated he was?"

Hennessey flatly commented, "He may have gotten off light." He mopped his neck and forehead several times with a handkerchief he then stuffed into his back pocket. "I'm telling you this whole thing is a cluster ..."

"Ah, what did you learn on the phone?" Allan Odom said, as he intentionally interrupted.

"John Embree, the head of the CAS unit, is quoted as saying, 'The camp's self-government is similar to a student government at a high school. It is pseudo-democratic, but all of the important decisions are made by the administration.' Well, that is pretty clear, don't you think?"

"About as clear as a bucket of mud."

"The Community Analysis Section was some pencil-pusher's idea. The CAS was supposed to gather data on internees so better management practices could be put in place. Social scientists were supposed to study how the forced communities responded and developed, how education continued, and how the internees adjusted to their new lives."

DuBois' grip tightened around his cup as he tensely added, "Yes, that is so important. We must find better ways to build better prisons. Maybe we should have them wear striped suits like prisoners on chain gangs."

"We don't need your sarcasm, DuBois. It's getting out of hand."

DuBois threw his cup at the nearest wall. "It already is out of hand! It should never have happened in the first place. Then we would not need to 'fix it' in the second place!" They stared at each other until DuBois walked over and slowly picked up the pieces of the cup. His shoulders sagged and he put his hand on Hennessey's shoulder. "Sorry, Thomas. This has been hard on all of us. Sorry."

Allan Odom was one of those guys who was always tampering with his pipe. After packing the pipe for the third time in 45 minutes, he said, "Some of those CAS science do-gooders just look at these internees as guinea pigs or lab rats. Just numbers. Others have been fighting this whole thing since the beginning, and their reports reflect that."

"Some challenged the incarceration process in their reports, but censors and lawyers redacted a number of their statements."

"Yes, and some of those reports read like the internees are at some kind of resort playing shuffleboard, golf, and sunbathing by swimming pools."

DuBois asked, "They have swimming pools in those camps?"

"If it rains."

Odom continued. "The WRA decided to 'Americanize' the

internees. American-style food rations, music, culture, education, newspapers, literature, movies, etcetera.”

“Don’t forget baseball.”

“Yes, and they’re even encouraging the young men to enlist in the U.S. Army. Myer and others believe the internees need to re-accept the American customs and culture, as most of them were already doing before their incarceration. The ‘problem’ internees are treated as troublemakers, and many have been jailed.”

DuBois said, “We’ve locked up people in a jail that was already inside a prison. No wonder they’re objecting to that kind of treatment.”

“The ‘good’ prisoners are recognized, rewarded, and asked to encourage others to get in line. It’s not working out as we hoped.”

“Those who are patted on the back and rewarded as model internees might then be beaten, stabbed, or robbed by other internees. Those who are ‘bad’ prisoners are isolated and rebuked, even if they are not jailed. Tensions continue to grow because of the deplorable housing, the low wages for the poor or non-existent work opportunities, the inactivity, the harassment by guards, and because of the rumors – the constant rumors that fuel uncertainty and feed people’s fear and anxiety.”

“Yeah, and education is shameful – if it even exists. There’s a lack of books, teachers, and proper facilities. Teachers are being assaulted and robbed, as though they have more than anyone else. It’s terrible conditions for both the students and the teachers.”

“And then came the Leave Clearance Registration process.”

"Internees called it the 'Loyalty Questionnaire.' What a screwed-up mess that was."

Hennessey laughed, then realized it was not appropriate. "Do you know that was supposed to be a recruiting tool for the War Department, to screen young men for the Army? It only took 28 questions to destroy a fragile relationship with so many of our citizens. They felt less like Americans and more like ... well, I don't know what. Many of them had not been born in Japan – had never even been to Japan!"

Odom remarked, "You called them citizens. I don't know when the last time was that I heard them called citizens."

DuBois added, "So many were upset about being asked to fight for a country that had locked up their families and them."

"What kind of reaction would the Nazis get if they asked the Jews not murdered yet and still locked up in those concentration camps to defend Germany?

"If it were you, how would you react?"

"We screwed up. We did not take into consideration how being locked up for a year would affect their thinking and how they would feel about their country. Then we dumped the questionnaire on them. We poured gasoline onto a grease fire."

"So, what do we do?"

"President Roosevelt wants a plan from us on resettlement."

"Another one?"

"The President says the Japanese Americans will be returned to their homes and businesses on the West Coast as soon as problems in the Pacific are reduced."

"Wonderful, just like it never happened."

Hennessey mopped his head again. "We are supposed to

work with the Office of War Information and come up with ideas for propaganda."

"Like?"

"Newspaper and magazine articles, radio shows and announcements, pictures, pamphlets, and even one-reel films shown before feature films."

DuBois asked, "And who are we trying to sell?"

Hennessey responded, "White America. Who do you think?"

Dan Milburn, an aide to Hennessey, said, "The Office of War Information is already working on some pamphlets like 'Myths and Facts about Japanese Americans.' Even the former U.S. Ambassador to Japan will be making tours on the West Coast and will be speaking on the subject."

Dubois suggested, "We may need some kind of pamphlet or presentation for schools, libraries, churches, and post offices. Maybe even a flyer that postal carriers could stuff in mailboxes."

"I know this may sound dumb, but what about Bugs Bunny, Daffy Duck, Mickey Mouse, Tom and Jerry, and Popeye? Maybe their cartoons can help," suggested Milburn. He wanted to add, *But I doubt it*. He thought better of it and kept his mouth shut.

Odom was at it again with his pipe. "We better be working on something to sell the internees on the idea of going home, if they still have one."

Hennessey added, "Right now many of the internees that answered 'NO' on the questionnaire are being locked up for re-indoctrination and re-education, and when finally deemed safe to re-enter society, they will be released. But they will have to attend required training on 'How to Make Friends with White Americans.'"

DuBois squeezed his eyes closed and rubbed his forehead. "Oh, brother, will there be one called 'How to Play Nice with the People that Locked You Up,' or 'How to Avoid Being Shot or Lynched'?"

"The problem is not just the Japanese Americans. It is the White Americans as well," said Odom.

"No, the problem is all Americans," said Hennessey. "White, Oriental, Latin, European – all Americans. This is not going to be easy, and it is not going to be quick."

DuBois said, "The children's game says, 'Olly olly oxen free,' but it won't be that easy. This may not resolve itself for years, if ever."

They all jumped when the phone rang. Hennessey started to pick up the receiver but hesitated long enough that the phone rang again. He flexed his hands, picked up the receiver, and announced, "Hennessey here." He listened for a few minutes without responding but pulled up a chair and heavily sat down. He started rubbing his forehead as if that would make the building headache disappear.

DuBois noticed Hennessey squeezing his wide-open eyes closed. "This is not good," he whispered to Odom.

After a few more minutes, Hennessey asked, "And how was it resolved?" His eyes went wide again, and he looked at the men in the room.

Odom commented, "Something has happened, and I fear it is serious."

"Casualties?" asked Hennessey with apprehension. He pursed his dry lips. "Thank you. No, I will call back after we discuss this further. Thank you." He slowly hung up the phone and said, "There has been a riot at the Tule Lake Relocation Center."

Milburn asked, "How bad?"

DuBois looked at Milburn and asked, "Is there such a thing as a good riot?"

"Knock it off," ordered Hennessey. Let's discuss this objectively and look for solutions."

"OK, what happened?"

Hennessey had not written anything down, so he was working to recall the events as described to him. "Let me back up and refresh all our minds. Tule Lake appears to be divided into two groups or mindsets. One group seems to have accepted their situation and tried to make the best of it."

"Despite what we did to them?"

"Yes, despite that. They were and are loyal Americans, patriotic Americans. There are Boy Scouts and American Legion veterans in those camps who encourage others to join them for the Pledge of Allegiance to the American flag when it is raised every morning. That group works hard, and they maintain healthy leisure and social activities. There is a Japanese phrase heard often in their circles – 'Shikata ga nai,' which means 'It cannot be helped.' Now many in this group are older or were already heavily vested in the American society and believe if they keep their heads down and their mouths shut, the situation might resolve itself. They are in denial."

Odom asked, "And the other group?"

"They are fuming. They resent what was done to them and how it was done. They sit, void of communication, and rail against anything and everything the government does, including the good things being attempted to alleviate some of their resentment. They feel the country has turned a cold shoulder to them, so they carry a big grudge against the soldiers, and even against the other internees who have accepted their fate. They are mostly younger men who don't work, refuse to work, or say they cannot find work. Vandalism started almost the first day some were incarcerated. Rocks through windows, disrupting laundry rooms and latrines, destroying plumbing, and food fights in the mess halls."

DuBois said, "Yes, and now that we are all on the same page, what has happened?"

Hennessey announced, "A riot."

Milburn gasped. "What? How? Who?"

"That questionnaire started a slow-burning fuse on a powder keg that finally exploded when some young men with nothing better to do started a fight with soldiers who were asking questions of young Nisei ladies."

DuBois asked, "Then what happened?"

Hennessey continued, "A lot of yelling mostly. One soldier was hit on the side of the head by a bottle of homemade sake. One Nisei man was shot in the arm, but that may have happened accidentally during the shoving and crowding around the outnumbered soldiers. The Army shut down everything and ordered a temporary but complete curfew for 48 hours. A homemade Japanese flag appeared out of nowhere, and was paraded through a small section of the camp, but then quickly disappeared. Soldiers were on full alert and conducted drills up and down the streets in the camp as a demonstration of force."

Odom exclaimed, "We cannot seem to do anything right!"

"It gets worse. Newspapers up and down the West Coast have blown this completely out of context. Some suggest that internees escaped and raped and murdered people on nearby farms. Some reported that internees escaped and burned a school bus full of children just outside Tulelake. Some reported half of the camp was burned to the ground and dozens of soldiers were murdered in their sleep. Some are calling for our boss to be fired, and I guess that also means us. And now Tokyo Rose is radio broadcasting support for the rioters at Tule Lake!"

Milburn asked, "So, what do we do? How do we deal with this?"

Hennessey announced, "Dillon Myer is on his way to meet with us right now, and I want us to have three good plans developed before he gets here. I'll get some sandwiches and coffee coming, so loosen your ties and open your minds, gentlemen. We have a lot of work to do in very little time."

Chapter 12
9:45 p.m., July 4, 1943
Tule Lake Segregation Center

July 4th, Independence Day, meant nothing to those inside the steel fencing and barbed wire. Captain Shackleford was conducting a staff meeting on some new developments and said, "Make sure there is no one outside that door and then close it." Williams did as he was ordered and sensed the other boot was about to fall. Shackleford continued, "Gentlemen, things are about to get dicey. Tule Lake is now designated as Tule Lake Segregation Center."

"We are now jailers in a concentration camp?"

"We will not use that word, and the next time I hear it, somebody will be on report and 48-hour guard duty. Is that understood?"

After silence indicated he had driven his point, Shackleford continued again. "This will become operational in two weeks. Fences will be doubled and made eight feet high. There will be more barbed wire, more searchlights, and more guard towers."

"Sir? May I ask why?"

"Two reasons were given me when I asked that same question, soldier. First, we have the room and the ability to increase our capacity. Second, there were more 'NO, NO' answers to the infamous questionnaire in this camp than anywhere else. Gentlemen, we will have many new guests joining us, all of the 'NO, NO' internees."

"This will turn the camp into a maximum-security prison!"

"Yes, it will. The WRA is going to put all of its rotten eggs in one basket. Here. And we will guard it. Two-thirds of our guests will be 'NO, NO' internees. So, the double fence will be escape-proof. Searchlights will be working all night on irregular schedules to prevent patterns. Later this year we will be joined by an entire battalion of MPs. We may even get more armored vehicles. But we must remember that the other one-third of detainees are hard-working, patriotic American citizens that unfortunately are here because of the way they look, not because of anything they have done or said."

"1,000 more men? Isn't that overkill, sir?"

A snicker came from the back of the room. Sergeant Weston said, "'Overkill?' How about just 'kill'?"

Private Escobar ignored Weston and asked, "Sir, why don't they just lock them up on Alcatraz?"

"I asked about that too, Escobar, and I got no answer." After considerable mumbling and side conversations, Shackleford said, "And we are getting a new boss." He pulled a piece of paper from his pocket and read, "Yes, Mr. Raymond Best will be the new Project Manager."

"He will be the third manager in two years."

"Well, my information says he has considerable experience with maximum security centers and jails, and he does not negotiate with prisoners. So, we will afford him all due respect and cooperation."

"Sir, I mean no disrespect, but ..."

"Go ahead. Spit it out."

"Sir, I joined the Army to fight for my country, not work as a jail cell guard. I respectfully request a transfer out of this birdcage."

"See my clerk when we are done. Anyone else want out?"

Two hands went up. "Yes, sir." "Me, too, sir."

"And you, Sergeant Weston?"

"Not on your life. I'm looking forward to a turkey shoot sometime in the future."

After listening to more rumbling and some grumbling, Shackleford had heard enough. He stood up and said, "Dismissed!"

It was hot and windy, and the air was depressing – heavy like everyone's mood. Bobby's voice said, *Well, I see the July weather here in 1943 is about the same as the July weather 70 years from now. You have to chew the air before you try to breathe it. Kemo Sabe, I bet we could spit chalk sticks! Wanna try?*

Ichiro was not paying attention. The Hisakawa family always gathered with other Japanese Americans around Tulelake to celebrate American Independence Day and honor the country that allowed them to be free. Saburo had often reminded the family that the racism they saw, heard, and dealt with in California was nothing compared to the racism in Japan. Chinese, Koreans, Thais, and others were considered lowly. The struggle between warlords, fiefdoms, and ranks of social classes made up of craftsmen, merchants, peasants, and warriors was constant in Japan. Saburo said, "This is the United States of America, and that cannot and will not happen here." He said that every July 4th, until last year.

Ichiro pounded a fist into the dirt. "This is terrible! We did nothing wrong, nothing to deserve this imprisonment and shame!"

Saburo placed his hand on his son's shoulder and said, "'Keizoku wa chikara nari,' and you know that means, 'Don't give up. Perseverance is power."

Yeah, well if perseverance is power, then we should be able to jump over the fence and run, cuz we have put up with a wagonload of horse crap!

"I am sorry, Otōsan. But I feel hopeless. Thoughts sometimes fill my mind with stupid ideas."

Uh-oh. I know who that was meant for. OK, I will shut up ... for a while.

"We must believe that things will improve, *Musukosan*. We must not give up hope, my son."

The tension had been palpable last year on Independence Day. Most of the internees had stayed indoors all day, many not even going to the mess hall for meals. Captain Andrews had ordered the guards to avoid almost any contact with internees to avert any potential conflict. Most of the guards resented this state-side assignment and felt they were told to hide from the very people they were guarding. They were in the Army to fight, not to babysit or coddle anyone.

That meant the guards looked for any chance to celebrate something, get drunk, and shoot off some fireworks. Last year, the guards on duty were disciplined for 'accidentally' firing rockets at the internees after two rockets blazed through a barrack's window and started fires. This year, the off-duty guards drove into Tulelake to get drunk and watch the fireworks, while those on duty just watched and listened to the fireworks from their duty posts ten miles from Tulelake. Not much of a view unless you were on duty in one of the 39 guard towers, 28 guarding the main camp and 11 surrounding the farms. The towers were 32 feet tall with a spotlight on top. Camp spotlight sweeps were kept irregular to prevent patterns. A trap door was latched from the inside of the tower to repel unexpected and unwanted intrusion.

But those on duty had new responsibilities now, to watch for and to log the location, date, and activities of three specific Japanese Americans named Juan Tu, Isao Hun, and Kaede Matsumuro. Their pictures were now posted in every guard tower along with an activity log for each. The three logs were collected from each guard tower when duty shifts changed. FBI agents, Captain Andrews, and Captain Shackleford then poured over the activity logs, searching for something they did not know they were looking for ... a commonality, a pattern, a plot. They knew something was going to happen, but they did not know what or when. But they knew the ringleader and his lieutenants were – Juan Tu and his stooges Isao Hun and Kaede Matsumuro.

They called themselves *Watashitachiha Chusetsudesu*, which in Japanese meant *We Are Loyal*. The soldiers just called them the *Loyalists*. The group shaved their heads, made shirts with a Japanese red sun on the back, wore white headbands with a red sun, and paraded around the camp. As head of the camp police, Sergeant Weston met with Captain Andrews earlier in the day to talk about the growing Loyalist group, which now made itself more visible in the camp of 12,000. "I think there are about five hundred of them," Sergeant Weston firmly stated.

"Their number is more like two hundred, but it is still a problem and getting worse by the day. What are your thoughts?" asked Captain Andrews. He wanted to hear the sergeant before he explained his own plan. The captain regretted asking as soon as Weston opened his mouth.

Sergeant Weston took the opportunity to take control of the conversation, or at least that's what he thought. Putting on his most serious face, he started counting the steps to his plan on his fingers. "First, I would double the number of internal police. Second, I would equip those men with gas grenades, submachine guns, and shotguns. Third, I would change the curfew from 10:00 p.m. to 7:00 p.m., before it gets dark. Fourth, I would have jeep patrols roaming the streets between barracks. Fifth, anyone caught outside after curfew would be shot on sight and the body left where it dropped. Sixth, any demonstrations or marches would be crushed. Seventh, barracks would be randomly inspected without notice to search for contraband. Eighth, any such troublemakers would be rounded up and isolated away from the other camp prisoners in the stockade, or maybe in the planned POW camp that will be built next door. Ninth, I would randomly reassign families to other barracks at unexpected times. That's how I would start, sir," Weston stated with an ominous, evil smirk.

It was obvious to Captain Andrews that Weston had been harboring considerable resentment and was intent on inflicting as much cruel punishment as he could get away with. After a few moments of stunned silence, he said, "That would not be much different than the conditions in the Italian and German POW camp next door, Sergeant. Do you really think these internees are as dangerous?"

"Absolutely, sir."

"Sergeant, I thank you for your insight and suggestions. I will let you know of my decision. Dismissed." *He is nuttier than Aunt Mabel's fruitcake and more dangerous than Uncle Buford's hair-trigger shotgun.*

Weston smiled and saluted. "Thank you, sir!" As he turned and left, he said to himself, *Oh, gee! I forgot to tell him Number Ten – how I'm going to start a riot.* The smile faded from his face when he thought about the leader of the *Loyalists*, Juan Tu.

Juan's mother, Tu Feng, a mild-mannered cook in a Japanese Chinese restaurant in Medford, Oregon, was half Chinese and half Japanese. Juan's father, Juan Carlos, was a bricklayer who snuck into the United States from Mexico. Juan Carlos was half Spanish, half Mexican Apache, and one hundred percent pissed off all the time. He easily carried a load of bricks on one shoulder and a big chip against everything and everybody on the other shoulder. Somehow, the incongruent couple met, married, and had a baby. Juan thought it would be memorable, or funny, to give the son his first name and his wife's first name, so Juan Tu was the name stuck on the kid. The father was killed in a drunken brawl in a Medford bar just a few months before Tu Feng and her son, now twenty-five years old, were rounded up and sent to the Tule Lake Relocation Camp. Tu Feng became one of the cooks for the camp. Juan Tu became the organizer and leader of the *Watashitachiha Chusetsudesu*, the *Loyalists*.

Juan did not discriminate – he hated every white person, and because he always felt he was being held back due to his ancestry, he hated Mexicans and blacks. The concept of creating his own army out of Japanese (sprinkled with a few mixed-race Chinese) gave him a purpose in the camp, and he modeled his organization after the Japanese military and its 'take no prisoners' vision. Initially, he organized them into squads of twenty-five men and two companies of four squads each. He realized that as the population of the camp grew, so would his army grow. The Loyalists were involved in robbery, theft, extortion, and contraband sales to the internees. They were involved in bribery, prostitution, and smuggling with the guards. Juan had his sights set on weapons as his next target. He saw a day coming when he would lead his army out the front gate and begin attacking whole towns and cities. He had a big chip on his shoulder, and it got bigger every day.

The guards turned their backs when the *Loyalists* were involved in major crimes, which was becoming more common. And as nasty and evil as Sergeant Weston was, he avoided any conflict with Juan Tu and his 'associates' as they ran roughshod over those inside the fences. Weston knew he was outnumbered, but he would never admit that he was afraid. Juan was almost six feet, three inches tall, a giant over most of the internees which afforded him additional prestige. His physique was chiseled from hard work at the loading dock and warehouse for a regional trucking company. The frequent beatings he got from his father before he died added to his resolve. He was the first to shave his head and parade around the camp. He had his followers make shirts with a Japanese rising red sun, *Kyokujitsu-ki*, on the back and make white headbands with a red sun. Every time he marched more internees joined the parade around the camp. Tension was growing, and Juan felt justified when he announced, "The soldiers have spit on us for the last time. The outsiders will no longer shove us around because they do not own us. The whites are not our slave masters. I will lead you to a better place in life. I am the Terror of Tulelake!"

The *Loyalists* started with small, diversionary tactics. An accident unloading a train would distract onlookers while other cases on the train were stolen for later sale to internees or soldiers. Internees who would not join the *Loyalists* might have an accident with a resulting personal injury that would be visible to other internees. Such 'accidents' minimized future resistance. One of the *Loyalists* might have the honor and privilege to have an arm or leg intentionally broken so they could be sent to the hospital and steal drugs. An entire squad of the *Loyalists* worked a month to create a basement under a barrack near the train depot so their treasure could be kept in one spot and guarded well. The walls and roof of this warehouse basement were reinforced with stolen railroad ties. Juan said to himself, *Someday we will dig a large tunnel from the warehouse and under the train depot to our freedom. The Terror will release more terror!*

Chapter 13
1:15 a.m., August 1, 1943
Tule Lake Segregation Center

The dream was always the same, and it came two or three times a week since they were locked up in this camp. The bedding was soaked in sweat, and it ended with a scream every time.

The three cars raced along a certain two-mile stretch of Volcano Road along Tule Lake. Well, two cars were trying to catch up with the 1934 Studebaker truck. Steve Corbin had the accelerator on his father's 1938 Plymouth 'Road King' mashed to the floor and almost through it. The Plymouth had bug-eyed headlights, which seemed appropriate, because so were Steve's eyes at that moment. When most of the residents in and around Tulelake struggled to put food on the table for their families during this depression, the Corbin family never seemed to want for anything, including a new car. Steve always felt entitled to get the best, be the first, constantly win, etcetera. It was unsure which would explode first, the Plymouth's radiator, the

Plymouth's engine, or Steve himself. He glanced in the rear-view mirror and saw steam or smoke coming from Skeeter Cummings' 1932 Ford convertible. Skeeter's 221-cubic-inch engine was always blowing a water pump, and today was no exception. He slowed the convertible down and pulled over. Steve sneered, but when he looked forward, his chin almost hit the steering wheel. "It's pulling away from me! How is that possible?"

Overhead, the sky was a bright blue with some fluffy white clouds and the temperature was just over 90 degrees. Perfect weather for a race. The Studebaker was a 'personally modified' 110hp Waukesha 6-cylinder, 358 cubic inches. Originally it was built to haul big loads on its 141-inch wheelbase, but much of the cab and engine had been redesigned by its engineer and driver, 15-year-old Tomoko Sazama. 'Tomoko' means 'wise child', but everybody called Tomoko 'Tommy.' Tommy did not care about the rusted right side of the truck, the missing right door, or the missing left windshield. Tommy focused more on the engine, keeping it in tip-top shape, and on improving its engineering and performance. Tommy was a top mechanic and a top driver, maybe the best in Northern California.

Tommy eased across the finish line where several classmates waited. Some cheered for Tommy, but many just stood in stunned silence because Steve lost. Big. Tommy was leaning on the Studebaker's cab with arms folded when Steve pulled up. Steve jumped out shouting, "You cheated! There is no way that pile of bolts could beat my new Plymouth!"

Tommy said, "You mean 'Your Daddy's new Plymouth' don't you?"

Steve clenched his fists. He was either about to take a swing at Tommy or shoot up into the sky like a rocket on the Fourth of July. He struggled to keep his emotions under control and said to himself, *I can't believe this has happened! My Plymouth Road-king lost to a Studebaker truck? I lost to a Jap? I lost to a ... a ... a girl?*

Tommy pursed her lips, scratched her head as if she were deep in thought, and said, "Maybe that silver spoon stickin' out of your mouth slowed you down. You know, too much extra wind resistance." That did it. Steve lunged at Tommy, but a few karate moves put him on the ground. Tommy stuck her hand out to help Steve to his feet. "I'm sorry, Steve. I guess we both over-reacted." Steve slapped her hand away and got to his feet by himself. As he dusted himself off, Tommy said, "How about this, Steve? The next two miles are more curved, and we will be more evenly matched. OK?"

It took Steve all of five seconds to think about it. The swagger came back and so did his sneer. "You're on. You're gonna eat my dust."

They were even at the first curve, then the Plymouth edged slightly ahead. The second curve was unusual because it curved right and banked left at the same time with a rolling drop-off to the left. Tommy punched the accelerator as she made the curve, but then felt the truck lose traction. The Studebaker truck went over the embankment and barreled down the hill. Tommy was thrown around the truck cab over and over and over. The dirt in the air mingled with the acrid smell of burnt tires and the smoke from the Studebaker's ruptured gas tank, the spilled gasoline trickled further down the hill with a ribbon of flame chasing after it. When the onlookers arrived, they did not find Tommy in the burning truck. "Where is she?" echoed several people. Others yelled, "She's not here either. Finally, someone frantically yelled, "She's here! She's alive! Help!" Tommy was wedged between two large boulders, unconscious and bleeding from several cuts. Her left eye was swollen shut and turning a bluish-purple color that matched bruises on both arms.

Steve and Skeeter worked to free her, and when she awoke, she could not stand. She was screaming because she was in pain and because she was scared out of her wits. "Help! I can't move! I can't feel my legs! I can't feel them! Oh, my God, help me!"

Tommy tried to jump out of bed and run, but since her legs did not work, she fell to the floor with a heavy thud. Her screaming interrupted this night's silence in Block 14, Barrack 14-6, as it had on numerous previous nights. Tommy and her grandmother, Yumi, lived in Apartment 5. People in apartments 3 and 4 begged to be relocated to other apartments because of Tommy's nightmares and outbursts, and the people in apartments 1 and 2 would now beg to also move. Yumi clutched the girl in her arms and let her cry some before she asked, "Tomoko, is it the same dream again?"

Through the tears and coughing, Tommy said, "Yes, Sobo (Grandmother), it is the same horrible dream. Nothing is different. It is still 1938, and it is so real. I don't feel the pain in my legs anymore, but I feel the pain when I have this nightmare!"

"It's been five years, and I wish your parents were here to

somehow help you. I wish we knew where they were and why no one can find them."

"They may be locked up in another camp, Sobo. The word 'internment' sounds no different from the word 'prison' if you are inside. They may be working to get us out." Tommy knew there was another option, but she dared not speak it aloud. *They may be dead, killed in this ridiculous roundup of Nisei. I cannot say anything though, Sobo is very fragile. She is all that I have now, and I am all that she has. I must stay strong for her.*

Two soldiers burst in. They had to check out any and every disturbance, but they knew what to expect here. One, Private Schmidt, matter-of-factly said, "Again, huh?

Tommy said, "Yes. I am so sorry, but there is nothing I can do to control a nightmare."

"Kid, there is something that we can do, but you ain't gonna like it. We can move you to an empty barrack next to the warehouses by the rail yard where the screaming won't bother no soldiers, no Japs, nobody." The soldier realized after he said it that he could have chosen different words to describe Japanese Americans, but the slang was used by everyone. He tilted his helmet a little and asked, "Did you have these nightmares before you were brought here?"

"Yes, but not as often. When my grandmother and I were at home with my parents; it still came, but not nearly as often."

"Have you heard from your parents yet?" Schmidt asked with a tinge of annoyance.

Tommy began to tear up. She responded softly, "No. We do not know where they are. We don't know if they are even alive."

Private Lawson had just been standing and listening to the

conversation. He pursed his lips and handed his small notepad to Tommy. "Here. Give me their names, your old address, and the names of any other relatives around the area."

Tommy started crying now, something she seldom did. "Thank you," was all she could say.

Private Lawson pointed to the notepad and said, "Now, I'm not making any promises. Hell, I don't know if I can find any of the people you write down."

Almost in unison, Tommy and her sobo said, "Thank you."

"Remember I do have other things to do around here. But I will try."

As they left the barracks, the first private flatly stated, "You are crazy! Why help those Japs?"

Lawson asked as they walked, "If they were not Japanese Americans, would you help them? What if they were German Americans? What if they were Irish Americans? Would you help them, George?"

Private George Schmidt said, "You know I am German American. Of course, I would."

Lawson stopped and looked at Schmidt. "That's my point. We are all Americans, Schmidt, so we should help all Americans. That's what we are about to fight for. The American way of life, not the German American way of life, not the Japanese American way of life, not for Protestants, Catholics, Jews, or atheists. Don't you see that?"

Schmidt thought about this for a few moments, smiled, and then asked, "Not even for the New York Yankees?"

Lawson chuckled and said, "I don't think they need

anybody's help. Let's go get a cup of Joe at the mess hall." Schmidt got a friendly swat to the back of his head.

* * *

Tommy called her transportation around the camp 'Yuni', which was short for 'Yunikōn,' a unicorn in Japanese. Yuni could carry Tommy everywhere, so long as someone was willing to push. The wheelchair had a fabric seat and back attached to a rickety wood and metal frame on four, 8-inch wood wheels, about the same size as those on a baby buggy. Tommy's grandmother was the first to push Tommy and the wheelchair to the mess hall for meals and for Tommy to get some fresh air. But over time, Tommy's grandmother became too feeble and simply could not move the chair anymore. Masako, her friend Miwa, and Momo no Hana, which means Peach Blossom, also helped. No one dared call Momo by either of those names, she preferred just 'Blossom.' Masako recruited three new 'volunteers', boys in the camp that she had gone to school with in Tulelake. Goro (known as 'Gordon'), Kenji (known as 'Ken'), and Ichiro were put to work. Ken and Gordon found four old 24-inch wheels, then found two Goodyear tires from a broken Schwinn bicycle discarded into a junk pile by the train warehouse and storage area.

With some help and some protection provided by Private Lawson, Tommy orchestrated the modification of her old wheelchair into better transportation. Her engineering skills were shown as she supervised Gordon, Ken, and Ichiro, who fitted the wheelchair with new axles and then made a hot patch for the tires. She had the wheels with the big tires put on the front. "Look! Yuni has new horseshoes! Maybe I can roll along by myself!" She beamed with pride and hope for her future when she announced, "Someday, I'm going to figure out how to attach a small engine to this chair and steer it with a joystick, like a boat. I'll call it a Yuni-mobile!"

Lawson smiled to himself. *And I'll bet she is successful, too.* He made sure no one tried to steal or confiscate the new chair. "You could call it the Tommy Cat Special."

Ichiro also admired Tommy. *No, I think it is a bit more than 'admire.' Why not tell her how you feel* came a voice inside his head.

Ichiro softly said, "It is not a proper time with everything that is happening. 'Shiranu ga hotoke,' Bobby. That means 'Ignorance is bliss.'"

Yeah, I know. We have another saying in 2017 that goes something like 'El toro poo poo!' Wanna know how that translates?

"Ah, no. I got it."

Seriously, tell her how you feel. If you get stuck, I'll be there to help.

"Yeah, that is exactly what I am afraid of." Ichiro walked over to where Tommy sat in the shade. It was not quite noon, and the thermometer was rapidly climbing to 95 degrees. Ichiro was already sweating enough, and now even more so by the sweltering heat. He blurted out, "I must talk to you while I can."

Tommy grabbed the side rails on Yuni and carefully responded. "OK. What's the problem? Is pushing me around becoming too much for you? Am I becoming a burden?"

Ichiro stared at her with wide eyes and some silence before he said, "No-no-no. That's not it at all." He started slowly walking around in circles, clenching and unclenching his fists. "No, actually it is the opposite." He stopped and sat on the ground in front of her and looked into her eyes. A thin smile crept across his face, but he swallowed hard several times.

He heard a soft voice whisper in his head, *Just say it, Kemo Sabe. Say what you feel.*

The smile grew some and he said, "I have no idea what's the best way to say this, and I will probably mess it up. I may be leaving the camp very soon and I'm not sure when or if I will return." He reached out and took her hand. "I don't know how long I will be gone or even where I will be, but I will find you again wherever I go or wherever you go. I like you very much, Tomoko Samaza. Maybe ... I ..." He stood up and walked away.

Tommy was stunned. Her pendulum of emotions was swinging from fear to an emotion she had never experienced before and could not name, with a stop between excitement and happiness. Her hand reached up to her face. She felt a blush on her face and shyly smiled.

Saburo was reading yesterday's copy of the *Tulean Dispatch*, the camp newspaper. The newspaper was usually six pages long, mimeographed after the Public Relations Officer edited (censored) all proposed articles. The paper was always in English. Printing in Japanese was strictly prohibited by the War Relocation Authority (WRA). Saburo could read about planned events, human-interest stories, camp baseball, entertainment, filtered news from other camps, poetry, and sometimes very filtered information about the war. The front page proclaimed that the school was short of furniture, women were needed for work on the camp's farm, and there was a call for workers on sugar beet farms in Oregon. The American Crystal Sugar Company was also looking for beet toppers, who would be paid $2 per ton. He looked up from his paper and smiled as Ichiro entered. His smile quickly faded when he saw Corporal Williams standing in the doorway. Saburo sternly looked at his son and asked, "What does this mean, My son? Why is a soldier in our meager home?" He turned his gaze to Corporal Williams, jumped to his feet, and demanded, "What has my son done wrong?"

Corporal Williams removed his hat and said, "To the contrary, I am here to praise your son. Sir, may I come in?"

"Please excuse my inhospitality. Of course, come and sit. May I offer you some of our poor tea?"

Corporal Williams had never gotten used to the weak taste of tea and he was sure the tea to be offered was used, reused, and re-reused. But he was smart and said, "I would be honored to share some tea with you. You are most kind."

Ichiro made the tea and served it in 6-ounce, earthen cups with different flowers painted on each cup. The cups had belonged to Etsuko's grandmother. Saburo said with a bit of embarrassment, "I must apologize. We have no sugar to offer you."

Williams thought, *Yuck. I have to get this down without sugar.* Instead, he said, "Oh, I prefer my tea without any. But thank you for the offer."

Ichiro heard Bobby's voice in his head say, *Hey, this guy is really good. I can read him like a cheap comic book, but I think your father is softening up a bit.*

Williams got busy. "As I said, I have come to say something positive about Ichiro. I see you are reading the front page of the *Tulean Dispatch*. Have you read the article at the bottom of the page about the job offer for employment?"

Saburo said, "Yes," and threw a questioningly look at his son.

"Oto-san, I want to go."

"Absolutely not!"

"Sir, if I might interject. Ichiro is the most responsible young man I have met in many years. He came to me to inquire about the jobs on the sugar beet farms, the amount of time away from here, transportation to and from here, housing at the farms, security, and safety, and wages he could expect. Mr. Hisakawa, a man twice his age asks fewer, less in-depth questions. I was thoroughly impressed. And I was completely honest with my answers. It is good but hard work, long hours but with good compensation. I also explained the work is not without possible danger, but that is why a security team will be with the workers all day, every day."

"I believe you have come to me in respect, and I do appreciate that, but I cannot allow our family to be broken up. My oldest son, Taro, was a college student and we do not know what has become of him."

"Otōsan, if I remain here, what am I to do? Empty barrack trash cans? Pick up litter? Watch the sun go up and come down? Join the *Loyalists*?"

"Ichiro, you are supposed to go to school and get an education!"

Bobby's voice said, *Look at the paper. Show him that article about school.*

Ichiro picked up the newspaper and pointed to the article. "Father, have you read this yet? It says the classrooms do not have enough desks. Did you know your daughter Masako sits on the floor at school because there are no chairs and tables? Our teachers write on the walls because there are no chalkboards. My science teacher only has one textbook, and many pages are missing from it. I do not call that an education!"

Silence filled the room and sadness filled Saburo's eyes. It was the first time Ichiro had ever raised his voice to his father.

"Sir, I am not sure the children are learning anything. I think the school acts more as a babysitter than as an educator," said Corporal Williams and let the thought hang in the air. Saburo looked to Williams for some kind of support, so the corporal offered reassurance. "Sir, I can offer two good reasons you should consider granting your permission. First, Ichiro may be younger in years, but he is older in maturity." He let that one sink in before continuing.

Saburo mulled that point over and agreed. "And the second point?"

Corporal Williams stood and smiled. "Mr. Hisakawa, Ichiro will get more protection than anyone going."

"And how will that happen?"

"Because, sir, I am personally leading the guard detail that will transport him there, watch over him while he works, and bring him home safely to you." The smile faded away and was replaced by commitment. "You have my word and bond on it."

Saburo looked at the hand extended to him by the big American soldier. The hand was bigger, whiter, and a bit softer, but the grip was firm when the two hands shook.

Saburo agreed with great sadness. But he agreed.

A voice in Ichiro's head said, *WOW! I have never seen anything like that. You owe that soldier a big hug.*

"I may owe him my life," was a soft reply.

You may owe him for an entirely new life!

Private Lawson knocked on the doorframe since there was not much of a door. "Please excuse this interruption. Corporal Williams? Captain Shackleford needs to speak with you ASAP at the hospital."

Williams put his cap back on and said, "Thank you, Private Lawson. My compliments to the captain and tell him I will be there presently." Lawson saluted and left as Williams said to Saburo, "I hope you will take into consideration what I have said, Mr. Hisakawa. Good day, sir."

Saburo thought over what had happened and what had been said. "I like that man, and I think he would be another good role model for you, my son." He put his hands on the shoulders of his son, then smiled. "I remember when I used to do this, I had to bend over to reach your shoulders. It seems like only yesterday."

Ichiro asked, "So may I go work in the sugar beet fields?"

"I will speak with your mother and somehow convince her it is a good idea. My answer is yes."

The voice inside Ichiro's head noted, *I see the sadness in his eyes. He is worried.*

Private Lawson was waiting for Corporal Williams outside the barrack, pacing back and forth. When he saw Williams, he looked around for anyone that might hear them.

Williams said, "Is there a problem? What are you in a tizzy over?"

"I'm not supposed to know this, but I overheard the doc talking with the captain."

"OK, spill it."

Once again, Lawson looked around. Then he whispered one word. "Typhus."

Chapter 14
3:25 p.m., August 1, 1943
Tule Lake Segregation Center

Thirty minutes later Corporal Williams joined Captain Shackleford and Sergeant Weston at the hospital. Captain Brewster, the camp medical officer, was very nervous and paced the small, cramped room. "This is very bad. This is very bad," he said over and over.

Captain Shackleford had a long list of things to do before lights out, so he asked, "What are we doing here? Why did you call this meeting?"

"Oh, this is very bad. This is very bad," came the reply.

"Doctor, please look at me. Thank you. If you don't stop pacing around, I will order Sergeant Weston to shoot you in the leg."

Weston laughed and said, "Yeah, and I may aim too high, Doc."

Brewster took a drink of water, dribbling some down onto his fatigues. "It's typhus."

Shackleford quietly asked, "Did you mean to say 'typhoid fever'?"

"Typhus fever and typhoid fever are not the same. Typhus has been described since the 1500s. In fact, in the late 1400s, the Spanish lost 17,000 troops during the siege of the Moorish city of Baza. In the mid-1600s, ten percent of the entire population of Germany died of typhus. 20,000 people died in Canada in the mid-1800s. 150,000 died in Serbia of typhus in the last big war! Why . . . "

"Thanks for the history lesson, Doc, but can we move this along?"

"I'm sorry. Yes. I'm sorry. This has me rattled; I've never dealt with things like this before. I was a podiatrist before I got drafted and put in charge here."

"A what?"

"Foot doctor," apologized Brewster.

The chair in the corner creaked and a thin, slightly haggard man rose. He took off his thick glasses and said, "Doctor Brew-ster, I will explain."

"Who the hell are you?" blurted Weston.

"I am Doctor Kei Harada, and yes, I am a real doctor."

"You look familiar. Have we met somewhere?" Weston said, trying to recall the man.

"Ah, yes. I have been here since I was arrested, right in the middle of performing an appendectomy at the hospital in Redding and thrown into this camp when it opened two years ago. I was chief physician here at the hospital until someone decided that a Jap doctor could not be trusted."

"I still don't remember where we met."

"You were bent over a treatment table. I treated you this past Christmas Holiday after you contracted syphilis from ..."

"Oh, yeah. Now I remember. No, we don't need to go into that stuff right now. Please continue."

Shackleford looked at Weston for several moments and then turned back to Dr. Harada. "Yes, please continue."

"There are three types of typhus. Murine typhus is spread by fleas and scrub typhus is spread by chiggers. I think we are seeing the third type, epidemic typhus, which is spread by body lice. Symptoms include headache, a sudden onset of fever, chills, and rashes usually after two weeks of exposure. Sometimes symptoms similar to influenza manifest themselves and the typhus is misdiagnosed. A week later that rash has exploded from the chest and belly to all extremities, but not the face and hands. That is the reason why people do not see it on other people if long-sleeved shirts and long pants are worn. By the third week, the brain is infected, which can lead to delirium, mental instability, and even coma. The eyes will become sensitive to the light, so many will stay indoors during the day. If left untreated, there will be a high percentage of death. I could speculate the death rate would be as high as sixty percent."

Corporal Williams suddenly realized he was absent-mindedly scratching his arm. He looked over to Private Lawson and saw him doing the same. Captain Shackleford was sitting on his hands to avoid scratching when he asked, "How do people get typhus?"

"By living in this camp, Captain. The answer to your question is that simple."

"Explain. And Brewster? Send someone to get Mr. Best, the camp director, over here right now."

Dr. Harada laughed and said, "That will do no good. I have explained some of the medical problems in this camp before to Mr. Best's assistant, Mr. Tackett, and he is either overwhelmed with other responsibilities, or he simply does not care enough to appraise Mr. Best."

Weston chimed in, "Hell, let them all die, then we can go somewhere else and kill Germans or Japs."

"Weston shut up, or you'll be cleaning latrines. Dr. Harada, please explain it to me," said Shackleford with some irritation in his voice.

"Very well. To be specific, the sanitary conditions in this camp are deplorable. Latrines don't always function, and water is often not available. That means people cannot wash their hands after they use the latrines, wash their dirty clothes, or properly wash themselves, especially their hair. People in this camp have body lice. That exacerbates the problem with the continued overcrowding of the camp. The conditions in the stockade are atrocious."

"And we continue to bring in more internees, which makes things worse. I see," said Captain Shackleford. "Doctor, you have laid out the problem very well, and may I say, very articulately. May I ask where you went to medical school?"

"Keck School of Medicine at the University of Southern California."

Doctor Brewster had remained silent after deferring the discussion to Doctor Harada. He asked the next question on everyone's mind, "How do we treat this typhus epidemic?"

"We don't."

Everyone spoke up at the same time. "What?" "We must do something!" "That can't be!" "Let's bring in experts from Washington." "There must be some shot that will treat it."

Harada put up his hands to quiet the uproar. "Quiet, please. We do not want to alarm the patients already in the hospital with rumors that they and their families are going to die."

"True. So, what do we do, Doctor Harada?"

"I said 'We don't' because I'm not convinced Washington or the WRA will give us what we need – or are even interested in our wellbeing."

Just then, Mr. Best came in and Dr. Harada reviewed the discussion thus far. Best occasionally looked at Brewster but got no comment or reaction from him. Finally, Mr. Best turned directly to Brewster and asked point-blank, "Why am I being briefed by this doctor and not by you?"

Doctor Brewster stood up and said, "Because he knows more than I do. I suggest that if you have any questions, you direct them to Doctor Harada." He closed the door as he slowly walked out.

Captain Shackleford said, "Mr. Best, that took a lot of guts for Brewster to swallow his pride and say that."

Best pursed his lips and said, "Yes, that is true. I will speak to him later. Now, Doctor Harada, what do we do?"

"We beg. There are treatments available for epidemic typhus, but I'm not sure we can get them. There are also preventative treatments available, but I'm not sure they would ever be shipped here."

Best had an angry and exasperated look on his face when he said, "I think you had better explain that statement."

"Certainly. There are medicines we have requisitioned that never seem to show up. The orders are canceled somewhere along the supply chain, or they are never shipped in the first place. When we pushed for reasons, we were flatly told that this camp and others like it are a low priority. Fighting men in the Pacific, Atlantic, and Europe get everything. Stateside hospitals and clinics are the second priority, and we are on the bottom rung of the medical supply ladder, which means we get very little – or just nothing. That is why I originally said, 'We don't' when asked how we treat and control this. Your predecessors tried to challenge that, but all they got was either a reprimand or empty air."

"Tell me what you need, and I will get it. I promise."

Harada responded, "There are antibiotics which may help treat the disease. Maybe penicillin. Prevention is the real key though. We need mandatory delousing stations built and repeat treatments required every seven days. We must require all clothes to be washed in a pyrethrum anti-louse powder called MYL. We need powder sprayers for every room, laundry, warehouse, mess hall, latrine, and supply boxcar to kill both the lice and their eggs. This includes every internee, soldier, and supplier that comes inside the camp."

Mr. Best furiously made notes and looked back over them. After a couple of questions to clarify what Harada said, he declared, "I will come through. I believe I have the clout to get this done. Doctor Harada and Captain Shackleford will work out a regimen for the entire camp to follow. In the meantime, I want a tight lid on this. We do not want a panic and we do not want to give our Japanese sympathizers in the camp any fuel for their fires."

Captain Shackleford said, "I have an idea. Everyone knows that the stockade is very crowded. Let's start our delousing there. We can say it is to prevent a body lice problem. Then we can expand it as a preventative for the entire camp."

Harada said, "That is a good idea. But it all falls apart if we do not get the needed supplies to address both treatment and prevention."

Raymond Best said, "Understood. Gentlemen, we have a lot of planning to do under a blanket of silence. We must not even inform our soldiers of what the problem truly is."

Weston had been quiet too long. "It ain't gonna work, boys."

Best marched up to Weston and emphatically said, "If you say one word of what was discussed in this room until you are so ordered, you will be living in the stockade and cleaning latrines there all day and every day until this camp closes forever. Do I make myself clear, Sergeant? Or would you prefer to be a buck private again?"

Weston was filled with rage so intense he could almost not contain it, but all that came out of his mouth was, "I understand, Mr. Best." Weston thought, *The day is coming when you won't be able to even manage your death. I will.*

Chapter 15
7:45 p.m., August 1, 1943
Tule Lake Segregation Center

A beautiful sunset was in progress, reds and purples streaking through clouds of orange and gold. A slight breeze moved the shades on the western window, but there was no movement from the shade on the eastern window. Captain Taggart Shackleford sat leaning back in his office chair with his hands laced behind his head, staring at the sunset as he tried to empty his mind and get rid of a monster headache. He was not sure which would kick in first, the three aspirins or the three fingers of bourbon he'd just downed. The news of the typhus epidemic seemed like the cherry on top of the lousy sundae he was having to shovel and swallow; the questionnaire, the outward flow of peaceful Japanese Americans to other camps, the incoming flow of dissident internees, and the lack of an end in sight. It was all a bitter, ugly, and terrible situation. He confessed to himself, *I'm just a jailer, a damn warden for trou-blemakers*. He poured himself another glass of bourbon and downed it quickly. *Come to think of it, I'm a prisoner here too!* He sat up and turned from the window to look at the only personal item on his desk. It was a framed photo of his grandfather on the left and his father on the right. He poured another drink and toasted the pictures. *Here's to the two of you. At least you contributed to your war efforts.* He came from a long line of commitment to the United States Army.

The hamlet of Norney, near the village of Shackleford in Surrey in southeastern England, was the home of Colin Shackleford until he sailed to the New World. Instead of focusing on making his fortune, he wanted to serve the country that had given him a new home and a new direction in life. He joined the Union Army during another dark chapter in American history – the Civil War. He served in the 6th Heavy Artillery Battalion formed at Sacket's Harbor near Watertown, New York. He was killed in action at Cedar Creek, Virginia around 19 October 1862, leaving a wife and a six-month-old son, Barrett.

His son, Trooper Barrett Shackleford served in the Spanish-American War in 1898 after many years in the United States Cavalry fighting Indians in the West. No one knows the real story, but Barrett ended up at the Menger Hotel in San Antonio, Texas joining the First United States Volunteer Cavalry. By the end of May, Barret and many other soldiers succumbed to and suffered from the heavy, wool uniforms not suited for the heat and humidity of Cuba, millions of mosquitoes, and malaria. Thirty-six-year-old Barret died as a Rough Rider, just before the Battle of Las Guasimas. His son, Robert, was four years old when he and his mother learned Barrett was killed, not by cannon fire from Spanish artillery but by malaria from mosquito bites.

Sergeant Robert Shackleford was a decorated soldier from World War I, the War to End All Wars, or so it was called. He was one of Major Jordan "Jordie" Baker's team, a joint American Expeditionary Force and French forces unit gathering intelligence on 2 July 1918. They were in a forward interrogation dugout, along the trench line, working hard to get terrified German prisoners to relax and be more open to talk. Then a wayward yellow German shell with Sulphur mustard exploded in the outside trench. The mustard gas blinded, burned, and killed 23 soldiers in that trench, but the explosion buried Major Baker, two other interrogators, one guard, and six prisoners in the dugout. Sergeant Robert Shackleford (the guard), and one prisoner were dug out still alive the next day; the others were dead. Shackleford had burns in his throat that made it difficult for him to breathe when he became stressed, and he was finally diagnosed with a lung disease similar to coal dust disease. He always said, "When I got 'mustered' out of the service, I really got 'mustard' out."

Captain Taggart Shackleford had started to pour himself another glass of bourbon. He looked at the glass and said, "Three generations of Army veterans before me served this country. And here I sit, rotting in my private jail!" He threw the glass and laughed when it shattered on the wall next to the door. He reached into the bottom drawer of his desk for another glass as his aide, Corporal Baines, carefully opened the door with a drawn pistol in his hand.

"Sir, is everything alright? I heard a crash."

"Everything is fine, Corporal. It was just an accident. Close the door, please, and come sit down." Shackleford retrieved another glass from the desk drawer and poured each of them a drink.

"Ah, Sir? I'm on duty. I'm not supposed to drink while I'm on duty."

"Then I will make it a direct order. Drink!"

Baines smiled and responded, "Sir, I make it a practice to never refuse an order. What shall we drink to?"

Shackleford held his glass up but had to think about a proper toast. After a few moments, he said, "I have it. Here's to getting out of this prison, into combat, making a difference, and getting home in one piece to the ones we love."

Baines became somber as he bit his lip. "I understand and feel the same way." He downed the drink in one big swallow and wiped his mouth. "Sir, is that possible, I mean is that possible, or are we stuck here playing babysitters?"

"Take the bars off, Andy, and let's just talk. Too many soldiers have requested transfers and left here; they wanted to fight an enemy. At first, it seemed everyone in uniform hated anyone with the look or sound of Japanese ancestry. 'Hate' may not even be a strong enough word."

"I must admit, I have filled out my own transfer request twice, but then torn them up. I have met some fine people here."

"Exactly. I lean one way one day and then lean the other way later. These people have lost everything. They have every right to be madder than hell, and yet so many are remaining calm and acting with kindness, trying hard to help each other survive. I have listened to their music and have listened to their stories of family. I played with the little kids on the school playground. I guess those are the ones who give me hope, who keep me here. I do see a better future in their eyes and their smiles, and I intend to make sure they have that future. The future for all Americans will be better because these imprisoned people are behaving with tolerance."

Baines smiled and said, "I think you just convinced yourself of whatever you were worrying about a few minutes ago."

Shackleford refilled their glasses and said, "Yes, I guess you are right. One for the road, Andy?" A knock on the door interrupted. "Better see who it is, Corporal."

Corporal Baines put his drink down on the desk, saluted with a smile and a wink, and said, "Yes, sir!"

Private Schmidt knocked again just as Baines reached the door. "I am sorry to disturb you, Captain Shackleford, but the train due at 1630 hours is now here at 2015 hours. Besides supplies, they have another 25 dissident internees for us. The squad responsible for delousing is now off duty. What are your orders, sir?"

"Corporal Baines, please give my compliments to Corporal Williams and Sergeant Weston. The delousing squad must quickly reassemble, or we will be up all night."

Baines and Schmidt left the captain's office and stopped at Baines' desk. "Here is a list of the delousing squad, George. Round them up. I'll notify Williams that he is in charge, with Sergeant Weston observing."

"Oh, boy. That will go over like a lead balloon, Andy."

"Yeah, I know, but a bunch of dissidents stuck on a train for four hours longer than planned will discover their prize in the Cracker Jacks box will be a free trip to the delousing station just might tear Sergeant Weston and his charming personality apart."

Schmidt smiled and said, "Is there time for us to sell tickets for that event?"

"Not today. Williams will be more, ah, amenable."

"A-what-able?"

"Agreeable, you knucklehead."

"Okay. Ah, Andy? On another issue, have you processed my transfer request yet?"

"Can we talk tomorrow about it?"

Chapter 16
7:30 p.m., August 2, 1943
Tule Lake Segregation Center Canteen

For some internees, morning meant another miserable day of jail time, on the inside looking out. Nothing changed except the calendar, and even then, who cared? Their release date, if it ever truly came, was completely unknown. Plus, the pain of lost lives and missed opportunities overshadowed all thoughts. For others, morning meant new challenging opportunities to find a way to make the best of their dismal situations. One thing both groups looked forward to was called Canteen Night.

The band was really hot on one particular night, music-wise and temperature-wise. August nights around Tule Lake were generally dusty, oppressive, and hot anyway, but tonight was exceptionally hot. The thermometer at the hospital registered 105 degrees in the afternoon and the temperature had not dropped much by evening, but the hot breeze had remained steady. And the music kept the joint jumping.

Noru "Izzie" Izukawa and his 13-piece band with two singers were in for a one-night-only appearance from Portland, Oregon. Izzie and his troupe played a location twice a year on a circuit that also included the camps in Manzanar, California; Heart Mountain, Wyoming; Poston, Arizona; and Gila River, Arizona. Before Pearl Harbor, they had played some big clubs, but since the war began this circuit was the only way they survived. Bands were not uncommonly formed with musicians from many of the camps, and some of those bands were allowed to tour, under constant guard, and at events outside and inside some of the other camps.

Izzie's singers were billed as the Ishikawa Sisters, Bunko "Bunny" and Susumu "SuSu", but their real names were Ume Kobayashi and Haruka Ikeda. Izzie got the crowd involved at each location by getting internees to play with the band. He had dance contests and music quizzes, all with prizes, to get everyone into a good mood and lift spirits, even though the beautiful music contrasted sharply with the stark reality of the barbed wire fences.

There were no microphones, no amplifiers, no speakers, and no air conditioning. Every door and window in the canteen were open so any breeze could help cool the crowd, but no one seemed to care about the heat if they were having a good time. The crowds heard the music of Glenn Miller, Duke Ellington, Woody Herman, Count Basie, Tommy Dorsey, and Benny Goodman. The band played ballroom music, swing music, and even some classical music. But the swing music, mostly, seemed to help the new Nisei hold on to their shallow American roots, a new generation struggling with Japanese heritage, culture, and traditional music with a shorter time length of American heritage, a melting pot of continually evolving culture, and a new musical sound.

Not all the internees were so accepting of this American music. Juan Tu sat with folded, defiant arms in the back of the large mess hall now decorated like a canteen. His stooges, Kaede Matsumuro and Isao Hun, sat on either side of him, watching the crowd, and in turn, the three were being observed by three dozen soldiers. Sergeant Weston had given the three squad leaders of the night's security detail some very special instructions. He ordered Corporal Williams, Private Lawson, and Private Escobar to "protect the mess hall first, the band second, and our camp residents third. If any of the *Loyalists* create any kind of disturbance, riot, fight, altercation, or destruction, your orders are specific. Shoot to kill. No arrests, no warnings, no confrontations. Kill them. Am I clear? Are there any questions?"

The three squad leaders were stunned. Williams started to say something but thought wiser and refrained. Lawson always deferred to Williams on judgment calls, so he remained mute. On the other hand, Escobar was delighted and said, "Message understood and will be followed, Sarge!" That's why the eyes of 36 men never strayed from the three men in the back of the canteen.

Masako and Ichiro held onto a table not too far from the dance floor. Masako said, "I've been thinking about making my name more American. What do you think of 'Missy'? How does that sound?"

Ichiro almost had to yell over the sounds of Tommy Dorsey's 'Marie.' "I think our mother will not like it at all."

And your pop will blow his top! Hey, that rhymes!

"But Ichiro, we must change so we are seen as more American and less Japanese. Don't you see that?"

"Yes, I see. I see it does not matter, though, because people will still see a short, beautiful, dark-haired, almond-eyed Japanese girl. Not a tall, blue-eyed, blonde German girl or an auburn-haired, athletic Texas cowgirl. You are Nisei, the second generation born in the United States of Japanese Americans born in the US, and your name is still Masako, which means 'elegant child' in Japanese. Just be yourself."

It was not the answer she wanted to hear, but she could live with it. A voice in Ichiro's head said, *That was well said! You are a good brother.*

They had been waiting for the rest of their party, and Ken and Gordon arrived pushing Tommy and her wheelchair. Sweat immediately popped onto Ken's forehead and he remarked, "It is hot in here!" He flopped into a chair, waving his hand to cool his face.

Yeah, even the snakes went north for the summer.

Ken was staring at Masako until she said, "Is my shirt on backward or something? Is there food stuck to it?"

Ken drank an entire glass of water and quickly stood up. He blurted out, "If I don't say it now, I never will be able to. Masako, will you dance with me?"

Kemo Sabe, you better catch him before he falls down. I think he's about to pass out!

Masako sat frozen in the moment with absolutely no expression in her eyes or on her face. Then slowly she smiled and replied, "I would love to, Kenji." She stood and extended her hand. Ken was not sure what to do next, but he figured it out as the band started playing Glenn Miller's 'Moonlight Serenade.'

Gordon stood up and said, "I think I gotta find something to drink. My throat just closed up."

He hurried off which left Ichiro and Tommy alone in a noisy, crowded, music-filled, hot canteen. It did not matter. Ichiro sat next to Tommy and said, "I wish we could dance." He patted her hand and had no idea what to say next.

"I wish we could too."

Now he was in conflict. The Bobby-voice stated the dilemma, *Do you announce you are going away for a few months and tell her to have a nice rest of the summer without you? Or do you completely change your plans, make your father happy you are staying, and piss off Corporal Williams?*

Ichiro took Tommy's hand and said, "We need to talk somewhere that is not so noisy. I have something to explain, Tomoko."

Uh oh, you are using her Japanese name. Sounds serious.

He struggled, but Ichiro got the wheelchair out of the crowded canteen and to the area where some trees and bushes had been planted two months ago and were beginning to take hold. He pushed her up to a park bench where he could sit. He started and stopped a couple of times, then just sat and looked at the ground. "I don't know what to say or how to say it."

"You are leaving," she said softly and evenly – not as a question, but as a statement.

It was as if a bolt of lightning hit him. He jumped to his feet and implored, "How? How did you know?"

"Remember when that man came to the camp and talked about workers helping with the sugar beet harvest north of here?

You have spoken about that several times recently and it seemed to weigh on your mind more and more."

That ain't all that has been on his mind, Ms. Kemo Sabe.

Ichiro thought, *Will you please stay out of this conversation? I'm having a hard enough time as is without your interference or assistance.* "Yes, that is it. I have no idea what it will offer, maybe some short-term work or maybe some longer-term work. I just don't know. But I do know I care very much for you and your opinion on that job opportunity matters very much to me. What do you think?"

The clear night sky was a brilliant mixture of the whitest stars on the blackest blanket overhead. Tommy pointed upward and said, "That's you up there, stable, secure, and shining brightly on everything and everybody." A shooting star crossed the sky. "See that? That's good timing. That shooting star represents somebody who is here one moment and gone the next. I want someone dependable."

Bobby's voice said, *Kiss her.*

"I will come back. I will earn some money so when this prison lets us out, we have something to live on, and by 'we' I mean you and I."

Kiss her.

"Alright, I will wait for you, and someday we will start a new life together."

Kiss her, you idiot!

"I leave in three days, and I promise I will write as often as I can, so you know what I am doing. Maybe I can learn some new skills that I can use later!"

God, Almighty, kiss her! The Lone Ranger even kissed his horse, Silver. Kiss her!

They kissed.

Finally! Miracles never cease!

There was noise to their left, the sound of hammers and saws. They turned to see some soldiers working under the bright camp lights, building a small hut on short stilts about 15 feet long, 8 feet high, and six feet wide with a strange box on top. After a few awkward minutes wondering what to do next, Tommy said, "Let's go back inside. Gordon is going to play the piano and be accompanied by the band on 'Rhapsody in Blue'."

Great! I love old classical music! Was that by The Rolling Stones or by The Beach Boys?

Private Escobar never noticed the young man and woman because his attention was focused on the project assigned to him. He was getting tired and cranky, and his clothes were full of sawdust. *Well, at least it's sawdust and not lice*, he said to himself. He shivered at that thought and barked out, "Come on you guys! We have five more of these damn contraptions to build tonight!"

Ichiro somehow had more strength than ever before and had no problem pushing the wheelchair across the dirt and into the canteen. Maybe his adrenaline was pumping. Tommy felt lighter than air, so maybe that was why. They found a place near the front, just in time to watch a very nervous Gordon begin playing. Soon he was lost in the mood and his fingers flew over the keyboard.

Kaede Matsumuro and Isao Hun both grinned. Isao leaned

closer to Juan Tu and said, "Now would be a great time for a fight to break out next to the bandstand."

Kaede jumped in, "Yes, let's do it! I'm getting bored."

Juan Tu saw something that stirred an emotion he had buried long ago when he saw Tomoko and Ichiro holding hands. Maybe Juan Tu remembered a similar situation from his past, or he had desired or dreamed of something like that happening to him. In any event, this was probably one of the few times his heart had ever softened, and probably never would again. "No, we are leaving." His departure was so unexpected that the stunned Isao Hun and Kaede Matsumuro almost had to run to catch up with him as he headed out the door.

Corporal Williams, Private Lawson, and Private Escobar saw Juan Tu and his cronies leaving in a hurry, so they jumped up to follow them. Williams paused at the door for a moment though when thunderous applause signaled the conclusion of 'Rhapsody in Blue' by the orchestra and Gordon. When the band started playing 'When You Wish Upon a Star,' he saw something happening on the dance floor, and he smiled.

Ichiro stood up and wheeled Tommy to the center of the crowded dance floor, and the other couples backed up to make room. Ichiro took Tommy's hands and deftly moved her and Yuni around to the music. Soon, they had the entire dance floor because everyone else stood, watched, and smiled. Kenji and Masako joined them after a few minutes, followed by more dancers. It didn't matter to Tomoko and Ichiro though – they were alone with each other.

Chapter 17
8:00 a.m., August 10, 1943
The Sweet Beet Farms, Malheur County, Oregon

The climate at the farm was very different from that at the camp. The climate was cool enough for the sugar beet seeds to germinate and flower, but warm enough to stimulate root growth. The plants' sugar reserves are stored in the roots, and the roots are harvested for their sugar in the fall. Ichiro had learned all that in a makeshift outdoor classroom beside one of the big equipment barns on the large, 1400-acre farm called Sweet Beet Farms. Ichiro and the other new workers learned what they were about to do and why they were going to do it. They learned how to help produce maximum sugar beet yields in a typical 120-day growing season. They learned that farmers plant their seeds one to two inches deep, early in the spring after tilling the soil.

A morning dew hung over the plants as the sun began its skyward climb. This particular morning, Ichiro sat on a hay bale eating a biscuit with jam, neither of which he had seen since his family got locked up in the camp. He thought he was growing up so he tried his first cup of coffee. As he spat it out, he wondered, *How and why do people drink this stuff. It's terrible!*

Bobby's voice quickly responded, *It's an acquired taste, like boiled pig snout or rhubarb pie; you just get used to it after it kills all the taste buds in your mouth.*

Ichiro had another biscuit in his pants pocket for later. He sat just looking at his new world and new adventure. Bobby's voice marveled, *Look how blue that sky is! Look how green those trees are next to the river! Look how dark brown the soil is!*

"This certainly looks different than the world inside the camp at Tule Lake."

And at Tulelake in 2017. It ain't no better then, Kemo Sabe.

"I wish you would stop calling me that," Ichiro said with a little mock exasperation.

"Call you what?" asked Corporal Williams as he walked up. "I'm sorry, I did not hear what you were saying, Ichiro."

"Sorry. I guess I was mumbling out loud."

"It sure is pretty here."

Ichiro laughed and said, "I was just saying the same thing."

Williams pulled some hay stalks from the bale and ran them under his nose. He stuck them in his mouth and chewed. "This smell reminds me a little of home. All that's missing is the smell of cow sh ... ah, cow manure." He surveyed the panorama and said, "My family has a farm in Iowa and we raise corn. After the war, I'm going home."

Ichiro said, "I guess I will be trying to put my family back together, but we have nothing to start with."

"You have your lives, and that is a very good start."

He's right, you know. And besides, you will probably have me to help, and Tomoko.

"Ichiro, I have an offer for you, but it has a big 'if' tied to it. If your family agrees and if you want to, my family will have a job for you on our farm. What do you say?"

Visions of what could be paraded across Ichiro's mind. *That could be a brand-new start for you. Maybe Tommy will join you.*

"That is an incredible offer, Corporal Williams."

"The name is Anthony. Anthony Williams."

Then the fantasy bubble burst and Ichiro was back on the ground. "I can't leave my family.

Don't say 'NO' just yet. Who knows how long the war will be, who will win, and how the country will change?

"Well, think about it. It's a genuine offer," said Corporal Williams as he turned to meet Yapadika, the farm foreman, just walking up.

Ichiro joined 35 other Nisei from the Tule Lake camp to help with the sugar beet crop on the farm. Yapadika, a full-blooded Northern Paiute Indian, knew a thing or two about racial discrimination, so he was sympathetic to these Japanese Americans and their plight. The 36 men formed a semi-circle around Yapadika and sat on the ground. He looked each man in the eyes and then smiled. "Good morning, men. My name is Yapadika, but please just call me Yap. It's easier. I am so thankful that you agreed to help us with the sugar beet crop this year. If your performance is good, there may be other work available to you on a more permanent basis. Or you could return next year to join us."

Someone in the crowd gently muttered, "If we are still locked up like criminals or rabid dogs."

"You may not know this, but Indians have a keen sense of hearing that comes from generations of listening for enemies in moccasins trying to sneak up on us. It didn't work for them then, and it will not work for you now." Yap turned and faced the man who had commented. "If you don't want to be here, you are welcome to leave. Now. But if you stay, you are expected to be civil." His eyes bore a hole through the man now wishing he had kept his mouth shut. "Or I will scalp you myself."

The workers were wide-eyed, uncertain if Yap's comment was real or just an attempt at Indian humor. Corporal Williams quickly stepped into the semicircle and quickly announced, "I am Corporal Williams; I will be squad leader for this duty assignment and lead Team One. Private Lawson, please stand and be recognized. Private Lawson will lead Team Two. Private Escobar, please stand. Private Escobar will lead Team Three. I will be completely upfront with you on something. We are not here to guard you and prevent you from escaping. To the contrary, our job will be to protect you from those who wish you harm. I'll bet there are eyes on us this very moment in the tree line over my shoulder, watching your every move, looking for an opportunity to pick you off one at a time."

The voice in Ichiro's head said, *Holy Guacamole! Is he serious? It's bad enough being a chicken locked in a cage, and now we gotta worry about foxes knocking off us chickens in the yard?*

Williams continued, "So, there is the first good reason to forget about trying to escape. And I'll throw in another reason that my boss, Sergeant Weston, wanted me to be sure and impress upon you. He said 'There ain't no extra room in the stockade, so you may become a permanent resident in the hospital', if you know what he means. Are there any questions for Yap or me?"

After several moments of silence, somebody asked, "When is lunch?" That got everyone laughing.

Williams put his hands on his hips and said, "Yeah, Yap? When do we eat lunch?"

"We'll get you out to the fields on three trucks and you will each work between two rows of beets, thinning the beets, removing any weeds, and moving forward. We don't expect you to come across any bugs, but if you do, leave one of these yellow flags where you found them. We will take care of them. The trucks will be waiting for you at the end of your rows and bring you in for lunch. How does stew and cornbread sound?"

Ichiro watched as the truck passed several International and John Deere beet harvesters parked beside the big tractor barn. The harvesters were being torn down, rebuilt, and prepared for their new use in 45 days. Four 1940 Farmall-A tractors were also getting a once-over.

Equipment maintenance must be happening all the time, said Bobby.

Yap was sitting next to Ichiro and noticed his interest in the harvesters. "They have shoes that go under the beets and dig them out. Then spiked wheels impale the beets, raise them, and the tops get sliced off."

Ichiro asked, "When does that happen?"

"We try to delay harvest as long as we can, maybe even into October, so the beets get as much sugar stored in their roots as they can. That's a good question you just asked, young man."

That's my Kemo Sabe.

Ichiro was nervous as the truck drove out to the fields. On the right were row after row after row of sugar beet plants in perfect alignment, their target for the day's work. But he was also afraid of the target on his back, and the possible trouble the tree line on the left might be concealing.

Don't look for a problem where it ain't. What was it that your father said? 'Shake a hickey' or 'Shikata ga nai', I think.

"He said, '*Shikata ga nai*' – 'it cannot be helped.'"

The trucks stopped, and everyone piled out. Yap announced loudly, "OK. Grab a shovel or a machete and spread out, men. Somebody every two rows now. Let's get busy thinning these plants."

Corporal Williams said, "Private Lawson? Take your team 500 yards ahead and position them to alternate standing your post with reconnoitering between your post and the tree line. Pick a time interval of your choosing to do that. Private Escobar? Take your team 500 yards back down the road and do the same. My team will start here. We don't want any surprises, do we? Let's get to work."

Sounds thorough, doesn't it?

Ichiro caught Williams' attention and said, "Thanks again for your help in getting me here. I won't let you down." Williams gave a short wave as Ichiro grabbed a machete and chose a couple of rows. He noticed the rows were almost perfectly straight, running ahead to within 100 yards of the river.

This doesn't look so tough. I'll sing songs to ya from 40 years into the future!

"No, thank you."

The sun felt bright, but the temperature was only 82 degrees.

Optimal sugar beet growing weather. Ichiro quickly got into a rhythm and began to quote what he had learned from Yap in the classroom yesterday. "Thinning the plants means we need to create not too much and not too little space between the plants so they can grow properly. If a hill-drop planter is used, then the plants grow in small clumps based on the interval set on the planter. So, we pick the best single plant in each hill and pull out the extras."

I think I would rather sing.

"A continuous-row planter places seeds continually in the ground and that's why it's called continuous."

'Syringe that tequila into those watermelons,
And we will party at the beach all night.
Yeah, yeah.
Spittin' seeds and smokin' weed.
Yeah, yeah.
Stick another syringe in the hot dogs too,
And the beach weenies will dance all night with the watermelons.
Yeah, yeah.
Pukin' and dukin' in the dunes.
Yeah, yeah.
Livin' and lovin' at the beach.
Yeah, yeah, oh, yeah!'

Ichiro stood up and quietly asked, "Are you alright? What was all that?"

What's the matter? Don't you like music?

"Is that what that was? I thought Sergeant Weston was here and had intentionally stepped on a cat's tail."

Hey, that was a crazy group out of Southern California called the Seedless Watermelons with Cantaloupe Cathie. No? Would you prefer some Elvis Presley?

"I have no idea who that is, so I would prefer the silence of the gentle winds."

Sorry, I don't know that one. Must be really old.

"Then just shut up. Please!"

Critics.

"Anyway, we find the best plants and encourage them to . . ."

Why did you stop? Is there a problem?

"I just saw light reflecting off something about a third of the way down the tree line."

Two men were doing what they could to conceal themselves in the scrub brush between the trees. Orson Parks, the leader of a small militia of 20 men called the *Oregon Owls*, surveyed the work party with a pair of 1940 Kershaw 6x30 Army-issued binoculars stolen in a raid on a National Guard Armory in Idaho, along with winter gear, slickers, boots, C-rations, and, of course, weapons and ammo. Orson said, "I think I count 32 workers – no wait, I count 36. This is going to be easier than I expected, Todd."

Todd took the binoculars and said, "Let me get a headcount and equipment status on the guards." After making a few notes and re-verifying his findings, he turned to Orson and said, "This may not be as easy as you wanted it to be."

"Why not? They're just a bunch of unarmed Japs! They will be easy to kill!"

"There may be 36 workers, but there are a dozen trained soldiers, knucklehead. I do not see any machine guns, but I do see four M1A1 Thompson sub-machine guns that fire about 700 rounds per minute. The other eight soldiers on duty are carrying M1 Garand, .30-caliber, semi-automatic rifles that can fire eight rounds from a clip and up to 50 rounds per minute. I didn't count side arms, because you will be dead before they need them!"

"We're not afraid."

Todd put his hand on Orson's shoulder and quietly said, "Of course you're not afraid. Stupid, but not afraid. Look, let's re-evaluate all this and come up with another plan that the *America for Americans* can support."

Orson Parks said nothing, but just belly-crawled away, thinking *Those guys in Klamath Falls just want the glory for themselves. They parade around and strut their stuff, but never actually do anything. We don't need them.*

* * *

Four weeks later, the workers got a late start. It started raining before dawn, rained until almost noon, and now the moisture hung in the air like a heavy wet blanket. It was hard to tell where the sky stopped, and the rows of sugar beets started. Visibility was down to 200 yards. The workers jumped out of the trucks at about 2:00 p.m. from the road between the river and the fields. Yap had told them today would be less thinning and more making sure there was no standing water on the rows. "We don't want our beets to drown, do we? Let's get in as much work as we can and hope the rain holds off." He knew that harvesting was just around the corner. Maybe three more weeks if they were lucky.

Yap smiled at Corporal Williams as he grabbed his elbow and quietly said, "Be ready with your whistle. See how the river is rising? I don't want to risk getting stuck out here and putting lives in danger."

Williams glanced over Yap's shoulder and swore he could see the river slowly rising. "Private Lawson and Private Escobar? Visibility is going to be at a premium this afternoon. Let's cut down our separation grid from 500 yards to 100 yards."

Ichiro heard that as he grabbed a machete and walked behind Williams to his rows. He said, "Corporal, I am glad you're watching out for us. I can't swim!"

"It's not the rain and the river that concern me. It's this fog. You could hide a tank in this stuff." And that was the moment that all hell broke loose.

Shortening the grid from 500 yards to 100 yards allowed ten members of the *Oregon Owls* militia to sweep in, undetected, from the northern tree line to within firing range. Shots rang out. Two soldiers and one worker went down in the first volley. Escobar's team returned fire but had no idea where they were shooting, they were just shooting. Corporal Williams could be heard above the noise ordering, "Hold your fire until you have a target! Don't waste your ammo! Lawson, take your team 20 yards closer to the south tree line, half of the team in a prone firing position and half kneeling. Hold your fire until the last possible moment! Go!" He did not even notice the bullet that grazed his right cheek and bloodied his shirt. Instead, he turned to Yap and yelled, "Get your workers back on the trucks and out of here!" An explosion knocked several to the ground as one of the trucks rose in the air before it flipped onto its back like a dying turtle. "Get them down! Into the furrows as low as possible and stay there! Move!"

Orson Parks could be heard yelling, "Forget the soldiers! Kill the workers!" Ten more of his militia swung into the assault from the southern tree line in the second part of a delayed pincer maneuver, hoping to divert the soldiers' attention from the intended targets, the workers. He heard rifle fire from the south and smiled. "Our boys caught them flat-footed!" Then he realized he was hearing semi-automatic fire, probably from the soldiers' M1 Garand rifles.

Ichiro screamed, "Get down! Get down!"

Bobby's voice added, *And stay down!*

Next, Parks heard two M1A1 Thompson sub-machine guns open up. In less than five minutes, he heard almost no sounds coming from the south, except for a few screams and loud moans. His ten militia lay dead or dying. Frustration crept into his voice as he screamed, "Homer, send in the last group!"

Homer yelled, "Charge!" and the remaining five militia screamed as they ran headlong into Williams' advancing team headed towards them. The screaming stopped, as did the militia when they saw the M1A1 Thompson in a soldier's hands. He cut down all five in little time. Three were dead before they fell to the ground. One lay on the ground trying to talk, but two bullets had removed most of his neck and his carotid arteries were pumping his blood over sugar beet plants nearing harvest.

Corporal Williams had his back to the still-charging Homer, who had a Springfield M1898 bolt action rifle his father had brought back from Europe at the end of World War I. He was now a one-man bayonet charge, and he had Williams as his target. He was five feet away from driving the bayonet between Williams' shoulders and into his heart or lungs when a machete, wielded by a 16-year old, terrified, Japanese American boy, sliced across Homer's mid-section, which released his stomach and bowels. Homer sat down on his knees and watched himself bleed to death. Ichiro had blood over his hands, forearms, shirt, and pants. He absentmindedly reached to his face and removed a sticky piece of Homer's gut.

Ichiro and Williams were both frozen where they stood. Ichiro had just killed another human being. He had read about these things and seen them in movies, but nothing prepared him for what just happened. Williams slowly came to realize that a 16-year-old boy, a boy like so many he was guarding as if they were the enemy, a boy that had no reason to do what he just did, had just saved his life. That boy just became a man.

Bobby's voice said, *I wonder if Williams' heart is pounding as hard as ours is. Can we sit for a few minutes and calm down? Please?*

The silence of death was almost as gut-wrenching and heart-stopping as the smell of the gun smoke.

Orson Parks was all alone, standing within 50 yards of Corporal Williams. He stood, mouth wide open, as if in a trance, swaying slowly back and forth. He closed his mouth and began walking to Williams, but not seeing him. As he neared, he drew his grandfather's Colt Single Action Army (SAA) 1873 Peacemaker. He had not fired a shot in this skirmish, the six .44-40 Winchester caliber cartridges were still in their chambers. He knew he had to do something, but he simply could not concentrate. He raised the antique pistol his grandfather had used in the

Oregon Indian Wars. A single shot rang out, and a large, circular hole appeared in Parks' forehead with an even larger hole in the back of his head. He stood still for a few seconds, dropped the pistol, fell to his knees, jerked, and rolled onto his back.

Private Escobar appeared out of the mist as the rain began falling again. He walked to Corporal Williams and dropped the M1 Garand he had just fired. "If you ask me, we were firing in the wrong direction. If I wasn't in uniform, I could easily have joined them." He spat on the ground next to Ichiro and walked back into the dissolving mist as the rain gave way to a torrent and the smell of death soaked into the earth.

The rain put out the fire of what was left of the shattered truck. Yap loaded up the workers into the remaining two trucks as Corporal Williams conducted a debrief while the events were still fresh on the minds of his squad. "Yap will send out another truck for us when he gets back to the barn. This was an unexpected, unprovoked attack, and you conducted yourselves admirably. Thank you for doing your duty. But right now, I want to know what you saw and what you did." He also wanted to find out how somebody got close enough to plant a bomb on that truck, who did it, and when they did it. He turned slightly and watched as Ichiro climbed into a truck. *And what about that boy? How do I thank him? What do I say?*

The tally was 27 militia dead with no survivors, two soldiers with minor gunshot wounds, one soldier injured when he fell over a row of plants and split his nose wide open, one worker with a gunshot wound in the upper leg, and one worker injured by wood and metal fragments from the exploded truck. The biggest casualty was the loss of all the workers and this farm's

sugar beet harvest. The workers wanted to go back to the internment camp – their home.

* * *

This grand experiment was a grand failure by mid-October. The workers had grudgingly agreed to stay through the harvest, even though they were scared out of their wits and constantly looking over their shoulders into the tree line for militia or at the riverbank for an assault from there. This hesitation slowed the work process, but not as much as what came from the skies. A late September Indian summer with clear skies and bright sunshine was replaced during the night of September 28 with 50-mile-an-hour winds, heavy clouds, and rapidly dropping temper-atures. A completely unexpected storm blew in from the Pacific Coast with substantial moisture pushed by the winds. As the front reached Klamath Falls, the moisture became a blizzard bringing a combination of high winds, a hard freeze, and heavy snow. The workers and soldiers stayed close to their quarters for two days because of the deep snow. Yap went out to the fields on October 5th and waded through the quagmire. He sadly knelt inspecting the rows and realized the sugar beet crop on Sweet Beet Farms was a total loss for 1943.

Corporal Williams watched as the workers and guards loaded into trucks to take them back to the Tule Lake Relocation Center. There was not much conversation and certainly no joking around. The workers had stepped out of their defeatist comfort zone to take a chance on a new life, albeit an uncertain one, to come here to work. They felt they had failed and were now returning to a dismal life behind the fences. They were trading fresh air and gentle breezes for a dusty, cramped, depressing lifestyle. The soldiers felt they were also returning to a prison of constant boredom and monotony. The skirmish had stirred something in them. They realized they had the skills of warriors, but not the opportunity to use those skills. They felt they were being wasted.

Ichiro stood in front of Yap and extended his hand. "I want to say thank you for showing us a new world of opportunities. I had never considered a life of farming before." He turned and looked at Corporal Williams as he said, "But I will now."

Yeah, once we get out of jail.

Yap bit his lower lip. "Some may say we failed, but an old saying describes how we learn from our failures. 'Far better it is to dare mighty things, to win glorious triumphs, even though checkered by failure, than to rank with those poor spirits who neither enjoy much nor suffer much, because they live in that grey twilight that knows neither victory nor defeat.'"

Ichiro thought about that and asked, "Who said that?"

George Washington? Lincoln? Confucius? Hiawatha? Who?

Corporal Williams and Yap exchanged smiles. Williams said, "My father had that quote framed and hung by the back door so he could see it every day when he went to work. He's gone now, but I remember that quote."

Yap said, "I think I would like to have met your father." He turned back to Ichiro and said, "That is from the man who also said, 'The only man that never makes a mistake is the man who never does anything.' The 26th President of these United States of America, Theodore Roosevelt."

"I learned a lot here. Thank you." Ichiro climbed up into the truck and they headed back to Tule Lake.

Two men were again crouched down in the scrub brush between the trees at the edge of the sugar beet fields. Some of the beets might be salvaged, but most of the failed crop would eventually be chopped up and turned under. Jared and Todd Hodges each had Kershaw binoculars to watch the departure of the trucks. Todd lowered his binoculars and turned to his father. "They will be in for a long, slow ride because the road in spots is more of a mud slop. I can make a phone call from that gas station back up the road and have a dozen men set an ambush to kill every one of those workers and soldiers. They will be sittin' ducks."

Jared never lowered his binoculars. "No, I have a plan to exploit a traitor within the camp for more information ... and maybe more. We cannot make the same stupid mistakes that Orson Parks made." He rolled onto his back and returned the binoculars to their case. He smiled at his oldest son and said, "Let's go home. We need to recruit more men."

Chapter 18
9:00 a.m., October 16, 1943
Tule Lake Segregation Center

An hour after sunrise, two trucks and two jeeps rumbled into the camp, followed by a large cloud of dust. The drive was about 39 miles, usually just over an hour, but because of the muddy roads and two washed-out road segments, it seemed like an all-day drive. Many of the workers felt dejected that they had failed to earn more money to support their families; others thought their hopes for a brighter future in general had been crushed. Some even felt their chances for escape were gone. The soldiers now realized their hopes for finally getting into the war were dashed. The silence in the trucks deepened as the camp came into view and depression set in. All were returning to a mundane monotony.

Sergeant Weston was standing at the entrance, hands on hips. "Welcome back from your vacation, ladies." The soldiers scrambled down from the trucks and jeeps and walked by Weston without offering a salute, and Weston did not offer any of them one. Privates Lawson and Escobar compared worker head counts to make sure all were present and accounted for, then they reported the count to Corporal Williams. As Williams grabbed his duffel and headed to the Personnel Quarters, Weston yelled out, "Corporal Williams! In my office, now!" Williams dropped his duffel at the door to the Military Police Offices, removed his cap, and followed Weston in. Weston sat down behind his desk and opened a file while Williams snapped to attention and saluted. Weston never looked up and did not return the salute. Williams waited him out, held the salute, and finally Weston had to return it.

"I have your action report here. Do you expect me to believe this pile of crap?"

"I'm not sure I understand what the sergeant is referring to."

"Oh, you know damn well what I mean. One of those Japs killed an American citizen, and you did not execute the murderer. Why not? Or would you like to be busted down to a private?"

"Sergeant, I don't believe that is what the report says."

Weston stood up and walked around the desk to stand almost nose-to-nose in front of Williams. He shook the report in Williams' face as he yelled from twelve inches away. "I know for a fact that that Jap kid killed an American citizen. You lied in this report, and I know it!"

Williams put on his best-perplexed face and asked, "But, Sergeant, you were not there, so how do you know what happened? I was there and experienced it. I wrote the only report you have on the incident. Without provocation, my men, and the workers we were guarding, were attacked by a group of hostiles under the cover of a heavy mist or fog. We did not know their identity, but we learned from the bullets they were firing that they meant business. They shot two of our men; we did not shoot ourselves. They shot one of the workers we were assigned to guard; we did not. They blew up a United States Army-issued truck; we did not. We were attacked. I ran out of ammo and grabbed the machete from the kid. He was scared to death and could not move. I threw the machete at a man who was about to stab me with a bayonet on a rifle, and I got lucky. The machete caught the man in the chest, and he went down. The boy did nothing. I will swear to this report in front of Captain Shackleford if you ask me to, Sergeant Weston. I would also be forced to ask Captain Shackleford about any conflicting report on the incident, and what unauthorized person or persons submitted that report without sending it through proper military channels. Sir."

It seemed as if ice hung from everything in the room, which matched the cold reception Weston was giving Williams. After several minutes of a staring match, Weston loudly exhaled and returned to his desk. Abruptly he said, "Dismissed, Corporal. Resume your duties pending further investigation and questioning by the FBI, the camp manager, and Captain Shackleford."

"I cannot do that again. I cannot and will not," said Masako emphatically. She walked to her bed and sat down with her back to her parents.

Etsuko did not know what to say or how to say it. She felt much the same way. She sat beside her daughter and sighed, "Oh, my Musume. I do understand."

Masako turned rapidly to her mother. "Do you? Did you have to completely undress in front of strangers so you could be sprayed with a powder as if you were covered in roaches or ants? Did you?"

"Yes, I was at the delousing station too. I gathered the pile of your clothes you dropped on the ground and boiled them. I hung them out to dry and then boiled them again. Then, I undressed in front of strangers for the same delousing treatment."

Masako whispered in shame, "Mother, there were men there when I undressed. I was so ashamed." She began to cry as she buried her face in her hands.

Saburo added, "I was here while soldiers and nurses sprayed that stuff in our clothes, beds, sheets, floors, chairs, everywhere.

Masako sobbed, "I was afraid I was about to die! I have heard rumors about Jews being forced to undress before they were gassed to death in German concentration camps. I thought I was about to die in this American concentration camp!"

Etsuko wrapped her arms around her daughter, and they cried together.

"Ah, hello, I am home," Ichiro announced sheepishly as he removed his cap and slowly walked into the little apartment.

Saburo, Etsuko, and Masako were surprised to see him, as they had no notice he was returning. "Has something happened?" asked Saburo as he stood up.

Bobby's voice said, *We could ask the same question, but I wouldn't dare if I were you. Change the subject. Quick!*

Etsuko ran to her son and embraced him. "You are whole? You are not sick?"

"We were doing well until the crop froze before we could

harvest it. They may salvage something out of it, but the crop is a loss."

"Ah, well, you did your best. That is all one can expect."

" *Shikata ga nai.* " *Right?*

Ichiro now hated that quotation. Bobby's voice said, *That's giving up, and it's not right. Especially since some men were trying to kill us!*

Ichiro agreed. "We might have been more successful if we had not been attacked."

Saburo and Etsuko stared at each other. Saburo demanded, "What are you talking about?"

"A local militia, the 25 men who attacked us with rifles and pistols." He looked at each of them as they stared back with their mouths open. "You were not told? You have not heard?"

"No! Told what? You say you were attacked? Who attacked you? Were you injured? All we know is that now you are back much sooner than expected."

"I am fine. I was scared, and things got crazy, but I wasn't hurt. We continued the harvest until the crop was lost to a bad freeze, which was not our fault. It was good work, and I learned a lot, Otōsan. I enjoyed working with my hands in the dirt."

Etsuko asked, "Did the guards protect you?"

"Let him speak!"

"Yes, they did. About two dozen armed men tried to kill us all, including the soldiers. We were working in the field in the early afternoon, between two storms, when one of our trucks blew up behind us, and gunfire came from two different directions. They had pistols and rifles and knives, and one even had a bayonet. We laid down as flat as we could between the rows of sugar beets we were working. And ... and ...”

Saburo put his arm on Ichiro’s shoulder and calmly said, “Take a breath and slow down. Easy, easy.”

“And I killed someone.”

Bobby’s voice said, *Oops. Now was probably not the right time to mention that little tidbit of information.*

Masako and Saburo stood frozen in their spots while Etsuko collapsed to the floor in a screaming pile of motherhood. Then everyone started talking at the same time.

Stop! Bobby’s voice pleaded.

Ichiro took Bobby’s cue and repeated it. “Stop!” Quiet!”

When all the screaming, talking, and crying had reduced to whimpers, Ichiro continued. “I had no choice. A man with a bayonet on a rifle was about to stab Corporal Williams, and I stood up where I hid and used a machete to stop him. He could have killed Corporal Williams and he could have killed me! I had to defend myself. I had to, I had to ...” and his voice trailed off.

Saburo asked after moments of excruciating quiet, “Who knows of this?”

“Most of the workers and some of the soldiers.”

“Did Williams say anything to you?”

“He smiled at me and said, ‘Thank You’.”

“Has he reported this?”

Ichiro scratched his head and said, “That’s very strange. Yes, he wrote up a report and Private Lawson co-signed it. But the odd thing is Williams said he killed the man; not me. Why would he do that? Why would Lawson agree to that and co-sign the report? Why?”

Saburo thought that over and said, "Perhaps he will try to use that against you at a later time and get you to do something or get you to do something against someone else."

Bobby's voice whispered, *I know why.*

Ichiro quickly blurted, "I don't know why ... but maybe, just maybe he is trying to cover for me, so Sergeant Weston does not use it against me."

Bingo, Kemo Sabe. Williams is trying to keep you out of trouble.

Saburo paced the floor from one end of the apartment to the other and back, with his hands clasped behind his back and looking at the ceiling. Finally, he stopped and softly said, "This conversation stays in this room. Absolutely no one can be told of this." He looked at Etsuko and said, "No one." He turned and pointed a finger at Masako and said, "Absolutely no friends or teachers." He turned finally to Ichiro, "And we do not discuss it with each other outside of this room. Does everyone understand and agree?"

All agreed. Bobby's voice said, *I promise I won't tell anybody. Cross Kemo Sabe's heart and hope to ... well, I may have already done the last part.*

"Oh, and that includes Tomoko. Not even her! Nothing will change, because nothing happened."

"Otōsan, it very definitely happened, and I must live with it, whether I speak of it or not. I must live with this the rest of my life because I took another's life."

"Yes, but you have the opportunity to also learn from it. You made a good choice in a terrible situation. It does not define you, but it can teach you. You must learn how to cope with choices made during traumatic situations, using your best judgment, now and in the future. Someday your life may depend upon it again."

I think I am also changing, Ichiro. I have a lot to apologize for and so many to apologize to. I hope someday I have the chance to make those apologies.

The Army placed the camp under martial law on November 13, 1943. The pot of boiling water now had a lid on it, and the water continued to boil, like the ones by the delousing stations. But now, the heat was turned up higher.

Chapter 19
1:30 p.m., October 17, 1943
Tule Lake Segregation Center

Saburo stood in front of his two children, one hand on Masako's shoulder and one on Ichiro's shoulder. He somberly said, "There will be no work today and there will be no school. Our family has an important function to attend."

"Otōsan, I promised to help with a calligraphy class at the school this evening. Did you forget?" asked Masako.

Ichiro added, "Father, what important function do you speak of? I am completely exhausted and don't want to go anywhere."

"Yes, you are going and there will be no discussion! We are going to a funeral."

"Who is dead? I heard nothing when I came back to camp."

Etsuko walked up and softly announced, "Someone very important. Someone you don't know and have never heard of, but someone that commands our respect."

Bobby's voice said, *Are they going to tell us, or do we have to play a 20-question guessing game?*

Saburo pursed his lips and reverently lowered his head as he said, "Miguel Takemura."

Masako and Ichiro at the same time asked, "Who is that?"

The voice in Ichiro's head chimed in with, *Did he say someone named Miguel?*

"You will find out at the funeral. Let's go."

Besides movies, dances, concerts, and plays the camp was becoming more American with gardens, mail-order catalogs, bingo games, churches, and even a funeral home. As they left their barracks, they joined a crowd slowly walking by the delousing stations and the boiling pots for clothes, toward the Catholic Church in part of Barrack 59, near the cemetery. By the time the Hisakawas walked into the church, they found no seats and stood in the back. More stood outside, and soon the crowd spilled into the edge of the cemetery.

Sergeant Weston was nervous. He whispered to Private Escobar, "Get Captain Shackleford here in a hurry! We may have a riot starting! And call out all the guards!"

"That won't be necessary, private, and we do not need more guards, sergeant," came a hushed voice from behind them. Weston turned and was about to challenge whoever was countermanding his order. "Oh, it's you, Captain. Why didn't somebody give us some warning about this unruly mob?"

"First of all, they are not unruly, and second, they are not a mob."

"But they are still Japs, sir."

"I think it's time you learned something new about these people. Come with me, both of you." They crammed themselves into a corner of the church, entering from a side door. Shackleford ordered, "Pull your caps, gentlemen. You are in a church."

There were no pews or kneelers, just folding chairs. A few chairs near the pulpit marked a separate place for the family of the deceased, but there was no family. The choir next to the high altar consisted of ten or twelve internee boys from eight years old to twelve. There was no organ or piano. The only music came from a man playing a guitar to accompany the choir. The church altar was filled with flowers, and the wonderful smells made everyone forget for a few moments where they were. Candles by the altar gave off a soft, comforting, peaceful flickering over the simple wooden casket covered in an American flag. An old Irish priest stood at the altar flanked by two younger priests, one a Nisei and the other a Latino. When it was time for the sermon, the old priest had to be helped to the pulpit by the Nisei priest.

"Why is there an American flag draped over that coffin? That is a disgrace!" said Weston, loud enough to be heard by those around him.

Shackleford grabbed his arm to silence him, but Weston was put in his place by a chorus of "Shh!" from all around him. The old priest sat down next to the pulpit in a chair the younger priest brought.

"I am Father Daniel O'Malley and I apologize for not standing. It is getting harder and harder for me to do that. This will be the last funeral I will preside over in my career, and yet this is probably the most important one ever. I have a story to share with you about an extraordinary man, whom many of you never knew or heard of. Let me introduce Miguel Takemura to all of you."

Bobby's voice almost yelled. *Did he say Miguel? Oh, my God!*

"Miguel Takemura was born on February 29, 1880, on a quiet dairy farm in Snohomish County, Washington to Hideki Takemura and Isabel Garcia. Hideki was a second-generation Japanese American, and the grandson of a railroad construction camp cook. Isabel was the daughter of a migrant farming family, and she was sold to a big farm to be a maid. I'm not sure how or where Hideki and Isabel met, but their respective families kicked them out and disowned them. They never saw their families again, but instead devoted their lives to each other and to raising their two children. Miguel was named for Isabel's father and Abella was named for Isabel's mother."

"Needing work and filled with patriotic fervor, Miguel joined the U.S. Army in 1917. By May 31, 1918, he was a 38-year-old mule wrangler for two munition caissons assigned to the U.S. Army, 3rd Division on the south bank of the Marne River. The American forces were ordered to cover a retreat by French forces as they fled to Chateau Thierry. His responsibility, those mules, were dead and his caissons were empty, but they were then used to block a bridge while the French soldiers planted explosives. The Germans had to be held."

"Maybe you've heard the expression 'There are no atheists in a foxhole.' Well, I was a 45-year-old battalion priest assigned elsewhere but got stuck in the open with part of the 3rd Division. I must confess I was beginning to question my own faith. The ground started to rumble and vibrate. One soldier peered over the barricade we had thrown together, and he got a bullet in his neck. He bled to death before I could even offer him The Last Rites. The soldiers were digging in as fast as they could for some protection, and I did the same, but one man held steady, and squatting, looked under the overturned caisson. He started counting aloud the number of approaching German soldiers but stopped when he reached nineteen. It was the first time I had ever heard the voice of Miguel Takemura, a soft-spoken and private individual. He turned to search for an officer but saw none. He saw me and said, 'It's a tank, and you and I are going to take it out.' I thought he was talking to somebody behind me, except there wasn't anybody behind me. There was no smile on his face – only a look of confident determination."

"He scurried over to a French soldier placing some of the explosives and said, 'I need to requisition some of this for a while,' took the explosives, and started to crawl back to the over-turned caisson when he turned back to the Frenchman and said, 'Merci.' He grabbed me by the arm and said, 'Into the river – now!' We made it across, me with a pseudo breaststroke dog paddle, and Miguel facing backward, using only his legs to kick because he held the precious cargo of dynamite sticks over his head to keep them dry. Then, we crawled over rocks and bodies to a close spot between the approaching tank and the barricade. He looked at me and said, 'Father, I'm not Catholic, but please remember me. There is no one else to remember me.'"

"I almost cried, and the only thing that came out of my mouth was as true then as it is true this very day. I said, 'God, knows you, loves you, and He will always remember you.' The German A7V tank looked like a giant shoebox. It was over twenty-four feet long, 9 feet wide, and over 10 feet high and had multiple machine guns and a cannon sticking out of the front. At least 20 soldiers followed the tank, using it as a shield. The tank clattered along at about 5 miles per hour. He crawled to the center of the road just as a bullet hit him in the head. At first, I thought he was dead."

"The approaching tank was about to crush him when he rolled sideways and attached the explosives to the underside of the tank. It passed over most of him but crushed his legs. He never screamed. The tank exploded; the German soldiers not killed or injured by the blast stood up and became sitting ducks for the American and French soldiers. The French soldiers successfully destroyed the bridge, and the American forces halted the Germans and forced their surrender."

"A few weeks later, I had the time to visit Private Miguel Takemura in the Army hospital before he was to ship out to England and then back to the United States. I offered to write a letter home for him since his arms now fell limp at his sides due to surgical complications from the operations on his legs, but he refused. He said there was no one at home, and that was one reason he joined the Army. I asked if any of his buddies had been by to see him, and he said no, that the only friends he had in the Army were his mules, and they were now dead. I noticed an offi-cial-looking box on a table next to his bed. When I asked him about it, he told me to look inside if I wanted to. So, I opened it to find a medal and a note saying this would be replaced in 90 days by the Citation Star. I closed the box and asked, 'Why did you choose me? How could I help you and your plan?'"

"He said, 'I picked you because I needed someone to

remember me, if ... you know ... if things went bad.' I never saw him again until too many years later on one Sunday here in this camp. I was walking out to my car, feeling like I was not making much difference to anyone here. I passed a barrack, where a very old-looking man sat in a wheelchair. At first, I thought he was sleeping, and then I heard him play a few notes on a flute, so I walked over to him and introduced myself. He looked so old, and yet we were about the same age. His eyes drifted up to meet mine. Once again, there was no smile on his face, but that same look of confident determination that I remembered 25 years ago. After a few minutes, he recalled our meeting, and we talked about his life. His physical needs were met at one of the National Homes for Disabled Soldiers, but his financial and mental needs were bounced around from the Bureau of Pensions of the Interior Department to the Veterans Bureau."

"He was arrested in the middle of the night at a nursing home, driven for hours to a racetrack, and thrown into a pile of soiled hay in a horse stall before he was shipped here. He did not get his wheelchair for two days, so he just laid on the dirty, hard floor." Father O'Malley had to stop and wipe his face, his tears were flowing down his cheeks. After he blew his nose, he continued, "Most of his remaining belongings, including that box for his medal, were thrown away or stolen. Ladies and gentlemen, that Citation Star is today called the Silver Star, but he never got it. His days here were filled with watching people go by without ever acknowledging him or speaking with him. Some days he would take the only possession he had and play it." Father O'Malley showed the crowd a musical instrument. "This is called a shakuhachi, or a Japanese flute, and Mr. Takemura carved it from bamboo. Buddhist monks play these to help themselves in their meditations. He would sit and play his flute for his own enjoyment and the enjoyment of others. Some days people would listen, and then help him get to the mess hall, or just bring him some food. But most days, he was alone." Father O'Malley stood and struggled to walk with his cane to the coffin where he rested his hand. "And he died alone, except for God."

"Ladies and Gentlemen, here in front of you lies a quiet, American hero – not a Japanese American hero or even a Jap. He was a 63-year-old decorated Army veteran of World War One, a silent patriot. I now ask you to join me in remembering a forgotten hero. That's all he ever asked for ... he just wanted to be remembered. God does; will you? Will you remember Miguel Takemura?"

The choir and Father O'Malley started singing 'Onward, Christian Soldiers', which Miguel had requested. After the Mass, many of the congregants walked behind a cart carrying the casket on its slow journey to Miguel's final resting place in the cemetery. Ichiro whispered, "What's the matter, Bobby? You were quiet during the service."

Ichiro, sometime I must tell you about another Miguel with a terrible disease who I made fun of. I am embarrassed right now, and I'm not happy with myself. I was cruel and insensitive.

The Hisakawa family fell in line with the crowd moving silently to the cemetery and singing 'Going Home.' The dust cloud rose skyward, along with the singing.

Isao Hun and Kaede Matsumuro sat on barrack steps watching the crowd move, straining at times to see through the dust. Kaede snickered and said, "We could lob a smoke bomb into the crowd and cause a lot of problems."

Isao jumped in, "Yeah, that is a good idea. Let's do it!"

Kaede said, "Wait! I have a much better idea. We could set off a few of the firecrackers we made and start a riot between the soldiers and the prisoners!"

Juan Tu was lying down in the shade and said, "No, no need. I thought about starting something while all those people were in the church, but after listening to that priest, I had a better idea. We ain't gonna do nothing." He stood up and said, "Everyone in that church heard how a war hero was treated like crap his whole life, including and especially right here. He never got a break."

Isao began to smile and said, "Now I get it! We can use his death to get people to join the Loyalists."

"Exactly! For now, though, we just let this day and its events sink into their minds, and then we spend time refreshing their memories of what happened to him and what has happened to them. Let them connect the dots. Then we act. Then we get revenge!"

Across the compound, Weston was standing in Captain Shackleford's office, shaking his head and looking at the floor. "No, that cannot be true. An Army veteran would never be treated that way. No. No!"

Shackleford was sitting on the edge of his desk, letting Weston ramble for a while before he said, "Sergeant Weston!" Weston froze. "Ah, Richard, I made you go to that funeral for a reason, and I think you get the point now. We cannot label these people for the sins committed by other people in Japan."

"No, that cannot be true. The Japs are our enemy!"

Shackleford decided to approach this from a different angle. He asked, "Are you left-handed or right-handed?"

"What?"

"It's a simple question, sergeant. Are you left-handed or right-handed?"

"I'm right-handed. Why?"

"Adolph Hitler is right-handed, so that means all right-handed people are evil, correct?"

"I'm a loyal American!" screamed Weston.

"Yeah? And so are some of these Japanese Americans. Loyal, and right-handed."

"I don't understand, sir," said Weston in a confused voice.

Shackleford leaned forward and whispered, "And some of them are left-handed too." He stood and walked around Weston and said, "You cannot label people, and I'll bet you don't want people to label you. Think this over, Sergeant Weston, and we can talk again another day."

Weston snapped to attention and saluted. "Sir," was all that came out of his mouth. Walking back to his office, his expression changed, and his eyes narrowed. "No, that cannot be true." He roughly cut through the crowd now circling the cemetery. He could still hear the song resonating in the afternoon.

> *Going home, going home,*
> *I'll be going home.*
> *See the Light! See the Sun!*
> *I'm just going home.*

I want out of here, whispered Bobby's voice.

Ichiro covered his mouth some and softly responded, "So do I."

No. I want out of this horrible dream! The wind changed direction, and a dust devil danced across the back of the cemetery, across the railyard, and disappeared. *That's what I want to do. If I ever get back home* ... and the voice trailed off.

Chapter 20
2:00 p.m., April 27, 1944
Tule Lake Segregation Center

The 'pot of boiling water' was turned down to a simmer between mid-October and mid-January, and on January 15, 1944, martial law was rescinded. However, more and more dissenters from other camps on the West Coast were shipped to the Tule Lake Segregation Center, now beginning to bulge at the seams with problem prisoners ready to take any kind of action they could against the soldiers. The first stop for new arrivals was the delousing stations. Some of their clothes were boiled, and others were thrown into a fire because they were beyond salvage. The wounds continued to fester, and the psychological wounds were far worse than the physical ones. Something was afoot, everyone in the camp could sense it, could almost smell it. An electrical storm the previous night woke everyone up, but the prayers for rain were not met. Perhaps today's diversion would calm things down some.

Baseball, America's game, was more universal than most

Americans would admit or wanted to admit. Professor Horace Wilson from *Kaisei Gakko* introduced the game in Japan between 1872 and 1873. Albert Bates organized the first game in 1873, and a railroad engineer named Hiroshi Hiraoa, a Boston Red Sox fan from his days as a student, organized the first team in 1878. By 1920, professional baseball, called *Puro Yakyū*, was a popular spectator sport in Japan.

Prejudice against Japanese Americans did not begin with World War II. Racism and distrust of Nisei and Issei were common in California in the 1920s and 1930s. Japanese Americans formed their own leagues and did not play against Caucasians. The war simply gave that racism an excuse to openly exist.

Eight teams, playing either softball or hardball, were formed within the Tule Lake Relocation Center. No outside teams, Caucasian or internment camp, were allowed to play any of the Tule Lake teams, so their league was an internal league without uniforms. Some teams wrote their camp block number on the back of shirts, but some teams were made up of players from more than one block of barracks. Most of the players were boys or men, but there were a few women who played, and the best was Riko Ishida. Riko was a lanky 22-year-old college student, outgoing and friendly, but kept a big secret from everyone in the camp. Her father's cousin was none other than Hideki Tōjō, the Prime Minister of Japan who ordered the attack on Pearl Harbor. Riko's family had moved to the United States when she was only six months old, and her father had last seen his cousin when Hideki was promoted in 1934 to major general as he was appointed the Chief of the Personnel Department in the Japanese

War Ministry. Not long after America's entrance into the war, her father had to endure months of grueling interrogation and separation from the family. He was kept in San Francisco, and the rest of the family was shipped to Tule Lake.

Riko learned baseball in Oregon and excelled at shortstop. Among her many talents was a great range of movement, anticipation, and a whip-like throwing motion. She was her team's biggest supporter and cheerleader. She was a great conversationalist and listener, but when the subject of families came up, she made excuses and walked away. She felt great shame, and she worked hard to hide it.

Today Block 4 was playing their best competitor, Block 2, and that meant the ballpark was crowded with almost 9,000 people sitting on the ground or standing. There were no bleachers, and the field had no grass, but that did not matter today. It would not have mattered if they were in Yankee Stadium. They came to watch shortstop Riko and the Block 4 team versus the Block 2 team featuring Goro Teruo and Kenji Haru, Gordon and Ken. Gordon, only 16, had a wicked curve ball that seemed to break hard into right-handed batters and then fall off the table. Ken played first base and could stretch out flat on the ground to catch a throw and tag out a runner.

Ichiro had gotten to the field early so he could save a spot for Tommy and her wheelchair. Gordon and Ken helped her get to the field, and Ichiro pushed her into the final position. He bent over to lock the wheels when Tommy placed her hand on his.

"Thank you, Ichiro. And thank you for coming back to me."

He did not have a clue about the next step, so he just looked at her and said, "Are you comfortable?"

It's a good thing I'm in your head instead of somewhere else in your body. I might just throw up or . . .

Ichiro whispered, "Best behavior, best behavior."

Tommy turned to him and asked, "I did not hear you. What did you say?"

Fortunately, Gordon and Ken said, "Cheer loud for us," and went to warm up. The awkward moment was gone.

After five innings, Block 4 was ahead 1 to 0. Riko laid down a bunt on a squeeze play in the 3rd inning that accounted for the only run. She was 2 for 3 so far for the day. Gordon had given up only three hits today, and two were to Riko. In the bottom of the 5th, Gordon gave up his first walk of the day, but the next batter hit a dribbler back to Gordon who spun and threw to the second baseman to cut off the lead runner. Then the second baseman spun and threw to Ken, who did a spread eagle to complete the double play. Side retired.

Ichiro, and so many others there, had forgotten the dismal surroundings, the confinement, and the lack of freedom for a while. He yelled, "This is exciting", so Tommy could hear him. He was also trying to talk to Bobby, who had not said anything in over an hour.

The always-stoic guards were even getting into watching the game. A few celebrated with some internees when a good play was made by the Block 2 team. Others shouted and cheered for the Block 4 team. Everyone was focused on the game, everyone except for Sergeant Weston and Juan Tu. Juan Tu was dictating notes to Kaede Matsumuro. Juan Tu kept his arms folded to prevent himself from pointing, but Sergeant Weston noted he pointed with his head, pointing in the direction of the Bull Pen,

the term used to identify the stockade for some of the worst prisoners in the camp. Juan Tu turned slightly to look in the direction
of the hospital and personnel quarters when he saw Sergeant
Weston. Their eyes locked and neither blinked or moved.

I've got it!

Ichiro turned to Tommy and asked, "Pardon me?"

*Me and Peter Bauch grew up together playing baseball. We
were back-to-back hitters, and we were called 'Pete' and 'Re-
Pete' in Little League. But what really impressed our coaches
was our skill at picking up signs from the other teams we played.
I remember once ...*

"I did not say anything," Tommy said, smiling back at Ichiro,
holding his gaze with her tender stare and searching for the right
words.

Here we go again. OMG! I think I may be sick!

Ichiro turned from Tommy and whispered, "What? What is
OMG?"

Oh, my God. It's puppy love!

Ichiro turned back to Tommy and asked, "Do you like dogs?"

"Why, yes, I do. Why do you ask? Can we have pets in the
camp?"

You know damn well what I'm talking about, said Bobby's
voice as it laughed. The voice softened after a few seconds and
Ichiro heard *Actually, Kemo Sabe, I am very happy for you.
Really.*

Ichiro smiled and then said to Tommy, "Maybe we can share
one."

"I'd like that," Tommy said shyly.

Back to business, Bro. I figured out the Block 2 team signals from 3rd base. See that? The 3rd base coach put his hand flat on his knee and left it there. That means 'Don't swing.' Watch this pitch.

Ken, batting with one out, held up and did not swing, even though he wanted to crush the pitch. The count was now three balls and one strike.

The coach's hand is on his knee again. Watch. And keep your hand off her knee.

Ken was a statue when the home plate umpire yelled, "Ball Four, take your base." Ken dropped his bat and trotted to first base. Yoshi was the next batter. Ken and Yoshi both watched the 3rd base coach for the signal, but he put his left hand in his pocket.

The hand is flat on the knee again. No swing, but the coach might be looking for a reaction from the catcher. Watch.

"Strike one," yelled the umpire when Yoshi kept his bat on his shoulder. The catcher quickly stood up anticipating a throw to 2nd base, but Ken just stood his ground.

Ah, his arms are folded. Yoshi will swing away, and Ken will take off for second base. Watch!

And that is what happened. Strike two on Yoshi, but the catcher's throw to second was late. Ken slid in face-first. The crowd jumped to their feet as Ken dusted himself off. Play stopped for a few moments as a dust devil lazily made its way from the left field fence, toward 3rd base and into the crowd.

See? I told ya. My school team got to go to Los Angeles and watch the Dodgers play the Mets once. My coach wanted me 'n Peter to watch the 3rd base coaches and learn signal calling.

Ichiro softly said. "Who are the Mets?"

The New York Mets. When the Dodgers moved to Los Angeles, the Mets became a National League team.

"The Dodgers are in Los Angeles in the future? Incredible! Next, you'll be telling me the Giants are in San Diego!"

No, the Giants are in San Francisco. The Padres are in San Diego, the Angels are also in Los Angeles, and the A's are in Oakland across from San Francisco.

Tommy said out loud, "I wonder what will happen next."

Ichiro responded, "Yeah, maybe there will be teams in Canada and games in Mexico."

Tommy asked, "What did you say?"

"Nothing important. I am getting a headache!"

Bobby's voice said, *There are. Sorry to break it to you.*

Ichiro rubbed his forehead and said, "Yes, I am getting a headache. A great big one."

Look at that coach. His arms are folded again.

Just before the pitcher released the pitch, Ken was headed to 3rd base as fast as he could. The air was punctuated by the loud *CRACK!* of Yoshi's bat. Except it was not Yoshi's bat, it was far too loud and came from another direction.

People along the 1st baseline started pointing toward the empty barracks beyond the cemetery. "Fire!" The sound of the explosion ricocheted off so many buildings that it was impossible to tell the direction it came from.

"It's a bomb!"

"It's the warehouses where winter blankets and fuel are stored!"

"No, somebody blew up the school!"

"The camp is being bombed!"

"No. It's a fire in the barracks!"

People began to run away from the ball field toward the west side of the camp and safety. Many tried to run into their barracks to salvage what few possessions they had. Ichiro shielded Tommy and her wheelchair. Large plumes of smoke began rising from the Bull Pen, as it was called by the guards, and came to be known by many of the troublesome internees. Many started choking and coughing from the strange smoke coming from the cramped stockade.

"It's poison gas!"

"Run!"

"The Army is going to execute us all!"

This stockade, the Bull Pen, housed the more undesirable, problematic dissident internees, many of whom answered 'no' on a loyalty questionnaire everyone in the camps completed in March and April earlier that year. The stockade jail, built to house 24, was gorged with 46 men when the fire broke out. There were some wooden buildings, but most of the prisoners, another 63, lived outdoors in tents without heat, protection from the brutal winter winds and snow, or the scorching summer heat. Bunks were on the cold ground, where ants and scorpions had easy access to human flesh. Unattended infections, pneumonia, frostbite, and heatstroke cruelly drove some to the brink of insanity. Several of the wooden buildings were completely engulfed, as were several tents, but the source of the smoke appeared to come from the delousing stations set up in the stockade. The cans of MYL powder seemed to mix with the smoke from the fire and drift with the wind across the camp. The camp firemen did not have adequate equipment or water to douse the fire, so they resorted to shovels and sand. Smoke now covered half of the camp.

Everyone had left the ball field to get a closer look at the fire or go back to their barracks, except three men. Juan Tu and Kaede Matsumuro stared at Sergeant Weston standing about fifty yards away. Isao Hun strolled up to Juan Tu from the direction of the Bull Pen and remarked, "Wow! I wonder how that fire got started." He winked.

Juan Tu leered at Sergeant Weston, a small trace of an evil smile slowly spreading across his face. "Your final days are starting now. Soon you will know The Terror of Tulelake when you face your death."

"Your time is coming," muttered Weston as he smiled back.

Neither heard the other, but each understood the message and threat being conveyed.

Chapter 21
7:00 p.m., May 30, 1944
Jared Hodges Farm outside Klamath Falls, Oregon

A picture sat on the mantle with a black ribbon taped diagonally across it from left to right, and top to bottom. The picture of Patrick Hodges was all that Jared had of his brother, Patrick's body was never recovered from his ship that was blown out of the water and sunk that horrible morning in December 1941 in Pearl Harbor. The picture and frame had sat there untouched for two and a half years. Dust covered everything inside the house, and outside, on this 250-acre farm. It had been a little jewel of a farm – plenty of pasture, a 1-acre garden for vegetables to feed the family and workers, 25 momma cows on 75 acres, and the remaining rich soil for wheat and barley.

Jared's wife, Theta, had always been a calming influence on him. She worked to keep him grounded in his faith and in those who sought his counsel. Many of the men he now included on the roles of America for Americans first came to him for marriage counseling, job counseling, or just someone to talk to and soften the daily burden of simply living. But a hard winter a few years ago in the late 30s drove Jared into a dark abyss. Theta was confined to bed, and as her condition worsened, so did his. She died an agonizing death, unable to breathe. He prayed over her coffin, surrounded by hundreds of candles in the church for three days, hoping against hope she would rise from the dead. The coffin was taken to the cemetery where Jared stood like a statue, never saying anything, but was led around by his sons. Later he tried to understand her death and did seem to improve some – until December 7, 1941.

When Patrick died, so did Jared on the inside. Quickly, that emptiness was filled with a burning hatred of anything Japanese, including Japanese Americans. He had found a focus for his holy rage. His internal storm matched the pace of the impending spring storm outside. High winds, lightning, thunder, and a downpour from a rapidly darkening sky became a death shroud.

Jared split his time between farming and preaching until December 7, 1941. His church, the Temple of Hope, was boarded up and closed a year ago, just like his heart and his mind. But the building still had a use.

"How soon will the work be completed on your new basement?" asked Jared Hodges over the telephone to his oldest son, Todd.

"Aww, I suspect this weather will delay the finish for another six months. We might have to redirect the water away from the church because we don't want anyone to get too close and be hurt," Todd said in a pre-arranged code. 'Six months' meant 'six days.' 'Redirecting the water' indicated a need to divert the attention of people away from the church. Jared said, "We can't afford any close scrutiny from snooping eyes." He was afraid that local, state, and even federal officials might be tapping telephone conversations, and he could not afford anyone interfering with the plans of *America for Americans*. Jared and his followers never used that name on any phone calls or written messages. Todd was not referring to his home's basement, but rather a new, secret basement in the old church building.

Jared Hodges was the leader of the *America for Americans* from around Klamath Falls, Oregon. Many of their 135 zealots had been members of the Oregon State Guard but split off to form a militia under Hodges, a charismatic former preacher-turned-Jap-hater after his brother was killed at Pearl Harbor. The Oregon State Guard pleaded with Hodges to bring his militia to reintegrate with the guard, trying to quell a possibly explosive situation. No luck. The *America for Americans*, formed in mid-1942, was made up of men from 20 to 60 years old, but most were in their early 40s'.

Everyone knew Hodges' old church, the Temple of Hope, was abandoned and then became the center for the militia's training and drills. It was an open secret that local law enforcement ignored, and maybe even envied. But only Jared Hodges and his two sons, Todd and Martin, and Jared's special squad called the Patriots' Shield knew that the basement was being built to house the militia's armory.

A donkey snort, followed by a short laugh, and then followed by fits of wheezing came from Martin Hodges, Jared's youngest son, as he reported, "I was at the feed store this morning, and everyone was grumbling about the easy life of luxury them Japs got at that camp. They're playing baseball instead of working. They're eating ham and eggs, steak and potatoes, and lots of vegetables that are all shipped in to feed them. And here we sit having to deal with all kinds of rationing and food shortages. It's just not right!"

Jared said, "Thanks for the information, Martin, but remember we must deal in facts, not speculation. Some of what you may hear is nothing more than rumor." Martin gritted his teeth and glanced at the flashing lightning and storm through the window. Jared continued, "But, Martin, also remember there is some truth even in a lie. Where there is smoke, there may be a fire starting." Martin smiled at his father.

The back door opened and closed behind Todd Hodges as he joined the discussion at the table. He sat down with a cup of coffee opposite his father and said, "Some of them don't have it so good, and for a big reason."

Jared's brow furrowed when he asked, "What are you talking about, Todd?"

Todd had an evil smile spread across his face. "It seems some of them Japs are locked up in a jail in the locked-up camp." Martin's wheezy laugh returned.

"What did you learn?"

"Any troublemakers are going into a stockade, and it doesn't matter if the Jap killed someone, stole food, spit on a guard, started a fight, or ended a fight. It doesn't matter, the man is headed to the stockade. Here's an Oregon newspaper called *The American Truth* that says a bunch of Japs escaped from that camp, killed a family, and burned their farm! We need to act soon!"

Jared stood and got himself another cup of coffee. He walked to the back door and watched the storm for a few moments. "We need to learn more about what is really happening inside that camp before we make a move. We cannot fight both the Japs and our own soldiers. We need more information so we can make a plan."

Martin asked, "And how are we going to get that information?"

Todd offered, "I know. We could turn Martin into a Jap and dump him at the camp's front door!"

"That ain't funny," and then Martin started to wheeze.

Jared Hodges' comments became a teaching opportunity for his two sons. "Orson Parks and his meager Oregon Owls failed for three reasons. First, they did not have enough men to complete their mission. Second, they did not have the right fire-power to get the job done. And third, they had no attack strategy."

Todd said, "I agree, but how do we get the information we need?"

"Two ways. We continue to recruit more men that think like us and are willing to act as we plan to do, we give the soldiers exactly what they are expecting us to do."

"Huh?"

"We are going on a reconnaissance mission, disguised as a demonstration, and almost force our way into the camp. I want one person to do nothing but count guard towers, and another to count military vehicles and identify their type. I want three people to identify the types of buildings, personnel housing, offices, warehouses, and barracks and then report their locations.

I want someone to sketch the camp. I want someone to identify military leadership beyond rank. I want to know who the leaders are behind the scenes, not just the ones issuing orders. I will generate an assignment list and you select the men, Todd."

Martin snorted and said, "Let's just bust in and kill 'em, and the ones we don't kill can die when we set fire to the camp. Those buildings are just wood, and they will easily burn everything and everyone in them!"

Jared responded, "Think, my son, think! They have over 500 firemen inside that camp! That's twice as many men as we have in *America for Americans*. They would have a fire out almost as soon as you could set a barrack ablaze. Use your head!"

"Oh," came the meek, single, soft-spoken word from Martin.

"Two."

Jared turned to Todd and asked, "What?"

"Two. You said you had two ways to get the information. What is the second way, Father?"

Jared said, "I am working on a rather unique way to get the info we need from an impeccable source."

Martin asked quicker than Todd, but with the same questions. "Who and where?"

"Inside the camp," Jared said flatly as his eyes narrowed. "Someone inside that hates the Japs as much as we do."

Chapter 22
9:30 a.m., June 28, 1944
Somewhere in Tuscany, Italy

Four soldiers sat in a huge bomb crater which four hours previously had been a farm's well house, or maybe its outhouse. Privates Eiji Namora, Taro Hisakawa, and Dai Irika were not sure, but whatever it had been it now made a hole deep and wide enough they could spread out a lovely meal of K-rations. Private Taro Hisakawa dug through knapsacks to inventory their food. The breakfast K-ration box had a brown printed label, the lunch K-ration box had blueprinting, and the dinner box was olive drab, just like it tasted.

Private Barry Chiba had lost his folding shovel, so he improvised with his helmet. "I knew it. I knew it. I knew it! If I lost that damn shovel, I would need it almost immediately. I lost it last night when that shell exploded, and we scrambled for cover. And now I need it." He dug a private foxhole deeper and wider, but the dirt kept sliding back and refilling the hole.

Private Irika observed the digging and said, "Please dig that end of the hole deeper. I'm taller than you are."

Hisakawa ignored that conversation and announced, "Gentlemen, wash up for dinner. No dirty hands and faces at this table, please."

Namora said, "Please inform the chef I would prefer my steak cooked medium rare with mushrooms. Oh, and a side order of tsukemono."

Irika chimed in, "I'll have the same, and Namora can have my tsukemono. Since we left Tule Lake, I have not missed those pickled vegetables and I hope I never see them again. Ever."

Chiba yelled, "I can't eat right now! I'm busy digging a hole I can hide in until the shelling stops or the war ends!"

Irika said, "No, it needs to be deeper on that other end, Barry. My whole head will stick out!"

A shovelful of dirt hit him in the back. "Shovel this, nōtarin!"

"Shame, shame. It's not nice to call me a dumbass."

A German artillery shell, fired from a hidden position in the little town of Belvedere, suddenly exploded a hundred yards to their right. Namora yelled, "Can somebody please close those windows, Sarge? How do you expect us to dine when so many flies are in our dining room!"

Sergeant Fujiko yelled, "Knock it off you clowns, and keep your heads down and attached to your shoulders!"

Three voices chimed in, "Yes, Sarge."

A fourth said, "And I'm digging, Sarge."

Fujiko added, "And Namora? Bob Hope, you ain't."

"I wish he was here, Sarge. That would mean it would be safe for him, and us!"

Hisakawa, rummaging through the knapsack, said, "Crap! Our cupboard is getting bare. We have one breakfast and three suppers left."

"No steaks?"

"Not even some Nigirizushi?"

Namora twisted his face and grimaced. "That's fine with me. I never have been able to eat octopus sushi. I even tried some with catsup once. Nope. I'll take one of the suppers."

Irika said, "Me too, please. I like the potted meat and the chocolate bar."

Namora said, "I tried rolling the bouillon powder in the chewing gum once. Not bad."

"You are one weird guy," Hisakawa said. "I guess I will enjoy the dried fruit on top of the biscuit after I have the canned ham and eggs as an appetizer."

Namora asked, "Will you trade me your chocolate bar for my biscuit?"

Hisakawa countered with, "Throw in your packet of toilet paper and it's a deal."

"Ooh, too steep for me. What if I throw in my four-pack of cigarettes?"

"Done."

"Good, 'cuz I don' smoke anyway."

"Neither do I. I use cigarettes as trade bait with some of the other guys."

Another shell exploded about 200 yards to the left, but it did not seem to disturb these soldiers. They were tough, and determined, and whether they would admit it or not, they all had a chip on their shoulders. The 442nd was fighting a war in Italy to prove they were worthy to be called Americans, but they knew they would face another war at home to repeat that burden of proof.

Originally, just over 1200 Nisei men from Hawaii and the mainland were inducted into the 100th Battalion, but another 3800 joined them during training at Camp Shelby near Hattiesburg, Mississippi. The 442nd Regimental Combat Team (RCT) included the 1st, 2nd, and 3rd Infantry Battalions, the 552nd Field Artillery Battalion, the 232nd Engineer Company, and a medical team. They even had their own band, the 206th Army Band and their own fight song called 'Go for Broke.' The 100th Battalion was shipped to North Africa to prepare for the invasion of Europe through Italy. The RCT with new replacements for the 100th shipped out from Hampton Roads on 1 May 1944 and landed at Anzio on 28 May. That chip on their shoulder became extra drive and determination, so much so that the 442nd became known as the 'Purple Heart Battalion.'

Irika asked, "Can someone explain this to me? Benito Mussolini, 'El Duck breath,' or whatever he is called, and his troops have been kicked out of North Africa. They were sent to the Eastern Front and got their butts shot off again. Even when they have the support of the Krauts, they can't beat the English or the Russians. Right?"

"Yep, and now we are here in Italy, and we will kick their butts into the Mediterranean," said Namora.

Hisakawa laughed and said, "Boy, I sure hope they know how to swim!"

"Well, then, why did the Krauts turn their backs on their former Spaghetti allies?"

"I think that was covered in the 'Stars and Stripes' a month or two ago. You didn't read it?"

"No, it got used at the latrine. Enlighten me, Professor Hisakawa."

"Okay, boys and girls, follow this, because this is very convoluted."

"Con ... what?"

"Screwed up! Now pay attention, you stupid Jap."

"Third-generation stupid Jap, if you please. Third," Irika said as he waved his hand in a mock salute with three fingers.

"The Italian people threw him out of office and into a prison. The Germans raided the prison and set him free. In the meantime, the Italians now in power signed an armistice with the Allies, which pissed off the Germans, so they sent thousands of troops into Italy to regain power. The new Italian government declared war on Nazi Germany and thousands of Italian troops got arms and munitions to fight the Germans, but many soldiers of the Royal Italian Army refused to change uniforms, so they joined the German forces. Hitler tried to arrest the Italian king, but he and his court were on the lam and not to be found."

Irika said, "Now I know that term." He turned to the enlarging hole beside him and called out, "Got any chewing gum left?"

No, sorry," replied Chiba.

Irika announced, "Meanwhile, Superman could not decide whether to burrow into the mine deep in the Rocky Mountains to save poor Lois Lane or swim under the North Pole to save Jimmy Olson trapped in the sinking submarine."

Namora rubbed his forehead and said, "I need an aspirin after that. And maybe a bottle of Italian wine. We got any left?"

"It busted yesterday when we were flanking the Germans and bottling them up in that town. The bag took a bullet."

"I'll put it in for a citation."

Another explosion to the left was closer and shook the ground, raining down stones, small tree limbs, and dirt into the foxhole/dining room – and the body of Private First Class Hayyim Yamaguchi. Namora and Hisakawa rushed to check for a pulse but feared he was already dead. "Get him off me! Help!" yelled Chiba.

Hisakawa wiped mud and dirt from Yamaguchi's face. Irika grabbed a canteen after pulling Chiba from his collapsed foxhole. Namora felt for a pulse and jumped backward when Yamaguchi sat bolt upright, gasping for air and screaming at the top of his lungs. Namora had to yell louder so Yamaguchi could hear. "It's okay, you are alive! Calm down and just breathe for a minute or two."

"What are you doing here? Aren't you supposed to stick with the captain and act as his emergency runner when the radio is out?" asked Hisakawa.

Yamaguchi looked first at his hands, arms, torso, legs, and feet before he searched the faces of his friends. "I'm alive?" He patted his chest and face and said, "I'm alive! Todah la'el!"

Irika shook his head and said, "I never would have imagined it. A Jewish Jap!"

"Probably the only one in Europe not in a zoo," speculated Namora.

"I'm still asking, why are you here?" pushed Hisakawa.

"Captain Newport got a message from Company F. They got clobbered in that fight yesterday. Now they sent a runner to inform the captain that Squad 2 just lost their squad leader. I was sent to inform Sergeant Fujiko, and now I am here to give you new orders. You are to take command of Squad 2 and move that squad to support Company C at the front door of the town. Company A is taking the back door. When all are in position, Company B will attack from the high ground on the Germans' east flank, splitting them, and driving them into Company A and Company C."

"We're gonna play billiards with the Germans caught in between! I like this!" said Namora as he slapped Hisakawa on the back. "And congratulations, Taro!"

Hisakawa did not like the sound of that order. "No, I'm just a lousy private! I have no real combat experience, but I'm supposed to take command of a squad?"

Namora said, "Taro, none of us have combat experience if you think about it for a second. Hell, the captain doesn't either!"

Hayyim continued, "To quote Captain Newport, 'The bar on Hisakawa's uniform may only identify him as a private, but he is a leader and an officer to the men that fight beside him.' He thinks a lot of you, Taro. Then he said, 'Now get your sorry ass and Squad 2 up to Company C.' And you are supposed to take these three clowns with you. The captain is afraid they will reflect badly on the Army if not under your direct supervision."

Irika said, "You could have some of the boys speak Japanese on the radio or over the loudspeakers. The dumb Krauts will think Tokyo Rose has sent them some reinforcements!"

Hayyim responded, "Good idea. I'll mention that to Ike the next time we share some tea and crumpets with Churchill."

✶ ✶ ✶

Two days later, everything was different – the mood, the location, and even the food changed. There was no food because supply lines had been bombed again by German Junkers JU 87, the Stuka dive-bombers. Privates Dai Irika, Eiji Namora, and Squad Leader Taro Hisakawa had found a bombed-out church in the village of Belvedere that had no roof or windows, but the walls cut down the wind. "I don't want to leave him out in the rain with the dead bodies of the Krauts," said Namora as the three men finished burying Private Barry Chiba in a safe corner inside the church. That morning, Chiba had been hit by a sniper's bullet, which made a clean hole through the back of his neck. "I'm leaving him my shovel since he lost his. When I see one of those folding shovels, I will think of him."

Irika said, "It seemed like we gave him a hard time so often. Do you think he ever understood it was because we liked him?"

Taro answered, "Sure. I want to believe he felt at home with us."

"He was sort of like family, wasn't he?"

After a few moments of silence, Taro said, "Let's get organized and squared away. Namora, you check with Sergeant Fujiko to find out if we can stand down for a while. We all need some sleep. Irika, can you run over to supply and find out if they have any K-rations yet? I need to write up an action report and our status."

Irika was already moving when he said, "Will do, boss. I'm so hungry I would even try some of Namora's chewing gum wrapped around bouillon powder!"

Quiet time. It was something they'd not had in at least a week. He reached into his knapsack for paper and pencil but came out of the bag with a handful of dog tags that represented the soldiers of Company C. Company C had lost all its officers and many of the non-commissioned officers, so Squad Leader Taro Hisakawa was in charge. He thought, *I never really knew most of these guys*. He dug deeper into the knapsack and came out with a letter home he had not mailed yet. He opened it and re-read it:

Aisuru chichi (loving father) and Kichona haha (precious mother),

I apologize for not having written since I left the United States, but so much has happened. Basic training was at Camp McCoy in Wisconsin, and before we got there, the base had been used as a detention center for Japanese American, German American, and Italian American dissenters. They were shipped out as we were shipped in. We were treated no different from the dissenters; we were all Japs, so we had to earn the respect of camp officers, drill sergeants, and other recruits being prepared for combat. And that was not easy. We were tested physically and psychologically to see if we could withstand the added pressure. The white officers and NCOs pushed us to our limits and then some, but most of us survived it, and we are better for it. We called the recruits from Hawaii 'buddaheads', something

*like the Japanese word for 'pighead,' and the Hawaiian
recruits call us from the mainland 'kotonks' which supposedly is the sound a coconut makes when it hits the ground.
The Hawaiian recruits often shot craps when off duty. They
said it was the #1 sport in Hawaii. They had a phrase they
used when they shot craps, 'Go for Broke,' and that has
become our motto. I am proud to be a member of the all-
Nisei 100th Infantry Battalion, but that sentence may be
censored and marked out of this letter when I mail it.*

*We shipped out to somewhere in Louisiana next for addi-
tional training, and I think some were still questioning our
loyalty even then. Gradually, every day, we are proving the
skeptics wrong. We are proudly fighting for our country, and
they all see it.*

I love and miss you.
Taro

Taro had read this letter several times since he wrote it, but
there always seemed to be a reason why he had not mailed it yet.
He folded it, carefully placed it in an envelope, and again stuffed
it into his knapsack. Thirty minutes later he had completed the
report and put it in a sack with the dog tags.

"That's not much of a tribute to good men who died for their
country," said Namora over Taro's shoulder.

"No, it isn't. I hope that someday people will remember the
sacrifices these men made, and I don't mean with just some
monument or plaque."

Irika shouted, "Hey give me a hand. I think I've dropped

some rations back there, but you can follow the trail to get 'em." He plopped his armful down in a pile by Hisakawa and said, "I heard you as I was walking up. I hope the folks at home don't forget the extra sacrifices we, the loyal American descendants of Japan, have made here. Some of those dog tags belonged to friends of ours from Camp Shelby."

Taro said, "The three of us will not forget, and that is a start." He turned to Namora and said, "You haven't mentioned what you learned from Sergeant Fujiko."

Namora kicked some of the stones on the floor of the old church. "Yeah, I was holding that back. We ain't standing down. We load up and head out in three hours. Sarge said for you to get 'em ready."

After informing the rest of Company C of the moveout and time, Taro joined Namora and Irika for some chow. Irika had scrounged through stuff and made them a hot meal. Namora tasted the food and quickly said, "Hey! What's in this?"

Irika was stirring his stew in his helmet over a fire when he said, "Well, we have the answer to a question that has haunted mankind for thousands and thousands of years."

Namora said, "OK, I'll bite. What question is that, pray tell?"

"Why did the chicken cross the road?"

"And?"

"The answer is 'To jump into this stew!'"

Taro said, "Good work, Irika!"

"Thanks, boss."

After they ate, Taro wiped his hands on his dirty shirt, took out paper and a pencil to write a new letter to his parents:

Dear Mom and Dad, (see how American I have become?)

I don't have much time to write this because we are moving out very soon. I think we are headed north, but I'm not sure, and I'm not supposed to put that kind of information in letters in case they fall into the hands of the Germans. That's why all my letters are in Japanese.

I want to mention two people you may remember from Tulelake, California. They are my foxhole buddies, and you may remember them. They are Privates Dai Irika and Eiji Namora. They both went to high school with me. Dai was a junior when Eiji and I were seniors. Please find their parents and let them know I said hello and that I am doing my best to watch out for them. They are always kidding around and making jokes but under their skin, they are scared to death. So am I, and so are all of us. That keeps us on our toes.

We met another recruit at Camp Shelby, Private Barry Chiba from San Mateo, and he was part of this squad, but we lost him yesterday, no wait, two days ago. A sniper in a crumbling church tower got him. We have had little sleep since the battle we were in, but we will sleep in the trucks taking us to our next stop.

We have heard stories of race riots by whites trying to kill Nisei. If both sides only knew how good they really have it back in the States, they might shut up and work together. They could be here.

I must take my leave of you, I must get my men loaded up

Taro set aside his private face and put on his official military façade. "Let's go, guys! Move out! Go! Go! Go! Today, ladies! Today!"

The first time the new Nisei RCT engaged the Germans was on 26 June 1944, in Belvedere, Tuscany. The fighting was intense. The Germans never figured out that they were flanked, and their doom sealed by a bunch of second and third-generation Japanese American soldiers; patriots all. The Germans were shelling the 2nd Battalion and never uncovered the trap. Some-times the troops had no artillery support, just each other – that and M-1 carbines, some M1A1 Thompson submachine guns, some Browning M1919A4 medium machine guns, bazookas, grenades, a few flamethrowers, and a lot of guts. They continued to drive the Germans north from Belvedere to Sassetta, to Cecina, and onto the Arno River.

The 442nd Regimental Combat Team even at full strength

only had 4500 men, but that RCT earned more decorations than any unit before or after them. 'Go for Broke' was the motto for the RCT, and every man believed it and lived it. In October 1944, the 141st Infantry Regiment of the 36th Texas Division was surrounded in the Vosges Mountains in Northern France by German troops. Hitler had ordered his troops to stand their ground and kill all enemies of the Third Reich, but General Clayton Dahlquist, commander of the 36th Texas Division, ordered the 442nd RCT to save this 'Lost Battalion.' By the end of the month, the battalion was saved, but at a very steep price.

General Dahlquist wanted to recognize the 442nd for its heroism, and at a special ceremony asked that they pass in review. When he saw only a few hundred men, he asked where the rest of the regiment was. It is said that Colonel Charles Pence replied, "But sir, this is the entire regiment!"

Chapter 23
6:30 a.m., July 19, 1944
Tule Lake Segregation Center

Things were getting out of hand again. Tensions rose like a thermometer in the California heat, and in the early summer of 1942, a group calling themselves *America for Americans* marched on the Tule Lake Relocation Center after the news about the Bataan Death March was all over the radio and in the newspapers. They demanded that the internees be turned over to them. Captain Shackleford listened to their demands and looked the group over. He then asked a question that the militia was not expecting. "I guess your group here numbers about 50, correct? We have about 14,000 internees at the moment, and the number is growing. It's Mr. Hodges, right? Mr. Hodges, how are 50 of you going to handle 14,000 internees? Oh, and don't forget the 1,000 armed soldiers that stand between the internees and you, and there are more soldiers on the way. How are you going to deal with all that, Mr. Hodges?" Hodges seemed to have a face full of doubt while he chewed on that chunk of information gristle. Captain Shackleford suggested, "Look, Hodges, I get it. You don't want these internees here, they don't want to be here, and my men would rather be fighting the Nazis and the Japs somewhere else. But think for a minute. You know you have heard how the Japs treated the survivors of the Bataan Death March. But if your militia dealt harshly with these internees, American POWs held by Japanese forces in the Pacific might be in danger of torture or even execution outright. I know you don't want that to happen, do you?"

The militia mulled that over as well and left empty-handed, except for the recon info they got. Hodges glared at Captain Shackleford and said, "We will be watching you." Hodges looked to the west and pointed to the tree line. "Guard your chicken house well, captain, there may be wolves in those woods." Hodges and his men slowly retreated to their trucks and cars. Hodges turned and stared one last time at Shackleford and thought, *And next time we will come when you least expect it, and with much larger numbers. This was a test, a scouting mission.* A young man riding with Hodges began to laugh, but the laughter soon changed to fits of wheezing.

Saburo, Ichiro, Masako, and many more internees watched in horror from inside barracks as this slow-motion, near train wreck unfolded. Saburo and Etsuko were both pacifists, always bending with whatever wind came from whichever direction. Ichiro honored and respected his father, but did not always agree on courses of action, or inaction. His older brother, Taro, was the only one who challenged Saburo.

Saburo noticed that Ichiro was intently watching Sergeant Weston nervously pacing around with his pistol drawn. He thought nothing good could come of conflict with the sergeant and urged everyone to move away from the spectacle. Ichiro, still staring at Weston, softly asked his Bobby conscience, *Why is he so nervous? What is he up to?* He got an unexpected reply.

Is Weston upset that those people are here, or is he upset that they are leaving without us? Bobby replied. *Or maybe he is upset that many of us did not die today.*

Saburo thought Ichiro was talking to him, so he said, "Shikata ga nai." This phrase was heard more and more often coming from the older internees. It loosely translated to "It cannot be helped," an indication that many were resigning themselves to their plight.

Ichiro said, "With respect, Otōsan, it cannot be helping if we just sit and do nothing to correct it."

My school principal said, 'If you never take action, then you will get the same outcome as you started with. Nothing.'

"A smart man, Bobby."

Ichiro trudged to his father's side as Masako joined them in a group hug in their apartment. Etsuko walked every morning to the post office for any mail. Usually, there was nothing because all mail was so heavily censored, but it gave her something to do in a daily routine. But now, she slowly walked into the apartment as if in a daze. Her eyes were glassy, and tears flowed down her face. She held two crumpled letters, one in each hand. Masako was leaving for a fast breakfast and then school, but she froze. She had never seen her mother like this. "Mother, what is wrong? Are you hurt?"

Saburo went to comfort her, but Etsuko pulled away and screamed, "They killed him!" She ran to the bed and buried her face in a pillow. She screamed and screamed, "They murdered him!"

Saburo peeled the letters from Etsuko's clenched fists. His eyes went from the one in his left hand to the other in his right hand. Back and forth, several times, as his eyes widened. Then he clenched his eyes shut and said with incredulity, "Taro."

Ichiro and Masako looked at their father with dread. "Otōsan, what is it?"

Words came out slowly. "Here are two letters about Taro. He wrote this one almost 18 months ago, but we only have received it now!" He held up the one in his right hand and read it aloud.

Aisuru chichi (Loving father) and Kichōna okāsan (Precious mother),

I know war is upon us, and I know that I am considered inferior by other Americans. I can either be bullied or killed while trying to go to school, or I can stand up and do something about it. I can stand up and do my part to help my country. I have decided to volunteer for a new regiment in the United States Army being formed of all Nisei soldiers. Think about that for a moment. Thousands of Japanese Americans standing to fight for their new country, despite so many Americans hating them and ridiculing them. I love this country, maybe even more than you do. I imagine after training we will be headed to Europe somewhere to fight. I am not sure when I will have a chance to write again, so I am writing now.

*Ichiro, you are now the young man in charge of the care
of our parents. Find the strength to do it. Find the strength to
help your sister, Masako.*

*Masako, you will grow into a wonderful young lady.
You're already smarter than me, so it might be easier than
you think to explore new possibilities.*

*I do not know if this letter will find its way to you, but I
am sure the love in my heart will.*

All my love.
Taro

After many sniffles and the frequent wiping of eyes, Saburo
coughed and cleared his throat to gain a semblance of composure. He announced, "Here is the other letter."

5 July 1944
Mr. and Mrs. Saburo Hisakawa
Tule Lake Relocation Center
California

Dear Mr. and Mrs. Hisakawa,

*It is with deep regret that I am writing to you to confirm
the recent telegram informing you of the death of your son,
Private First-Class Taro Hisakawa, 442nd Regimental
Combat Team, 1st Battalion. It may be some comfort to you
to know your son died trying to save two wounded comrades
near Hill 140, nicknamed 'Little Cassino', in Italy. I am told*

Etsuko gave out a blood-curdling scream of anguish. Masako
tried in vain to comfort her mother. Saburo recrumpled the letters
and quietly cried, "What telegram? There has not been a
telegram!" Ichiro ran out the door. He did not know where he ran
or where he was going. He just ran. Bobby's conscience had no
idea how to react or what to say, but he felt such pain, pain that
he had not experienced since his mother left him.

He softly said to Ichiro, *Slow down. Please. Let's find a place
to talk.* They ended up at the barracks where Issei dissenters had
lived but were transferred out last week to the Bull Pen stockade.
Ichiro half-fell and half-sat on the doorstep. A cloud of dust he
had kicked up running now surrounded him. *Ichiro, I am feeling*

your pain too. I feel your thoughts about your brother; he must have been a special guy.

"Please just shut up and leave me alone," sobbed Ichiro. "Go away!"

I wish I could. Believe me, I wish I could! I do understand what you are going through. But where you go, I go.

"Yeah? How do you understand?" Ichiro barked.

I never had a brother or a sister. My loss was my mother. Ichiro's mind grew quiet for several minutes before Bobby continued. *She left my father and me one day when Dad was at work, and I was at school. She left a note on the kitchen counter that said she was going away with a guy who promised her a carefree life. Never heard another word from her, ever. I felt guilt, that I was at fault and I drove her away 'cuz of something I did wrong, or maybe 'cuz of something I didn't do. And 'cuz she left, I pretty much lost my father right after that. Our relationship fell apart, and I don't see any way to fix it. So, I sort of understand how you feel. I am sorry, my brother.*

"What? What did you call me?" Ichiro blurted out.

I said, 'I am sorry, my brother.' I guess I feel close to you now like the brother I never had. Maybe like your brother, Taro, was.

Ichiro took a deep breath, and a small smile appeared. "Well, Taro was never inside my head, that's for sure." He wiped the tears from his eyes.

That's better. We'll take this one step at a time, Kemo Sabe.

"Confucius once said, 'Susumitsudukete sae ireba, osoku tomo kankei nai.'"

Great, I'm stuck in the head of a Japanese American kid who now quotes Confucius in Japanese! I wonder if I ever get back into my own body again if I will still understand Japanese. That could be a handy skill to have.

"Confucius said, 'It does not matter how slowly you go, as long as you do not stop.'"

Oh, Okay. In 2017, we say 'Just keep on keepin' on.' So, we will do this together.

Chapter 24
8:30 p.m., July 25, 1944
Tulelake Diner

The dinner crowd had thinned out to just seven customers in the diner. The dinner crowd had not been much bigger as business these days was bad. A truck driver sat at the counter finishing off a piece of cherry pie and a cup of coffee before he jumped back into his rig and continued his trip to Salem, Oregon. He had to get this load to two Salem warehouses by midnight, and he would probably be an hour late, but he didn't seem to care. A doctor and his nurse sat in a booth discussing an emergency case they had dealt with right before they left the hospital. A bearded old man sat at a table near the doctor and nurse, sipping on his cold coffee, between dozing off occasionally. A younger man sat across from him and just stared out the window. A burly man with hard eyes sat in the booth near the diner's side door and faced the front door. He stirred little whirlpools in his coffee as it got colder. A man sat in the last booth with his back to the 'whirlpool stirrer', and he faced the side door. The waitress behind the counter was counting her tips as she waited for another pot of coffee to brew. The cook was searching through the want ads in the *Medford News* for a new job while he burned his dinner – a chunk of ham he had dug out of the trash and two eggs.

'Whirlpool stirrer' looked straight ahead and whispered, "What news do you have for me tonight?"

"What you did last week was very stupid."

"That's your opinion, and opinions are like belly buttons. Everybody has one."

"You are missing the point. You alerted the camp brass that your group exists, specifically who you are, and that you are willing to confront the camp."

"The demonstration was done for multiple reasons, and we got what we really went after."

"I hope so, because you may be getting a visit soon from those snoops from the FBI. How will you deal with that?"

'Whirlpool stirrer' concentrated on his coffee for a few moments. "Okay, good point. Thanks for the tip, but I will be ready for them."

The man behind him quietly said, "I have a plan for you, Hodges."

Jared Hodges sipped some of his coffee but was cautiously looking around to see who was in the diner, who could see him through the windows, and who might be within earshot of the conversation. The leader of the *America for Americans* group was already paranoid about their actions and plans being discovered, and now some of his 135 zealots were joining him on the paranoia carousel. They were tired of the constant training and wanted action and promised results, tired of looking over their shoulders, and were determined to charge ahead. The commander of the Oregon State Guard had showed up on his front porch before noon and had once again pleaded with Hodges to bring his militia back into the guard. He promised he would discuss it at their next meeting and bring it up for a vote. He lied – he was stalling for whatever tonight's meeting would result in.

"I'm listening."

"Imagine that camp as a big rectangle, with the rail line entering the rectangle at the bottom right side, referred to as 'Point Alpha', and exiting the center right side, referred to as 'Point Bravo'."

"Yes, we now have maps of the place from our visit last week."

"I suggest two tactical thrusts into the camp. Half of your men will attack each point."

Hodges interrupted the man, "I don't see any reason to split my forces and double my exposure. No."

"My plan calls for 'Alpha' to be attacked at 1245 hours, followed by 'Bravo' being attacked at 1300 hours, Hodges. I chose the time because so many Japs will be out in the open and easily exposed to gunfire. Attacking 'Alpha' first will herd people to 'Bravo' where you catch them in a pincer movement and avoid as much conflict with the troops."

The bearded old man noisily stirred as the waitress made her way around pouring more coffee. Conversation at the back two booths ceased. After she walked off, Hodges looked out the window as he said, "Interesting. But how do we prevent losing the element of surprise when we storm the rail entrance?"

"Because at 1230 hours Juan Tu will be leading another hate parade through the camp. They always seem to begin near the rail yard depot."

Hodges thought about the plan for a few moments. "Hmm. Now I think you may have something. The guards will be forced to move toward the parade to maintain order."

"If they are still there."

Hodges said a little louder than he intended, "What does that mean?" He heard a chuckle behind him.

"There will be an explosion and fire on the far northwest side of the camp, north of Border Street, at 1245 hours that will further split forces in the camp."

An evil, sadistic smile spread over Hodges' face. "I like it, all of it. When?"

"Today is Tuesday. That troop reduction I told you about probably will happen Wednesday night or Thursday morning. A big shipment comes in early Friday morning and will be off-loaded all day. How about Saturday?"

"We'll be ready."

The old man coughed again, and the conversation stopped. The waitress gave Hodges his check and said, "You didn't like the coffee?"

"Darlin', my mind was on other things. Not your fault." He paid the waitress a dime for the coffee but left a quarter tip. "Sorry to take up your time."

She was a little stunned at getting such a large tip on just a cup of joe. She walked to the next booth and slid the check on the table. "You had the roasted chicken, cornbread dressing, and coffee. That'll be 50 cents."

The man looked at the ticket and stood up. "Here's a dollar. I feel generous tonight, Daisy."

"I sure do appreciate it! I just noticed you are wearing civvies tonight. Going to a dance somewhere, Sergeant Weston? Need a dance partner or something tonight?"

No, my uniform is being cleaned," he lied and started to walk away. He bent over and acted as if he had picked up a napkin. "Oh, mister? I think you dropped this." Weston handed Hodges the napkin, which had a picture folded inside. The waitress walked to another table and Weston quietly said, "If you don't kill but one person, this is the man. Make sure every one of your men gets a copy and memorizes the face."

He headed for the door as Hodges said, "Oh, how clumsy of me. Thanks, mister!" Then he thought to himself, *If Weston thinks this guy is such a threat, maybe I can twist that to our favor. Or maybe I can kill the guy in the picture, or maybe both of them. Maybe this guy wants Weston dead as well. Maybe I can play that angle. There are several possibilities.*

The young man walked in front of Hodges to the door. The old, bearded man waited to make sure no one followed, then he brought up the rear. The young man and the old, bearded man met Hodges at a truck parked a block away from the diner on a side street. The young man asked, "Well?"

Hodges smiled and said, "If you have anything planned for Saturday or Sunday morning, Martin, cancel it."

The young man smiled. The smile displayed his two missing front teeth, a souvenir from a raid on a munitions warehouse three months ago in Oregon. He had a wheezy laugh, preceded by a donkey snort. "Sounds like fun, Dad. I would not miss this for anything!"

"Swing by the feed store tomorrow at noon, pick up your brother, and bring him to the church."

"Sure, Dad. What's he doin' at the feed store?"

"He's watching the train station for incoming freight cars and checking schedules inside the dispatcher's office. Our friend inside the camp said 750 of the 1,000 soldiers who came in last year are being shipped out any day. That will dramatically reduce their numbers and firepower."

"Oh, I didn't know. I'll hurry him to the church." Martin started to snort, which then resulted in a wheezing fit.

Hodges turned and grabbed his son by the shoulders. "No! If you hurry, you will alert the town that something is happening, which it ain't, or at least not at this very moment. Just casually pick him up." Martin jumped into the back of the pickup, and the donkey snort returned.

Old Man Karnes climbed into the cab of the pickup with Hodges, and asked, "Now what?"

"Can you get more firecrackers?"

Old Man Karnes' smile revealed tobacco-stained teeth that matched the beard around his chin. His eyes seemed lifeless and colorless.

* * *

As State Highway 139 leaves California and enters Oregon, it became Highway 39, the Hatfield Highway. East of Merrill,

Oregon, the Hatfield Highway curved west and merged into Highway 50. Every winter somebody always took that curve too fast, especially when it had ice or snow. Late December 1943 was no exception. A truck hauling chickens to Klamath Falls rolled on its side, scattered chickens, and feathers, and removed 12 6-foot timber guardrail posts from along the highway. A month later, a week of quasi-decent weather meant the Klamath County Road crew could re-grade the shoulder of the damaged road, and place new posts before the weather turned foul again. It was still cold, but at least there was no snow or ice that the four-man crew had to deal with.

Casper Walston said, "It's so cold, I just saw four Bigfoots playing strip poker."

Garth Linden was picking up the old broken posts and laughed, "That's nothing. It's so cold, that my wife's divorce lawyer has his hands in his own pockets for a change."

Ray Hayden was laying out the new posts and flagging spots that needed special attention. "It's so cold, me and my neighbor had to chisel his dog off a lamppost last night."

'Moose' Elkins looked up and saw a familiar old car coming to the highway curve from California. "Looks like we got company. I think it is Old Man Karnes."

A 1932 Ford Model 18 flat-head 8-cylinder coupe ground to a halt after taking 100 feet to stop. The four men could almost see the rust falling off the car as it finally quit moving. 'Moose' said, "Ouch, that hurt my ears! It sounds like my old teacher when she scratched her fingers down the chalkboard. Ain't it about time to fix them brakes?"

Old Man Karnes stretched as he got out of the car and spit

tobacco juice, some of which dribbled down his beard. "Yeah, one of these days." He turned and pointed to his two passengers. "Y'all know the Barclay Boys, don't 'cha?"

Howdies were exchanged, and one of the Barclay Boys walked behind the road crew truck to take a pee. Casper Walston warned, "Be careful. That could freeze before it hits the ground!"

The other Barclay, Alton, separated from the work crew and overdid his laugh. He slapped his knee and said, "Now that's a good 'un, all right." The road crew all turned and looked at Alton as if he were a little crazy, which meant the diversion had worked. Alvin Barclay reached into the road crew truck and grabbed two cases of dynamite. He quickly put them in the Ford before being detected.

Old Man Karnes reached into his coat and pulled out a bottle. "Maybe this stuff will keep you warm for a while. Here."

'Moose' accepted the bottle of rotgut whiskey as Walston, Hayden, and Linden crowded around for their turn at a swig or two. They did not even notice as Old Man Karnes and the Barclay Boys drove away.

"I'll drop you off at the Hodges Farm. I gotta pick up Jared and then go store these 24 firecrackers in a special place."

Two hours later, Old Man Karnes and Jared Hodges were driving to the old church. Jared was reviewing a lengthy list as he said, "I'll need your help to go over our inventory against this list so we can identify what else we need to shop for."

"We need transportation, for sure," observed Karnes as he drove. We don't want to use any of our own vehicles to prevent being recognized. My guess is we need about a dozen trucks."

"Where can you shop for trucks?"

"I think we will visit Edgewood, Yreka, and Hornbrook, then slip over to Keno and Dorris before we get back to Newell and Alturas. Then home."

"Pick-ups, we need pick-up trucks. We could also use bread trucks, dairy trucks, or lumber trucks."

"Sounds logical, Jared, we will get it done. We'll paint over any logos or signs."

Hodges thought another moment and smiled. "Find me a plumber's truck. I have an idea for it."

They pulled up next to the back door as the sun retreated below the cold horizon. They walked around the truck to stretch their legs, but mostly to scan the area for any people who should not see what came out of the truck. When they were satisfied, they removed the tarp which was almost frozen to the truck bed. Karnes grabbed the two boxes as Hodges unbolted the door. Just inside the door were two light switches, one for lights and the other to trigger an explosion in 30 seconds. By turning on the light switch first, the second switch was disabled. The two men made several trips to bring in the cases of dynamite stolen from the road crew truck, as well as the 500 rounds of ammunition stolen from an armory in Utah, and one submachine gun stolen from an Army supply depot near Pasco, Washington. Hodges commented, "We have to forage for supplies farther and farther from home, so we aren't accused and the locals in those areas are."

Once they had moved everything to the basement, Hodges locked all the doors behind them. "We don't want to be disturbed, now do we?" The basement had flags, boxes of church stuff, some World War I rusted rifles, pickaxe handles, worn-out boots, pistol parts, and some old, busted gas masks. Junk. They moved a tall bookshelf loaded with old hymnals aside and revealed a chained and locked metal door. After opening it, Hodges repeated the light switch procedure. "And we don't want to blow ourselves up either."

When the light did come on, it illuminated a concrete vault 100 feet by 100 feet cut under the hillside behind the church. Karnes knew of this place but had never seen it before, and it took several moments to grasp it all. There were rows of rifles and pistols, ammunition of different calibers, stolen uniforms, bayonets, knives, mortars, and medical supplies. Karnes was looking at gas masks when Hodges said, "We keep the gas canisters in a pond down the road so they can stay cool."

"This is amazing! How you kept the construction crew quiet is also amazing."

"We brought in a crew from New Mexico. They had an accident driving back, and unfortunately, all were killed. Tsk, tsk. Too bad."

"Yes, how unfortunate. You seem to have everything to start your own army."

"We are still short on a few items. We need mortar shells for those mortars over there, and we need ammo for the submachine gun we just acquired. We also need food rations in case we are in a prolonged fight. But most of all we need men, men to use these weapons and prevent the Japs from invading our coast."

"Just seeing this will get you men."

"No," Hodges said as he re-sequenced the timer switch and the lights. "Only Todd, Martin, and I know of this stash. The construction crew knew of this, but they tragically can't share that with anyone anymore. And now you have seen it."

"I am honored. Now what?"

"We wait; wait until the right moment to strike. But first, we need to gather intelligence and recruit men who believe in what we stand for and who are willing to fight for it."

Chapter 25
12:15 p.m., July 29, 1944
Tule Lake Segregation Center

Tommy was at the command of her Yuni, with assistance from Ichiro and Masako. Private Lawson had secured permission for grandmother and her to move into Barrack 41, an empty barrack in Block 5, just across from the rail depot. He told her, "It will be noisy during the day when teams are unloading train cars and moving things into storage, but it will be quiet at night." He knelt and said, "And no one will hassle you if you … you know … if you have another nightmare."

This was the nicest thing that had happened to her since she came to the camp. She never showed any emotion, well, except to Ichiro. But now she could not disguise the tear trickling down her cheek. "Thank you, Private Lawson. John. Thank you."

The moment became awkward, so Lawson stood up. "You are welcome, miss."

"The name is Tomoko, but I prefer 'Tommy.' Have you found out anything about my parents?"

"I had a lead about them being assigned to the temporary assembly areas at the Stanislaus County Fairgrounds in Turlock, but I lost them from there. I am not done though."

"Oh. My grandmother, my Sobo, is so frail. She has lost her courage; I think she just wants to die. I don't know what to do."

"I said that I am not done. Give me a little more time."

"Waa, waa, waa! Look at the little kid thrown into a wheelbarrow to be dumped on the trash pile. Waa, waa, waa!" exclaimed Juan Tu, leaning against a tree and pretending to cry. He balled up his fists and pretended to rub his eyes for more dramatic effect.

His buddies joined in, and they all began to cry, "Waa, waa, waa!"

"It's not enough that you hate the guards, but now you hate your own people?" Ichiro said as he walked up. "She has done nothing to you, Juan Tu."

The Bobby-voice exclaimed, *Oh, my God! That is almost exactly what I did to Sandra Rodriguez and her brother, Miguel. He was stuck in a wheelchair because of MS. I'm as big an asshole as this asshole!*

Private Lawson turned to face Juan Tu and said, "That's enough. Leave her alone."

Juan Tu snapped upright and slowly lowered his fists to his side. "And if I don't? What are you going to do about it?"

Lawson walked up to Juan Tu and quietly said, "I think on my day off tomorrow I will show up right where we are standing, and I won't be in uniform. I'll be waiting for you, tough guy. If you show up with your gang, then everyone will know you're not a leader of men, but just a bully leading other bullies. If you do not show up at all, then everyone will know you're a coward."

Bobby's voice said, *This is hard to listen to. Did people think that way about me? I don't like this at all, Ichiro.*

Juan Tu smiled and said, "And if I show up by myself?"

"Then you are more stupid than I thought."

"How's that?"

"You will get your butt kicked from one end of this compound to the other, and everyone will know you're all talk and no action. Any way you look at it, you're going to lose face." Out of the corner of his eye, Lawson saw Ichiro move slightly to his left to get a better angle on Juan Tu. When Ichiro clenched his fists to take a fighting position, Lawson thought, *This kid is overmatched, but he sure has guts. I could probably count on him for a few blows at the start, but I'll have to finish it.*

There was no smile on Juan Tu's face, and his eyes looked like those of a shark before closing in on its prey. "We have a rally tomorrow to protest the terrible treatment of all Asians here and in other slave camps by you, your murdering soldiers, and all others that enslave us." He noticed Ichiro moving but made no move.

"Wow, big words from a Jap coward," came words from the side. All turned to see Sergeant Weston stride up, smile, and say, "Now, break it up before I break you up."

Juan Tu tried to regain his position of power to his buddies by saying, "You plan to take all of us on?"

"Nope. Just you. I'm gonna smash your head like a pumpkin after a Halloween party. And I will do it with my uniform still on." He looked at Lawson and asked, "Private, don't you have something to do? If you don't have something to do, I will find you some work, maybe patching barrack roofs or emptying bedpans at the hospital."

Juan Tu hesitated, then said to his group, "Come on. We have to prepare." He led them toward the north section of the compound where trains exited the camp. Private Lawson walked off toward the center of the camp. Sergeant Weston walked toward the incoming rail gates as he looked at his watch.

Ichiro thought of a question for Bobby. *Why are you usually so quiet when we encounter Juan Tu? Are you that afraid of him?*

There was silence for a couple of minutes before Bobby's voice replied, *I see my old self in that guy, and I don't like what I see. I see what he does to people, and how they react. I feel inside what it does to you, and I don't like it. I guess I am ashamed.*

It was almost 1230 hours and there was an uncomfortable sensation in the air. Tommy in her wheelchair, Masako, and Ichiro were all quiet as if they smelled trouble. Ichiro heard a quiet voice in his head almost whispering, *This is not good. You and I need to talk.*

Ichiro thought quickly and said, "Masako, help me get Tommy to some place safe. I think trouble is coming, and I want her out of the way. None of her things are here yet, and until we move them over this won't be a comfortable place for her to stay."

"I've been called many things, but never 'trouble,'" said Ken as he walked up with Gordon.

Ken asked, "What are you up to?"

"We need your help. We need to move Tommy into the shade," said Ichiro as he winked at Ken and Gordon. "How about one of the barracks in Block 1?"

At the dance last year, Tommy began to look at Ichiro through eyes that had a different focus. She was usually self-reliant and refused help. She usually viewed her friends as just that, friends. But since the dance at the canteen, she looked at Ichiro very differently, and her heart felt something a bit stronger every day. She softly smiled as their eyes met. Ichiro matched her soft smile with one of his own. The silence was broken by Masako when she said, "Oh, brother, I think I am going to vomit." She shook her head as she grabbed the handgrips on the wheelchair. "Let's get her moved."

Gordon recognized the awkward moment and inquired, "How does the ramp work into your barrack that we all built?"

Ken added, "Yeah, it works great. We had you to supervise us, Tommy."

Ichiro suddenly felt like a naked man standing with one foot on an ant bed and the other foot in a tub of honey. He swallowed hard. "Ah, yeah. Let me help you." He also heard a faint laugh in his head as they quickly pushed Tommy down the dirt street between barracks.

Kemo Sabe, now we really gotta talk. Jesus H. Christ on a pogo stick. Or, maybe I should have said, 'Buddha on a broomstick.' Is that better?

* * *

The protest march started ten minutes late, at 1240 hours, at the warehouses beside the high school. The confrontation with Sergeant Weston continued to gnaw at Juan Tu. He felt confident he could deal with Private Lawson, but Weston was a man with nothing to lose and much to gain. And right now, Juan Tu could not afford to lose any power. *After all, I am The Terror of Tule-lake!* He was more alert than usual during the march, searching for an opportunity and a way to deal once and for all with Weston.

The group of 63 *Loyalists* had started marching from the edge of the warehouse platforms, turned on 5th Street, but slowed as they turned north on Main Street. Ahead, soldiers were blocking the planned route and were guarding several technicians working on 3rd Street and the intersection with Main. A quiet alarm went off in Juan Tu's mind. *That is very strange. There is a lot of activity, but no one is really doing any work.*

Usually, they marched north on Main Street up to North Street and across the camp, but today because of the street work they were blocked at Main Street and 3rd Street. More men joined them. Juan Tu thought, *We could double back to 5th Street, or we could back up to 4th Street and turn east heading toward Main Street, and more men could join us there.* A sea of shaved heads wearing white headbands called *hachimaki* with red spots representing the Imperial Red Sun walked and chanted slogans. They each wore a white shirt with another Imperial Rising Sun on the back. Many had grabbed trashcan lids and used them as clashing cymbals. "Go back to 4th Street and turn east," barked Juan Tu. As the group turned around on Main Street their numbers were approaching 195, and they had grown into a loud, angry mob. That's when all hell broke loose.

Homemade smoke bombs were lobbed into the camp at Point Alpha, where the rail line entered the camp. Fifty armed members of the *America for Americans* began screaming, "Death to murdering Japs!" and rushed into the camp. Only 20 carried guns, but the rest carried baseball bats, axes, and knives. Hodges waved a Civil War sword that he had stolen from a neighbor's house. They fired a few shots overhead but then started firing at anyone they encountered, internees and soldiers. Someone at the Reception Center turned on the claxon air raid siren. Now everyone in the camp panicked, but the guard towers remained silent.

Masako and Ichiro were sitting on the steps of the now-empty Block 1 Barracks 10 after they had pushed Tommy just inside the door and into the shade. The hot winds blew sand and dust into their eyes, noses, and mouths. It was getting hot quickly. They jumped to their feet when they heard the commotion. They did not know what it was, but they knew it was not any good. The claxon siren told them something horrible was happening. Ichiro looked south of the schoolyard towards the railyard and warehouses and saw the smoke. The fighting started. Bobby yelled in Ichiro's head, *Get Tommy out of that wheelchair and on the floor!*

Ichiro pushed the wheelchair away from the door and lifted Tommy as though she were a small, fragile doll. Ichiro gently placed Tommy flat on the ground using the wheelchair as an extra shield and covered her with his own body. Tommy's eyes were closed tightly, and her lips suppressed a scream. When she opened her eyes, Ichiro's face was just inches from her own, and his eyes were as wide as hers. The fighting and yelling seemed to fade into the background. Ichiro gave her a smile, a quick kiss, and she was no longer terrified. Their relief didn't last long, however. The two windows in the barrack wall nearest the street exploded when bottles of gasoline with lighted rags were tossed into the barrack. The fire quickly spread across the barrack's dry wooden floor and consumed the doorway – the very doorway they had only moments before been sitting by. Bobby's voice yelled, *Get out the other side!*

Ichiro assessed the situation and said, "Masako, get the wheelchair out the far window and I will carry Tommy out to you." With a strength he never knew he had, Ichiro lifted Tommy again, as if she were the most precious thing in his life. She smiled at him, placed her arms around his neck, and kissed his cheek.

There was no door at the opposite end of the barrack, just two similar, thankfully wide and tall windows. Ichiro shoved the wheelchair through the window; then he laid Tommy across the sill of the window and then climbed out the next. He pulled her through the window and set her in the waiting wheelchair. Ichiro looked at his sister and said, "Get her away from here. Take her to our barrack and tell our parents what is happening. Tell them I am safe but hiding until I can return. Now, go!"

Bobby's voice said, *You are growing up very fast, Kemo Sabe. Let's go save the wagon train!*

Masako saw something in her brother that was not there the day before. "Be careful, Ichiro. I have lost one brother and I cannot lose another."

Bobby's voice yelled, *Enough of this duck and cover crap! Let's do something!*

Ichiro agreed, hugged his sister, and looked over her shoulder at Tommy. He held her in his eyes and winked. "Ken and Gordon, watch over them and protect them." And then he was gone.

Juan Tu and his *Loyalists* turned and ran toward the commotion at the railhead but were stopped by the rushing human tidal wave coming at them. They ran down a small path between barracks, intending to get to Central Street. Some of the *Loyalists* wanted to turn south and run to the railhead to defend internees, but others wanted to turn right and join the flow headed north. There was confusion at the blockade created by the street work. Suddenly, the soldiers turned and began firing at the onrushing, fleeing internees. The soldiers who were firing were joined by the street repair workers who suddenly had weapons as well. "You can't escape!" was the last thing many Nisei and Issei heard as bullets tore through their flesh. Internees in the central part of the camp were now trapped between the *Loyalists* and the charging *America for Americans.*

Juan Tu was running, searching, and screaming, "Isao Hun! Kaede Matsumuro! Pass out our weapons!" Barracks were torn apart. Flooring, rafters, showers, and toilets revealed rifles and pistols that had been smuggled into the camp in pieces, reassembled, and hidden for such an emergency, or even a possible mass escape.

Kaede handed Juan Tu a 1935 Berretta semi-automatic pistol and extra ammunition. It had been stolen from a retired bookkeeper's garage two years ago and had been smuggled into the camp last year. Juan Tu only took a few moments to decide where to take the fight. He knew how many were in the group blocking the street, but he did not know how large the force was coming at him from the railhead. He turned and fired into the soldiers and repair workers on the street. Others of the *Loyalists* quickly followed suit, and the nine soldiers and workers were no longer blocking anything. "This way to freedom!" he shouted, running east on 3rd Street with the *Loyalists* behind him, the internees behind them, and the *America for Americans* now charging north on Main Street about 500 yards from them. The charge stopped, however, at the bodies of the soldiers and workers. Hodges knew the street repair workers were a special group of *America for Americans* he had chosen specifically for this task, led by his oldest son, Todd, with additional orders to shoot the soldiers in the back so it could later be blamed on the *Loyalists*. His face turned ash white when he saw the body of his first convert, his most devout follower, his son, Todd, with a bullet hole in his chest. His face turned red with anger, then a dark purple with hate. He stood and yelled to all around him, "Kill every man, woman, and child you come across. Leave no one alive!"

An explosion rocked the eastern end of the camp.

The old, bearded man from the diner had stolen two cases of dynamite from a highway repair crew in January and no one had ever solved the robbery. Now four sticks of that stolen dynamite had exploded and ripped a gaping hole in the fences near where the railhead exited the camp. The hole was so big a truck could be driven through it, which is exactly what the *America for Americans* did. Ten pickup trucks poured through the opening, each with many armed *America for Americans*, firing and shouting, "Death to all Japanese!" Like a flood during a dam breach, they spread out. Most drove northbound on Rail Road Street, then headed to Central to meet the protestors head-on. But a few trucks drove westbound on 5th Street, to push internees into the fire and also to support the first wave of invaders. Internees were diving for any cover they could find.

Juan Tu heard the trucks coming before he saw them. He looked around for protection and then had a different idea. He yelled an order, "Get those rain barrels and line them up across the road. Quickly!" His men jumped into action. Two men started to empty a barrel to make it easier to move, but Juan Tu screamed, "Leave the water in! The extra weight can give us more protection!" The trucks were less than 50 yards away when he yelled, "Don't shoot until after they hit the barrels and run from the trucks!"

The *Loyalists* did not have to wait very long. Four pickup trucks, driving side-by-side, slammed into the barrels. Each truck had six armed men in the bed of the truck and three in the cab. Sheets of spray shot skyward from the collisions, and the men in the truck beds went flying. They were still groggy as they tried to stand and were easily picked off by the *Loyalists*. Their cheer was short-lived when they saw fifty more armed *America for Americans* charging in from behind the pickups. Many of Juan Tu's men fell as rifle and pistol shots were fired. They all heard what sounded like more trucks coming, so Juan Tu turned to give the order to retreat, but the words never left his lips. His eyes went completely wide, and then he yelled, "Quick! Get under the barracks!" The rumbling sounds were not coming from behind the pickups, they were behind Juan Tu and his men. It was not the sound of pickup trucks; it was the sound of just one vehicle.

Captain Shackleford had gotten a strange Christmas present last year from California Governor Earl Warren. The governor thought it might be a good idea to station a M1917 Light Tank of the 40th Tank Company of the California National Guard at the camp, though his exact reasoning was never made clear. No one thought it would run. It did. No one thought it had ammunition. It did. Shackleford had ordered it to be covered until he could figure out what to do with the monstrosity. He said to himself, *This belongs on a courthouse square or in a park for kids to climb on. Not here.* Now he thought differently.

The six and one-half ton tank, powered by a modified four-cylinder, gasoline engine, could do a whopping five miles per hour but smoked more than a train engine. Private Lawson was inside the light tank feverishly maneuvering the metal beast and learning as he drove. So far, he had only hit two buildings as he got the tank to make turns. The M1917 Light Tank was 16 feet long, almost six feet wide, and seven feet in height, which meant even an experienced driver would have some difficulty in the narrow streets of the camp. Captain Shackleford commanded the crew, comprised of just Lawson, and was ready to fire the .30 caliber Marlin machine gun. The tank was less than 100 yards from the skirmish line on 3rd Street created by the rain barrels when he opened fire. The *America for Americans* were told there would be no resistance, and now they found out differently. Their numbers were quickly dwindling. "Faster," ordered Shackleford over the radio headset to Lawson. "We cannot let any escape."

Lawson wondered, *Does he mean Japanese or does he mean*

the militia? "Sir, this tank might go faster, but I can barely steer it now!"

"Just keep us moving forward, Private!" Two pickup trucks suddenly appeared, coming between the barracks on the right. The first one was driven by the old, bearded man from the diner. He lit a single stick of dynamite with his cigar and started to throw it when bullets fired from a Thompson submachine gun, manned by Corporal Williams, blasted away most of his shoulder. The dynamite fell to the truck floor and wedged under the accelerator. Old Man Karnes sat in disbelief and stared at the dynamite as it exploded, sending truck shrapnel and militia body parts through barrack windows, doors, walls, and even into some of Juan Tu's men.

Now there was confusion in what was left of Karnes' group, who spoke up at the same time, "Where did those soldiers come from?" "I thought they were supposed to be on our side?" "Yeah, that's what Hodges told us!"

"First Squad! Assume a kneeling position! Second Squad! Assume a prone firing position! Fire on my command! First Squad, fire and reload! Second Squad, fire and reload! First and Second Squad advance 50 yards and repeat positions! First Squad, fire and reload! Second Squad, fire and reload! First and Second Squad advance 50 yards and repeat positions!" Methodically and without a single injury, Corporal Williams and his men cleared two blocks of 3rd Street of protestors and militia. "Hold your positions here!" They were now the front vanguard for the tank.

Another truck cab tried to cut across in front of the tank, but the truck bed took the weight of the tank treads, and all five men were crushed. A third truck driven by a neighbor of the young man from the diner was directly behind the second truck. Captain Shackleford turned the machine gun, and suddenly all seven men in the truck were gunned down. "Keep moving," was Shackleford's order. "Williams, great job! Now take a team and sweep behind us to prevent a counterattack." Williams took three men and ran toward the open field at West and American to make sure the militia was not regrouping behind them. When the tank was within fifteen yards of what was left of the rain barrels, Shackleford opened up with the machine gun on the militia caught unawares. They did not know whether to shoot, surrender, or run, so they stood where they were and died. The tank went up and over the crushed rain barrels and the pickups, still with militia inside. The Marlin machine gun stopped firing sometime before Shackleford realized he was out of ammo. As he turned to retrieve another box of ammo from behind him, he yelled out over the headset, "Keep moving. Continue north on Main Street to 2nd Street and head toward Central, Private."

"Yes, Sir!" When they reached 2nd, the tank was rocked by a massive explosion to the northwest. Lawson saw through his small windshield considerable smoke from the direction of the fencing on the edge of the camp.

Shackleford said over the headset, "Change in plans, son. Head to that plume of smoke!"

Lawson saw that the militia had blown a huge hole in the fence, and now militia and internees were escaping from the camp. He yelled over the headset, "Sir. Shall I radio for an attachment to come to guard what is left of the fence?"

"Great idea, Private! Do it; we can block their escape their escape." *Or minimize it. There's gonna be hell to pay for this, and I will probably get stuck with the check! Where are my soldiers?*

Lawson smiled a little and thought, *Maybe I will make a good soldier after all if I get out of here alive.* He queued his radio and said, "Reception. We need two squads with rifles and a machine gun to the southeast corner, where the rail lines leave the camp."

The radio from Reception crackled, "This is Sergeant Weston. Inform Captain Shackleford I will personally bring two squads as ordered, and on the double! I will lead one squad and Private Escobar will lead the other. Out." Weston needed some time to think. *This has not gone as I planned, but I think I can salvage the plan,* he thought as he grabbed his helmet, a walkie-talkie, and his rifle. As he burst out the door, he yelled, "Third Squad! Fifth Squad! On the double! Our objective is the southeast fence. Today, ladies! Now! Move it!"

Private Escobar and the Fifth Squad poured out of the soldiers' barracks located within the southwest corner of the camp next to the Military Police Compound, the Military Motor Pool, and the Camp Power Station. The eleven-man squad was not combat-ready – some were fresh from their initial training. They hurried out of their bunks, the latrines, and the doors half-dressed. They ran north on West Street, some with weapons at the ready and some who had forgotten their weapons.

The radio crackled again. "Fourth Squad, be ready to move on my command when I give you the destination. Be ready," ordered Captain Shackleford in a much more confident and authoritative voice than Weston's screams. Another massive explosion rocked the camp as the Power Station was shredded by dynamite. Four militiamen began lobbing lighted sticks of dynamite over the fence and into the military motor pool sheds, the Military Police compound, and the 'Bull Pen' stockade. A radical, anti-anyone-non-white named Mitch Glass, who owned 'Gas by Glass', the gas station in Tulelake, was running. He had a knapsack over his shoulder, and moments before lit and thrown a stick of dynamite that took out an Army truck filled with several soldiers who had failed to scramble away in time. A soldier in a guard tower shot him before he could lob a third stick he had just lit. He fell to the ground on top of the dynamite and was blown to pieces.

The sounds of trucks, screaming, gunfire, and explosions could still be heard in the barracks in Block 4 where they hid. Smoke from smoke bombs and buildings now on fire limited their vision. "We can't stay here!" yelled Tommy over the explosions when she noticed the next barrack was on fire.

Ken coughed from the smoke now pouring in the broken windows. He said, "But Ichiro said we should protect you, and this looks like a pretty good place to do just that."

"Not me. I'm out of here!" said Tommy. "I think I will take 6th Street west to Border Street and head north. The crowd is on West Street, so Border might be better, easier rolling for Yuni and me. Anyone want to join us?"

Masako quickly said, "You lead, and I will push."

Tommy smiled and said, "Alright! Three cheers for Girl

Power!" She turned in her chair and said, "Do either of you scaredy-cats wish to join us?"

Ken was now equally mad and embarrassed. He said, "Move over, Masako. Let Gordon and me show you Man Power and how fast we can push this wheelchair." He smiled at Masako and said, "Stay low and behind us. I don't want anything to happen to you."

Chapter 26
6:35 p.m., July 29, 1944
Tule Lake Segregation Center

Sergeant Weston and the Third Squad sauntered north on West Street as if out for a Sunday stroll in the park. His squad wanted to engage the enemy, any enemy, and fight. Some moved ahead of Weston, but he ordered them back into formation. "We can't just 'Ride to the sound of the guns' as some old general once said – right before he got shot. If we do that, we might leave Japs behind us that can attack from the rear. Carefully inspect every side street and building as we move forward, men."

"But what about these others that started this whole thing?"

"What others? Oh, you mean the townspeople trying to help us! Yes, we spare them. They ain't the problem."

Further ahead, Private Escobar and the Fifth Squad moved up West Street in an attempt to cut off internees making a run for freedom, and any militia still trying to shoot internees. He turned a corner at 2nd Street that ran along the northwest fence line and quite literally fell on top of Jared Hodges, whose face was deeply creased by a bullet and now had blood along his jaw. Escobar looked at the man in an out-of-place World War I military uniform, and asked, "Who the hell are you and where did you come from?"

"We are from *America for Americans*. The militia? Sergeant Weston asked us to help you prevent these murderin' Japs from escaping!"

Escobar smelled a rat. "Show me some identification, right now!"

He was looking at Hodges' Oregon driver's license and casually said, "I appreciate your help, sir. There certainly are more of them than there are of us. When did Sergeant Weston contact you about helping us with this riot?" He smiled as he held out Hodges' wallet but did not release it.

"Ah, well, ah, he called us a while ago."

"So, he called you, and you just happened to be passing by with your entire group of armed men and equipment?"

"Well, ah, well, ah, he told me the other night at the diner that he had heard from an informant that something might be happening soon. Yeah, that's it."

"That's amazing! You got here from Klamath Falls right after Weston called you." He threw Hodges' wallet in his face. "You are lying through your teeth, which is where I'm thinking to insert the butt of my pistol."

Weston and the Third Squad had caught up with Escobar and the Fifth Squad. Weston panicked when he saw Hodges being interrogated by Escobar and realized his little kingdom was about to tumble. He ordered half his squad to move east on 2nd Street, and half to move back and then west on 3rd Street. That left Weston and Escobar to question Hodges.

"Sergeant Weston, there is a problem here. This man claims you called him to come help prevent this riot even before it happened."

Weston pulled his service revolver and pointed it at Hodges. "He did? Well, there won't be a problem anymore." Weston turned and fired point-blank into Escobar's chest. Even after Escobar fell, his eyes stared at Weston as if pleading, 'Why?'

Hodges stared at the still-open eyes of Private Escobar and screamed, "Are you crazy?"

Weston turned the pistol back toward Hodges and ordered, "Complete your mission or I promise the next bullet goes into your head. Understand?" With complete clarity, Hodges understood as he frantically nodded his head.

Border Street curved beside the fencing as it intersected with an open lot at 3rd Street. Masako, Tommy, Ken, and Gordon witnessed Sergeant Weston shoot Private Escobar. Masako screamed. Weston and Hodges both turned, and Weston said, "More trash to get rid of."

"Not if we can help it," came a determined voice from another side street. Weston's eyes almost bulged from their sockets. Hodges was unsure of his own future, and now even that seemed a bit weaker as he stared at a Japanese American man and a young man covered in dirt, mud, and blood. They stood alone but the two projected the strength of an army.

Masako yelled, "Otōsan!"

Tommy smiled and softly said, "Ichiro."

* * *

Just 90 minutes ago, Ichiro ducked into doorways, rolled under ramps, flattened himself against barrack walls, and even crawled under a latrine as he scrambled to reach his parents. Their apartment in Block 4 was just across Central Avenue from where he had taken shelter the first time with Masako, Tommy, Ken, and Gordon in Barrack 40. But that 'short trip' had taken an hour and a half! Once he even had to do something very regrettable, he smeared some of the blood of a dead internee on himself, laid on the ground, and rolled the body onto himself to hide as some of the *Loyalists* and some of the militia battled on Central. He thought he saw a wheelchair moving quickly and beyond the high school, but he could not move his head to get a good look and risk allowing detection. After several minutes, the fight moved down the street. He crawled across the street to Block 4 and ran to Barracks 4-8.

He found his parents huddled in the corner of Apartment C under a window. He panicked when he saw blood smeared over his mother's face and down the front of her dress. He feared the worst when he yelled, "Where is all that blood from, Okāsan! What's wrong? Is she hurt, Otōsan?"

Saburo turned to see his son and sighed with relief. Ichiro saw his father was holding a towel to his mother's head. Saburo said, "It is a simple cut right at the hairline. It bleeds excessively, but she will be fine."

Ichiro hurriedly devised a plan of action. "Okāsan, please find Tomoko's grandmother and the two of you stay hidden until we come back. Otōsan, I need your help."

Bobby's voice cautioned, *Are you sure you want to leave her here? Wouldn't she be safer with us?*

Ichiro thought, *No, because I do not know what kind of danger lies in store for us. It is a risk either way, but I think this is a smaller risk.*

Etsuko smiled as she saw her young son becoming a man. "Yes, Ichiro, I will," was her only response.

"Otōsan, I think I saw Masako, Ken, and Gordon pushing Tomoko as fast as they could toward the west side of the camp. We must find them. Is there anything here we could use for weapons?"

Saburo smiled and said, "I have always found these as my best weapons." He was showing his hands to his son and turning them slowly.

Your father is pretty cool, but he ain't bulletproof, Kemo Sabe. There is a saying in 2017, 'Never take a knife to a gunfight,' but that may be all we have. Find something!

"Let's take any knives we have here in the apartment, just in case."

From a box under her bed, Etsuko retrieved a chef knife and a small paring knife, both stuffed into a pair of cotton socks. "I borrowed them from the kitchen, and I guess I forgot to return them," confessed Etsuko with a slight smile.

Ichiro looked at his mother with surprise, and Saburo snickered, "After all these years, you never cease to amaze me."

Ichiro hugged his mother and walked to the door. Saburo held Etsuko at arm's length and read her mind. "Yes, I will bring him home safely. Yes, I will come home as well. Find Tomoko's grandmother, as Ichiro said, and find shelter. Stay there." He read her mind once again. "And I love you too, my tsuma." He followed Ichiro out the door.

Bobby's voice said, *I am jealous of you. I cannot ever remember my mother and father doing that. Maybe I would have turned out differently.*

Ichiro softly responded, "Maybe, but certainly you are here now, and I need you now."

* * *

Masako yelled, "Otōsan!"

Tommy smiled and softly said, "Ichiro."

Weston with hate dripping from his mouth like saliva declared, "Now we have more Japs to kill."

Hodges panicked and fired at Saburo, who tried to sidestep the path of the bullet from Hodge's pistol. The bullet skidded across Saburo's chest. He was bloodied, and dropped the chef's knife, but was still standing. Saburo wiped some of the blood from his chest and through clenched teeth he shouted, "Is that the best you can do, or do you have the courage to face me man-to-man without weapons?"

Bobby's voice added, *Like I said, he ain't bulletproof. He's got more guts than brains.*

Quiet!

Hodges raised his pistol to fire when a red flower blossomed on his chest, followed by the sound of a small explosion. He first looked at the blood squirting from the wound and spreading across his old uniform, then he looked up at the approaching Corporal Williams holding his Thompson submachine gun. As

Hodges collapsed to the ground, Williams replaced his 30-round magazine clip and was ready for more action.

"Hold it!" came the scream from another direction. "Drop your weapons, you white dogs!" Isao Hun yelled as he crawled from under a barrack as Kaede Matsumuro provided cover. Isao pointed a cocked Smith and Wesson at Weston's head as Kaede held a rifle to Williams' chest. Both soldiers froze and dropped their weapons to the ground.

Kaede began to gather the weapons as Juan Tu emerged from under the barracks. "I must speak to the management of this facility some time." He made a spectacle of dusting himself off as he announced, "The sanitary conditions in this place are deplorable." He walked over to Weston, but first took a moment to flip Hodges over onto his back. He scooped up a large handful of dirt and sprinkled it over Hodges as he said, "What is it you Christians say at a funeral? Oh, yes. Ashes to ashes and dust to dust." He kicked the body and added, "You white dogs will die. It is a must!"

Kaede piled up the weapons and ammo belts as Isao softly asked for orders, "Now what, Juan Tu?"

Juan Tu walked around as if he were a general inspecting his troops. "Let's take an inventory of the living and the dead, shall we? First, we have two boys and two girls who are minor players in all this. I think they were simply trying to leave. Next, we have Corporal Williams. He hates Sergeant Weston as much as any of us, which is a redeeming value to his soul, and I must honestly confess to him he did truly care for those locked up in this prison." He strode up to Williams and said, "I do thank you for that." Juan Tu's actions and speech now revealed an educated mind that he had never displayed since his arrival in the camp. No one inside the camp knew he had a Masters' Degree in Asian Studies from San Francisco State University. Since that level of education would not serve him in his chosen role in the camp as a rabble-rouser and hate-monger, he kept it buried until another day. Today was that day.

He walked towards Saburo and Ichiro. "Here's an old man and my lil' Jap friend, as Weston called him, who's trying so hard to grow up. Boy, do you know you will probably die in this place? Maybe we all will." He returned to the body of Jared Hodges and nudged it with his foot. "I still have no idea who this guest is, but I'm sure Sergeant Weston can enlighten us all, so a proper name can be placed on his tombstone."

Weston could not hold his temper any longer. "Are you crazy? I have no idea!"

"Oh, yes you do. We were under that barrack and could see you talking to him." Juan Tu slowly walked toward Weston as he said, "And lastly, we have Sergeant Weston, a man who hates everyone and who is hated by everyone."

Weston looked at his watch and slightly took a linebacker's squat just before he plowed through Juan Tu, which sent him flying backward into a hard landing on his back. The group stared in disbelief at Weston's rapid retreat – marveling at the speed with which he ran – simultaneously wondering where he thought he could go to escape a certain court martial.

Suddenly, a blast sent half of Barrack 34 in Block 3 into the air and knocked everyone down.

Chapter 27
7:10 p.m., July 29, 1944
Along the Northwest Fence, Tule Lake
Segregation Center

The growing sunset added streaks of red and gold to the graying skies. There were clouds of fire and smoke over much of the camp, but the worst at the moment was the explosion in Barrack 34 which sent wood and metal fragments in every direction for several hundred yards. The falling debris in turn ignited fires in Barracks 32, 33, and 35. Those unchecked fires would soon spread farther, like falling dominos. But presently, no one could see those fires because they all were standing in a fog of dust and shrapnel, with flames surrounding them. Masako was coughing enough to make her retch and fall to her knees. She could hear others around her groaning.

Ichiro called out, "Otōsan! Where are you?"

"Here, Ichiro." Ichiro almost fell over him as he stumbled in the direction the voice came from. "Here, son," came the voice faintly. As the thick smoke and dust settled, Ichiro could see his father had a small piece of burning metal in his leg just below the knee.

Bobby's voice helped assess the wound. *He is not bleeding, probably because the metal that burned off his pant leg also seared the wound.*

Ichiro agreed. "I think you will be fine, but we do need to get you to the camp hospital."

If it is still there.

"Ichiro!" He turned to see Masako tending to Corporal Williams, unconscious on his back. Ken was helping her.

Gordon was standing beside Tommy's wheelchair, just looking down. When he looked up at Ichiro tears were rolling down his cheeks. "Ichiro, I think ... I am afraid she's ... I don't know what to do."

Ichiro ran to her and all that could come out of his mouth was, "No!" He took her hand, placed it to his face, and then jumped back. "She's alive! I feel a pulse! She is just unconscious!" As he spoke, he saw Juan Tu bent over what was left of the body of Kaede Matsumuro. Isao Hun tried to crawl away to who knew where but collapsed.

Juan Tu, the academic turned internee thug boss, seemed to have a transformative moment as he looked from Kaede to Ichiro and pleaded, "What have I done? What has my hate done to my friends? I should have been a source of inspiration to other internees, not a source of fear and hate."

Bobby's voice lamented, *It looks like he is no longer the Terror of Tulelake.* After a few moments, he added, *And I guess I don't want to be that any longer myself.*

Tommy stirred in the wheelchair. Gordon said, "She's coming around."

As Ichiro turned back to Tommy, he noticed Sergeant Weston was missing.

* * *

It had finally happened, and Sergeant Weston's big plan was working, but not exactly the way he had envisioned it. No one ever figured out that the *America for Americans* militia had been paying Sergeant Weston for information for over a year. The militia never knew that Weston's information was often tainted or slanted to incite hatred and tension against the internees. No one ever figured out that Weston was filling his pockets at the same time he was pushing and pushing the internees to a point that they made mistakes – angry reactions that kept them defensive. No one figured out that Weston was playing both groups against each other so that when that inevitable boiling point was reached, and tensions became open conflict, Sergeant Weston could lead soldiers to squash rebellion, kill many of the Japanese Americans, and look the other way as the *America for Americans* militia scurried in retreat. Then he could tell his superiors, and the press, that these internees were not to be trusted. No one figured out his plan. No one except Private Escobar, and now he was dead. *And I don't think anyone back in that field will live to tell anything they might have learned. Besides, who would believe them? They have no proof!*

He stopped to rest in a culvert about 200 yards outside the fence. "That old guy, Karnes, that stole all that dynamite did a good job with a delayed timer on an entire case. That blast took out 100 yards of fence and a bunch of barracks. I hope they were filled with Japs scared silly and trying to hide." He mopped some blood from his face and his right arm. *Mine?* He snickered as he realized, *The camp's fire department won't be able to put out any of these fires, so bodies will be burnt beyond recognition, including those people I just left.* He checked his ammo belt and discovered he was out. He checked his pistol and found he had two bullets left. He spoke aloud, "I just have two regrets that one of these bullets didn't go into Juan Tu's head and the other into Captain Shackleford's head."

"Save it for yourself, Sergeant Weston."

Weston jumped up, surprised to see a 5-foot, 10-inch young man staring at him. Ichiro was bloody over most of his body, which covered the dust and mud he had crawled through to get across the camp hours ago. His hair was still smoking as he felt the heat of what remained of a burning ember on his scalp.

Bobby's voice warned, *Remember what I said about a knife at a gunfight, Kemo Sabe. You ain't got no silver bullets. Be very careful, my brother.*

"Well, well. It comes down to me and you, lil' Jap."

"I guess it does. When the authorities find out what you planned and unleashed on the innocent people here, you will be tried for treason."

"Who says they will figure it out? You ain't gonna tell nobody."

"Maybe I will and maybe I won't. But the others you left behind will."

Weston swallowed hard and tried to maintain his superiority

over the Jap kid. "What others are you talking about, boy?" He took a few casual steps toward Ichiro.

"My friends, my father, Juan Tu, and Corporal Williams."

"That ain't possible; they are all dead. You're trying to confuse me."

"No, I'm not. In truth, they are bruised, battered, and a little bloody, but they are all alive, just as alive as you and I are. You must really have some kind of superiority complex to assume you were the only one in that group to survive that blast. You didn't run that far before it detonated. Yes, and there's another offense to add to your growing list of criminal charges. You were behind that explosion since you knew it was going to happen. Kinda dumb that you didn't even take the time to go back and check the bodies. Seriously, what kind of military badass are you?" Ichiro scoffed and said, "Sorry. You screwed up big time, Kemo Sabe."

Hey, that's my line!

Ichiro took a few steps toward Weston.

That's it. We gotta get close.

"So, what do you suppose we oughta do?"

Ichiro spread his hands some and took a few more steps. They were now 15 feet apart. "That sort of depends upon you. I guess you could run away and hide, but then you would be hunted down like a rabid skunk. You might be shot on sight, or they might have a big trial followed by a hanging."

I vote for that one.

"Or you could surrender and maybe the Army would go easy on you."

Hell, no, they won't! insisted Bobby's voice.

Weston took another step and said, "There is another possibility. If Escobar's body got real toasty, there would be no way to identify him except for my charred dog tags I can put around his neck." He made a big show as he pulled his tags over his head and held them in his sweaty grip. "I can just assume a new identity somewhere else. Hey, I might even join the service, maybe the Navy. I ain't never been on no big boat."

Crap and corruption! He already had an escape plan.

"So, all I have to do is kill you and disappear, kid."

"That won't work either," came a voice from beside a tree about 50 feet to Weston's left. "I like Ichiro's idea about you surrendering."

Ichiro exclaimed, "Corporal Williams! I'm glad you were here to witness Weston's confession!"

He looks terrible; he is ash-white.

Weston was stunned to see him. "How did you survive that blast, corporal?"

"I could ask you the same thing, Sergeant Weston. Ichiro, come over here, and away from that maniac."

"Don't move, kid. I've got a bullet right here with your name on it," Weston said.

Ichiro was ten feet away when he saw the blood oozing from a wound in Williams' side. Blood was dripping from his hand as he shakily held a pistol pointed at Weston.

"Ichiro, come over here," Williams calmly said in a very even tone tinged with command.

Ichiro moved and was about three feet away from the tree when Williams began to crumple as if he were about to pass out.

Ichiro turned to face Weston, and his hand slowly went behind his back.

"Goodbye, Corporal Williams," Weston said with conviction.

The paring knife flew out of Ichiro's hand as he dove in front of Corporal Williams.

No! screamed Bobby's voice as the gun exploded. Then there was darkness, darkness like the bottom of a deep well at midnight. Then, total silence.

Chapter 28
2:55 a.m., March 6, 2017
Tulelake, California

Bobby woke up breathing heavily as if he had been running from something terrible. *Wait, I wasn't running; I was jumping in front of Corporal Williams. The America for Americans or the Loyalists or everybody was running through the huge hole in the camp's fence. And the soldiers were chasing them. They had been shooting at us from the back of pickup trucks!* He sat on the edge of his bed and dazedly thought, *I am soaked in blood!* The memory of what had happened filled his mind. *Ichiro and I were shot by Weston!* Bobby switched on the light by his bed and then realized to his relief that he was soaked in sweat, not blood. *Ichiro, where the hell are we?* There was no response. *How did we get inside? Where is everybody? Where is Tommy? Is she okay? We were trying to run and push Tommy's wheelchair to the woods when we were hit by a huge explosion. Then we started chasing Sergeant Weston. Isn't that right, Kemo Sabe?* Still no response from Ichiro. Bobby staggered absentmindedly into the bathroom and splashed water on his face. As he looked up, he saw a familiar reflection in the mirror. *OH MY GOD!* His breathing stopped as he stared at his reflection and the same look of shock. *I am Bobby again! I'm back in my house! I'm back in Tulelake!* After a few moments of celebration mixed with confusion, he thought, *But when is this? Am I back in 2017? Where is Ichiro?*

He walked to the kitchen and checked the gimme calendar they got from the feed store. The calendar showed the right month and the right year. Relief flooded his body until he heard his father cough behind him in the living room. Usually, Ed King sat in his busted easy chair with beer cans strewn everywhere. He would drink beer until he passed out watching old westerns. Ed coughed again and said, "You can't sleep either?"

"No, I guess not," Bobby said as he turned around, expecting a blow to the back of his head or a slap to his face. But what he saw stunned him. The TV was off, there were no beer cans on the floor, and his father looked as if he had been crying. "I guess things got out of hand," Bobby said, really unsure where the conversation would lead.

"For both of us, son, for both of us," Ed said in a voice tinged with regret, remorse, and sincerity. "If you are completely awake, maybe we should talk."

Bobby very carefully sat down opposite his father. He wanted to make sure he was out of swinging distance and had an escape route to either the front door or the back door. "Okay."

Ed started his confession, "I'm not happy with the way things are, but I don't want you to go." He started two or three sentences, but words just did not come out of his mouth. Finally, he blurted out, "Bobby, I have failed you as a father. I should have been more supportive of you. I should have set a better example for you. Instead, I blamed you for your mother leaving. I know that all your delinquency is due to the way your life has been since your ma left. I remember what a nice boy you were before she left; you were kind, and you did well in school. I hate myself so much for what I've done or not done to further destroy your life. Maybe that's why I drink so much. And when I see how angry and mean you are, I feel such guilt and remorse for what could have been, I drink even more."

Now the tears were running down his cheeks. "Please forgive me. We need each other. We can help each other, and I need you, son. I've got some of your grandpa's old guns that I'm gonna sell to pay old man Simmons to drop the charges against you for burning his smokehouse. It's time for us to make a fresh start. I owe that to you. Please stay!" Ed's mouth continued to work, but words eluded him.

Bobby could not speak. He always had a glib retort for anything, but not this time. Something had changed in his father. *Hell, something changed me, too! Ichiro, are you hearing this? Ichiro?* Still no response. They made serious talk until 5:30 am, when Ed surprised his son by asking, "Bobby, I'm getting hungry. If you will pop some bacon into the microwave, I'll scramble us a mess of eggs." For the first time in an unimaginable time, Ed smiled at his son.

Bobby returned the smile and said, "Great idea. I'll make us some toast and set the table."

Ed said, "I think there is still some of that jalapeno jam in the refrigerator."

* * *

An hour later, Ed was leaving for work. "We can talk more later if you want."

"I'd like that very much. Dad."

Ed liked the sound of that word, that word he had not heard in too many years. His feet barely touched the ground walking out to the truck. Bobby did the dishes and got cleaned up. In the bathroom, he brushed his teeth for the first time in he didn't know how long and took a quick look for some aspirin he knew he would not find. *This headache is killin' me*. He was about to head to school when he remembered the suspension. *I've got a tough talk ahead with the principal to get back into school. I've never groveled for nuthin' before – in fact, I'm not sure that is the right word to use. But I've gotta do it. Ichiro, you ain't said a word since I woke up, but I just know you are still there. Come with me to school. I need your support, Kemo Sabe.*

* * *

Bobby walked quickly down the street because, for the first time in a long time, he did not want to be late for school. *I've wasted a lot of my time and the time of so many others, but maybe, just maybe, it ain't too late. Correction, maybe it isn't too late.* He stopped when he saw Abdul Mohammad across the street. Bobby waved and said, "Abdul! May I speak with you for a moment?" He got to the center of the street and realized that Abdul was ignoring him. "Abdul, wait, please!"

Abdul turned to face Bobby with fists clenched expecting a

verbal fight or a physical one. He was ready for either. "What insults do you have for me today, infidel?"

Bobby slowly stepped up onto the curb with his hands deep in his pockets. He shrugged his shoulders and said, "No insults, but an apology. A real apology this time, Abdul." Of all the things Abdul envisioned that could come out of Bobby's mouth, he never thought he would hear this. "I have come to realize that it is wrong to despise or hate, or whatever you call it, a person or a group of people because of what they look like or their religion."

"What brought on this epiphany?" came a softer question from Abdul as he unclenched his fists.

"Huh?"

"Why and why now?"

"Oh, I've been studying what happened at that old, deserted camp outside of town. I've learned that all those people were Americans but were still locked up, thousands of them. They hadn't shot anyone, beat anyone up, robbed a bank, or nothin'. They were all thrown into a concentration camp just because of what they looked like, not because of anything they'd done.

Abdul now looked differently at Bobby, and said, "Let's sit on this bench for a minute. Bobby, have you ever heard of the U.S. Army's 442nd Regiment?"

"Yes, but I don't know much."

"That regiment was made up of almost all Japanese American soldiers, and they fought in Italy to help win the war in Europe. They became the most decorated combat unit in the history of the U.S. Army. Real American heroes."

Bobby thought about the letter Taro sent his family. "Yes, I think I knew of someone in that regiment."

"What?"

"I mean I read about one of those soldiers."

"The point I am trying to make, Bobby, is that there are about 10,000 Muslim-Americans right now in the U.S. Army fighting to preserve and protect the American way of life, just like the Japanese American soldiers of the U.S. Army's 442nd Regiment during World War II."

Bobby's eyes went wide, "Oh my God, this could be happening all over again! That's horrible!"

"Why the concern now?"

Bobby knew what to say but had to be careful how he said it. "Abdul, have you ever seen the same picture a bunch of times, but then you look at it in a different light and you see something different? I don't know, maybe I'm not explaining it right."

"Interesting analogy."

"Huh? Oh, yeah, a 'ganalogee."

"A-nal-o-gee, Bobby," Abdul said with a friendly smile.

"Yeah, I get it, we learned that word it in English class. Well, I guess something I read about the people in that camp made me look at what is happening to Muslim Americans differently. So that is why I need to apologize. I was wrong, Abdul."

Abdul smiled and said, "My grandfather taught me an interesting proverb. It says 'The first to apologize is the bravest. The first to forgive is the strongest. And the first to forget is the happiest.' Perhaps we have both learned something that we can build a new friendship on. Do you agree?"

Bobby extended his arm, and they shook hands. "I'd like that very much, Abdul. Ahh, can we include your sister, Sara, in this new friendship?"

Abdul laughed and said, "One step at a time, young infidel. One step at a time. Sara is smart and proud, and you haven't done anything so far to make her feel anything towards you but disgust and loathing."

"Well, I have to try. She is a very strong young lady, and I admire that in her."

"Perhaps we can work on that – with supervision, of course."

"How would that work?"

"The two of you can sit on our porch and talk while I sharpen my sword." Booby's eyes almost bulged out until he saw Abdul wink at him and say, "I believe the expression is 'Got you.'"

Bobby looked at his watch when he saw the sun peeking under some low clouds in the east. "I gotta git. Thanks for your time, Abdul. And again, I'm sorry for the way I have acted. I was a stupid idiot."

"Assalaam-O-Alaikum, my new friend. That means 'Peace and blessings be with you.'"

* * *

Like clockwork, Mr. Stevens' 1999 blue Sebring pulled into the parking lot at Tulelake High School at 7:45 a.m. Bobby was sitting on the curb at the head of Mr. Stevens' reserved spot. Mr. Stevens was unsure if he should get out or just wait for raw eggs to fly in his direction, which is what happened about a year ago. He looked around for Bobby's Three Stooges, but they were not to be seen. He carefully got out of the car but made sure he could duck back in if he needed an escape route. Bobby slowly stood, opened his arms, and said, "I have really screwed up. Big time. I owe you an apology, I owe Mrs. Carson an apology like I owe so many other teachers. I owe so many of my classmates an apology. It has been a night of serious thinking, and I'm not very happy with what I figured out. I can start by saying 'I'm sorry, Mr. Stevens.'"

Instead of saying 'HUH?' when his jaw hit the ground, Mr. Stevens said, "And you are saying all this so you can just get back into school? Right? Is that it? Did your father beat you into submission to make such a statement?" He started edging his way to his office.

"No, he didn't. I'm here on my own, and I don't expect you to let me back into class. Someone recently taught me that the first to apologize is the bravest, but right now I just feel pretty da ... ah, pretty darn stupid. I'm ready to turn my life around, sir; I want to join the Army or Marines after high school. I know that the first thing I have to do is to tell those I've hurt that I am really sorry for what I have done. 'One step at a time' is what an old friend once said to me." *Did you catch that, Ichiro?*

Mr. Stevens turned to take a good look at Bobby. Something is different. "Do you think either of the armed forces will have you, considering your background?"

"Mr. Stevens, I may not have had total control of the Stupid Market, but I guess I was heavily invested in it. Yeah, I've made a lot of mistakes. Oh, boy, lots of 'em, and some are unforgivable. I've had ... ah ... an experience, let's say, and my eyes may be open for the first time to the real world. I have got to find ways to make things right with you, my teachers, my classmates, and ... my father. Am I making any sense to you?"

Something has definitely changed; something powerful happened last night. Self-realization? A 'Come-to-Jesus' meeting with his father? Fear? An epiphany? He reached into his pocket for the keys to his office as he juggled his briefcase and sack lunch. He looked at them for a few moments and said, "Well, you are still suspended." He slightly raised his eyes to watch Bobby's reaction.

"I understand, sir." He turned to head home and said as he walked away, "It was still important that I apologize, Mr. Stevens. Goodbye."

Mr. Stevens saw what he was looking for, a complete and thoroughly repentant Bobby King. A smile slowly spread across his face as Mr. Stevens announced, "You didn't ask how long the suspension was for. Don't you want to know?"

Bobby stopped and did a half-turn. "Sir?"

I just heard him call me 'sir' three times, and Bobby has never done that! "Yes, your suspension. It ends at 8:00 am this morning and you better not be late for class, young man!" Mr. Stevens detected Bobby's eyes getting misty.

"S-s-s-sir?"

"You heard me! Now get going before I change my mind!"

* * *

Bobby seemed to walk in a haze of not-quite reality. *I still don't understand what happened, but something did happen. I guess I have a new way of looking at everything and everybody,*

Bobby thought as he walked down the hall of Tulelake High School. No one spoke to him, out of fear of being the recipient of a verbal or physical assault. Carl, Jason, and Andy did not know what to say to an unusually quiet, seemingly retrospective Bobby, so they just stayed mum and went in separate directions as quickly as they could. Larry O'Shaughnessy instinctively reached into his pocket for his wallet to pull money out. *I think I owe Larry some money – and an apology.* He saw Darrell and Wayne once again standing in front of Arthur's locker. Arthur slammed the locker door shut, glared, and walked away. *Well, it looks like I have some heavy work to do to make that right.* He passed by Mr. Robertson's classroom and saw Peter Bauch. "Hey, Pete, can I speak to you for a minute before your class starts?"

If looks could kill, Pete's eyes were sending lasers. "Why?" was all he said, as he defiantly crossed his arms.

"Because I found something that belongs to you."

Pete turned to Mr. Robertson and asked, "Five minutes, please?"

Robertson looked at his watch and then the clock on the wall. He raised his fingers in a victory sign and said, "Two."

Pete walked up to Bobby and said, "What." Not so much a question, as a demand.

Bobby extended a wallet to Pete and said, "I found it. Make sure everything is in there."

"You found it?"

Bobby sheepishly said, "Well, sort of. I was mad at you, and I threw it and your clothes into a storm drain. I went by there early this morning, and the wallet and your clothes were still there.

Everything was pretty moldy and disgusting – including your wallet. I'll pay to replace everything as soon as I can make some money. I threw the clothes away, but here's your wallet."

Pete searched his wallet and pulled something from a secret compartment. "It's still here and it's dry."

"What is it?"

"An old picture of me and you when we were best friends. We were at that baseball tournament in Medford. Remember?"

"Hell, yeah, I remember! You went three for three that day. You were on fire!"

"And you hit a home run so far that the ball got back to Tulelake before we did."

They laughed until Mr. Robertson said, OK, guys, class is starting."

Peter looked up at Bobby and asked, "What happened to us?"

"I got stupid," Bobby said with a lump in his throat. He rubbed his forehead.

"Then let's start today to fix that. Okay?"

"You're the only real friend I've ever had, Pete. I don't want to lose you." Bobby thought, *I've already lost another good friend somehow and somewhere. I cannot afford to lose another.*

Bobby turned to walk back to Mrs. O'Malley's English class, but after three or four steps, the lights went out. When he awoke, Larry O'Shaughnessy was crouched down beside him, waving a tablet like a fan. "Are you OK, Bobby?"

A woozy Bobby replied, "I think so." Larry helped him to his feet as laughter erupted from the crowd, especially from Arthur, Darrell, and Wayne standing in the front. The hall began to spin as did the laughter, and Bobby collapsed again.

* * *

When he awoke again, he found himself on a couch in the nurse's office. "Wow! What happened?" When he could focus, he saw Mr. Stevens with his arms folded, standing behind the school nurse, who was applying a cold compress to Bobby's head.

Bobby started to sit up, but the nurse pushed him back onto the couch. "Not yet, young man. You can get up when I say so." After 15 minutes, the nurse took his temperature again. "The temperature looks fine, but I suggest he goes home. Can someone call his parent?"

Mr. Stevens had not moved since Bobby was brought to the nurse's office. Without hesitation, he said, "I'll take him home myself."

* * *

As they pulled up in front of Bobby's house, Mr. Stevens said, "I called Doc Wilson before we left the school. He should be here any minute, and he will check you out. If he releases you, then you can come to school tomorrow. Otherwise, you'll stay here until Monday and recuperate. Agreed?"

Bobby rubbed his forehead again and meekly said, "Yes, sir."

"Bobby, I need you to shoot straight with me on something. Can you?" He was afraid to ask if his father had beaten him during the night, but he had to find out for the boy's own good.

"Okay."

"Did something happen last night? Were you hurt last night?"

Bobby just stared at Mr. Stevens. He did not know whether to cry, laugh, bang his head on the car's dashboard, or just go nuts. So, he calmly said, "Yes, something did happen, but I don't know if I can explain it because I didn't understand it myself. Maybe it was a dream. Maybe it was what I wished would happen. I just don't know. It was something that happened to me – inside me, in my mind – and it's changed me. But my dad didn't hurt me if that is what you're asking about. He was going to, for sure, but he didn't. Somehow, he changed too. We had a good, long talk for the first time since my mom left. We agreed to start over and take care of each other."

Bobby was looking for an excuse to stop explaining when he saw Doc Wilson pull up. Doc opened Bobby's door of the car and announced, "Pat, thanks for not letting him walk home. I'm going to get him inside and to bed."

At the door to the house, Bobby turned and said, "Thanks, Mr. Stevens. And thanks for asking about ... well, you know."

Chapter 29
6:15 a.m., March 6, 2017
Tulelake High School

The concussion bothered Bobby all day Saturday, or maybe the events running through his mind were so complex that his head hurt from trying to remember or trying to analyze the how and why of what happened. Things were getting better at home. Bobby and Ed played cribbage and canasta Sunday afternoon and listened to a basketball game on the radio. The fact that they were even talking overshadowed much of the content of their discussion. Just talking was a huge step for them.

Monday morning found Ed up before the sun. Bobby was awakened by the smell of biscuits baking in the oven. Bobby walked into the kitchen rubbing his eyes and saying, "Wow, that smells terrific! I had no idea you could make biscuits!"

"Well, then don't look at the empty biscuit package in the trash can. I got these at the store." Laughter and small talk made for the start of a good day. Bobby was washing dishes when his father said, "I'll try to get home early for dinner. We can talk about your joining the Marines then. You're not old enough yet, so we can figure out what you need to do to get ready when you turn 18."

"Thanks, Dad."

"I'm in luck. He's here," said Bobby as he ran to school by way of Pauley's Produce. Most of the lights in the store were off, but he said, "Hey, Mr. Pauley?"

A shadow in the middle of the store responded, "Yes, Bobby? I'm not open just yet, but what can I do for you?"

Bobby pursed his lips and abruptly said, "Hire me! Please, sir."

"What?"

"I need a job, sir. I can work every morning before I go to school and every afternoon after school. I can work all day Saturday. I don't have any skills, but I do have a strong back and a weak mind, sir."

His grin was returned by Mr. Pauley, who said, "Bobby, you're smarter than you give yourself credit for. You've got yourself a deal."

Bobby was almost jumping up and down when he said, "Thank you so much, Mr. Pauley! I will not let you down. When can I start?"

"This afternoon will be good. We will talk about the mathematics of retail pricing, marketing different produce at different times and seasons, and the local history of farming and produce that ends up right here on these shelves."

"I'll get here as fast as I can, sir! Thank you!"

As he ran down the street, Mr. Pauley wondered, *Now what is suddenly so different about him?*

At the main doors of the school, the thresholds are old and worn. He saw Sandra Rodriguez struggling to push her brother, Miguel, in his wheelchair across the rough spots in the doorway. "Hi, Sandra. May I help?"

"Why? Do you need to earn a Jerk of the Year Merit Badge or something?" She did not need the sarcasm and verbal abuse of Bobby King today – or any other day.

"I'll tell you why – 'cuz I've been way out of line with you and your brother, and I want – no, I must make amends. That's why."

Sandra just stood and stared at Bobby with her mouth open. "Huh?"

"You'd better close that mouth or you'll catch flies." Bobby's attempt at humor missed the target, but Sandra caught the intent when she noticed the smile Bobby gave her was genuine. Bobby knelt by Miguel's side and said, "How are you today, Miguel?" Miguel mimicked the stare his sister had. Bobby patted him on the shoulder and said, "If you need anything, and I mean anything, you let me know. Okay?"

Bobby left two stunned people and found a third, Larry O'Shaughnessy. Larry froze in the hallway and started looking for an escape route as he said under his breath, "Oh, crap!"

"Hey, Larry," Bobby said with a sheepish smile. "How are you doing? Ah, just so you know, I won't be stealing your lunch money anymore. Those days are over and done with. So, you can relax."

Larry was already reaching for his wallet to pay Bobby. He had decided the previous weekend to carry his real wallet in his backpack and to carry a second one with two dollars in his hip pocket, which he could pull to give Bobby every day. "What did you say?" Larry stammered.

Bobby swallowed hard and confessed, "I said I'm done being a thug, and I'm not going to harass or steal from you anymore. I'm sorry I was mean to you. I was kinda messed up for a while. I hope you'll accept my apologies, Larry."

A stunned Larry stared at Bobby for a couple of moments before he responded, "Yeah, sure thing, Bobby." He shoved his hand into his hip pocket as he said, "Hey, I've got an extra couple of bucks today if you need it for lunch."

Bobby smiled and chuckled, "No, man – I'm good. But thanks; that's nice of you to offer."

After lunch, he saw Ned and Nancy, the Simmons twins. Nancy was walking into Mrs. O'Malley's English class and Ned was headed to Mrs. Carson's History class. *I don't know yet how to fix that one, but I'll find a way. Ichiro? Are you getting all this, Kemo Sabe? I may need your input on this one.*

Mrs. Carson was in the hall outside her classroom, talking to an older woman in a wheelchair. Mrs. Carson saw him coming and motioned him over. "Bobby, I want you to meet someone who had a big influence on me when I first started teaching here." As Bobby turned to face the older woman, he saw she was of Asian descent. "Bobby, let me introduce you to Ms. Tomoko Sazama. Her family lived here in town as far back as the 1930s' including during the Japanese American nightmare that happened during World War II. Ms. Sazama, this is Bobby King, one of my students."

Tomoko and Bobby stared at each other. Neither spoke for many seconds, and the silence became awkward. Then, at the same time, they both said in unison, "Have we met before?" That broke the tension and they all laughed.

Tomoko saw something familiar in the way Bobby stood – in his expression, but it seemed a faded memory, a frayed remembrance, that she could just not connect. *I'm just getting older and more fanciful*, she thought to herself. The name 'King' did not register, but then she looked closer at Bobby. *There is something in his eyes? Or is it his expression? Yes, this young man somehow reminds me of another young man from many years ago. How very strange.*

Her hair was gray; her life history was echoed in the wrinkles and lines on her face, and her hands showed that life had thrown many obstacles in her way. But Bobby remembered exactly who she was. At first, he felt he was seeing a long-lost friend, but then he was perplexed by a huge question. *If that camp stuff was all just a dream, then how is this reality possible? This is Ichiro's very special friend he always kept in his heart.* He squatted down and softly said, "I am pleased to meet you. If you influenced Mrs. Carson, I do thank you for that. She is my favorite teacher, and I am probably her worst student."

Mrs. Carson was still getting used to the new Bobby King, Version 2. But she smiled and said, "Ms. Sazama is here today at my invitation, as a guest speaker for our class. She will share her personal insights into the Tule Lake War Relocation Center and the consequences of the internment of Japanese Americans. You know it is the 75th anniversary of those internments."

Bobby nervously worked hard to conceal his shock. He said, "May I help you into the classroom, Ms. Sazama?" Bobby pushed her wheelchair into the room, as he had done so many years ago. *Or was it just yesterday?* The bell sounded for class to begin.

* * *

After class, many students were asking Tomoko questions, so Bobby stayed seated, watching and listening. The room was almost empty when he rose from his desk and asked if he could speak with her privately for a few moments. When she agreed, Bobby closed the door and turned to face her. "I don't know how to begin."

Tomoko smiled. "Try the beginning. You seem to have something of great importance to say. What is on your mind, young man?"

"I am afraid you would not believe me, so let me try this as a starting point." He took a deep breath and pointed at the wheelchair. "Is this Yuni #4, #5, or #6?"

Tomoko's eyes flashed with surprise and she stuttered, "This is Yuni #6, but how ... did ... you ... know? How did you know that name?"

"I know because I knew about the first one. But here comes the big question, Ms. Tomoko Sazama. Or would you prefer I call you 'Tommy?'"

Her mouth was working but no words came out, only a quiet gasp.

Bobby pressed on. "Where is Ichiro?"

Her mouth dropped open, her eyes shone bright, the blood drained from her face, and fear gripped her as hard as her hands gripped the wheelchair handles, so tightly that her knuckles turned white. All she could get out was, "How?" Her heart was about to explode from her chest or just stop beating altogether.

Chapter 30
6:15 p.m., March 6, 2017
The Tulelake Diner

he place had not changed much in its 80 years of service. There were the same booths and the same tables, some with newer chairs. There was the same old kitchen with some new equipment, plates, and silverware. Plastic glasses and coffee cups replaced real glasses and coffee cups. On the lunch specials board, there was the same old menu item of roasted chicken and cornbread dressing, except it was now $7.99 instead of 50 cents. New faces and new paint.

Their discussion at the school had been very brief. Ms. Carson had reentered her classroom shortly after the dismissal of Bobby's class, and this conversation required both privacy and delicacy. Bobby suggested they go to the diner, and Tomoko's interest was piqued enough that she agreed. Besides, Bobby seemed to have Ms. Carson's trust, so she did not feel she was in any danger. Bobby realized then that a little kindness does go a long way in people's attitudes and perceptions of you.

Bobby wheeled her up as close as he could to a table reserved for the handicapped near the window. They watched the sun slowly reaching the horizon more than they looked at the menus. A waitress brought Tomoko hot tea and a soda for Bobby.

Tomoko asked herself, *Can I believe this boy? Can I allow painful old memories to be dredged back up? Can I allow my defenses to be lowered and revisit the old camp, go through those old fences, and kindle the memories of the horrors that happened behind them?* She turned and gazed out the window without really focusing on any single thing. She turned back to Bobby and announced, "So, talk, young man. Let me hear you explain in detail how you know my name, who Yuni is, and how the hell you know who Ichiro is?"

Bobby sat bolt upright and froze. "Wait! You said, 'who Ichiro is!' Did you say 'is'? Is he still alive?"

Tommy sighed and said, "I meant 'was,' I guess. I don't know if he is alive. I assume he physically died so long ago, but he is still alive in my heart."

"Oh," is all that came from Bobby. "I thought …, I hoped you meant he was still alive somehow, somewhere. He is still alive in my heart too. Tell me what happened that day. Please."

"How could somebody who died almost 75 years ago be alive in your heart?"

"Please."

Tommy looked forlornly out the window as if she was looking through time to a place and an event where she did not want to travel. She looked back at the table and confessed, "We were always told to not speak of what happened at Tule Lake, or any other such place. Parents, relatives, and friends all instructed us to never reveal our past, never speak Japanese, only speak English, avoid eating Japanese food, never listen to Japanese music, and certainly never wear anything Japanese in public or even in the privacy of our own homes. We were told to never display Japanese art, Japanese books, or magazines, and never furnish an apartment or house with Japanese furniture. We were told to peel away everything Japanese from our minds and hearts, and never discuss that terrible time with anyone. It was our shame, so we were to treat it as if it never happened. Throw your past away, live your life now, and build a better future for your family and yourself, they all said." Tommy looked at Bobby with misty eyes and pleaded, "Now you want me to go back seventy-plus years and relive those horrible experiences?"

Bobby softly begged, "Please."

Tommy searched the face across the table from her, and across 75 years. "I don't know. It still hurts."

"I promise I will tell you how I know you if you tell me what happened. I will tell you, but you will think I'm insane. Please tell me what you know first about the big riot and the explosions."

"Well, that is the big problem. You see, I was injured when one explosion ripped a hole in the fencing on the northwest side of the camp on July 29, 1944."

"Yes. Gordo and Kenji helped you. Go on."

Tommy had a look of incredulity on her face. "Yes, that's true. It felt as if a giant rock was on my chest. But how ...?"

"Later. Please go on."

Ichiro's father ... "

"Yes, Saburo."

"Yes, Saburo also needed some medical attention. About 20 feet away was the leader of the *Loyalists*, Juan Tu ..."

"Yes, he called himself The Terror of Tulelake."

"Yes. He was holding his dead friend in his lap and rocking back and forth. I heard he ended up in an insane asylum in Oregon. But that day, he sat there, holding his friend, and singing a sad, old Japanese song; I think it was called the Takeda Lullaby. The song goes like this:

'Hayo-mo yuki-taya, Kono zaisho koete
Mukou ni mieru wa, Oya no uchi
Mukou ni mieru wa, Oya no uchi.'

"That translates to:

'Today, I'm going back to my home over the mountain.
I can see my parent's humble house over there.
I can see my parent's humble house over there.'

"He was singing it when they picked him up and supposedly, he was still singing it until the day he died in the insane asylum." Tommy shivered and said, "How horrible!"

Bobby pressed on. "But what of Ichiro?"

Tommy was growing uncomfortable with the conversation. She fidgeted, shifted her weight in the chair, rubbed her hands, and said, "When I finally regained my wits, I realized that that evil sergeant ..."

"Sergeant Weston."

"Yes, that evil man was gone."

"And Corporal Williams was dead."

Tommy now just stared at Bobby as her mouth opened and closed without saying anything. Finally, she asked, "If you know all these people and you know what happened, why are you asking about Ichiro?"

"I'll explain everything later. I promise … just continue. Please."

She pursed her lips, trying to decide if she should do as asked. She read Bobby's face and saw a pleading look, someone needing to know the answer to some burning question. She sighed and continued. "Sergeant Weston was gone, and so was Ichiro. We all assumed he must have followed Weston or Weston followed Ichiro."

"Then what happened?"

"Private Lawson and two squads of soldiers arrested so many, including us. The camp was put under a complete lockdown, a total 24-hour a day curfew. Dozens of soldiers were shipped in, and most of the previous soldiers were shipped out. The following week, trucks showed up every day; and internees were rounded up without any notice and were shipped to other camps. Gordon and Ken were shipped somewhere, I don't know where. I never again saw or heard from either one. My Sobo, my grand-mother, was shipped to Manzanar while I was helping at the camp hospital. If Private Lawson had not told me, I would never have known where she went."

Tommy paused as a few tears rolled down her cheeks. "She died there alone, confused, and afraid." Tomoko used a table napkin to dab at her eyes as she recovered some composure. "Can we stop now?"

"Saburo?"

"I think both Saburo and Etsuko were shipped out to the camp at Heart Mountain in Wyoming, but I don't know for certain. I saw him once while I was in the hospital. I saw Masako just once also, and I don't know what became of her."

"And Ichiro?"

A pained, elongated pause intensified the silence, so much so that dishes clanking as they were washed in the kitchen could be heard in the dining area. Bobby could tell this hurt Tommy to relive this horrible chapter in her life. He said nothing, allowing her to take her time.

"Ichiro had disappeared, as so many others did. I assumed that he'd been sent to another camp but had no way to know for sure. I hoped he was at another camp, and that after the war he might try to find me. Everything after that day was chaos, and everyone was scattered apart. We were just surviving, and every moment was absolute heartache. I never heard from Ichiro again. I have prayed that he stayed safe and has lived a happy life all these years."

"What about Corporal Williams?"

"I never saw or heard from Corporal Williams again after that day, until much later, when he was an old man. He told me he had read a magazine article that mentioned a speech I made at a community college about the camps, and that it prompted him to seek some closure to that episode of his life."

"A few years later, in 1972, there was a somber ceremony at what was left of the camp for the 50th anniversary of the – I still don't know what to call it, the tragedy, I guess. After some speeches and a reception, I was trying to roll my chair around what was left of the camp, but it was hard physically, and emotionally. I felt someone take the handles of my chair and help me. A man leaned over and said, 'I remember you.' I turned and stared into the face of a 70-year-old man with the eyes and the smile of the 20-year-old man I remembered as one of the few soldiers all of us could trust. It was Corporal Williams! He had retired from the U.S. Army as a captain after the war and had become a counselor at a camp for troubled youth in Iowa, near his corn farm. He retired from that when he was 65 and started trying to find old Army buddies. He learned that Private Lawson died in Europe as Captain Lawson, leading a platoon crossing a river during the final push into Germany."

"And since then?"

"Nothing."

"What did he say about Ichiro?"

"I tried to bring that up and he him-hawed around it. He never said."

The silence returned and became deafening. Finally, Bobby could not stand it any longer and said, "I told you that you would think I am insane. But how else would I know all those details that you just shared? How would I know names? How would I know about Yuni?"

Tomoko drank some of her hot tea and set the cup back on its saucer. She turned the cup in circles and seemed to concentrate on a distant memory. She looked up into Bobby's eyes searching for answers and said, "Alright, I will listen. How do you know all this?"

"Because I was there," Bobby spoke softly, yet expressively, for over an hour, and told her everything. Occasionally, he would have to backtrack his thoughts to add important points. He would stop talking when the waitress would walk by or stop to ask if they needed anything. Tomoko leaned forward when Bobby talked about the better times but pushed back into her chair when he mentioned the harder times. It was as if she was riding a roller coaster.

"And then I woke up in a pool of sweat in my own bed – in my own house – in 2017. I think that is everything." His hand shook as he picked up his soda, dribbling some down his shirt. He wiped his mouth with the back of his shirt sleeve and said, "He loved you."

"He never said that to me." She acted surprised, but she knew it then and still felt it now.

"You lost a loved one. I lost two people." He gulped more soda.

"How?"

"I lost the worst part of myself, the 2017 version of The Terror of Tulelake. Yes, that's what I used to call myself, but I have no regrets about losing that piece of me. But I also lost the best part of me – Ichiro." His eyes narrowed to a scowl. "But we still don't know exactly what happened to him!"

Her lips pursed and her eyes looked determined. "Then let's ask someone who does." She dug into her purse and pulled out her cell phone. After she found the number in its contact list, she pressed the call button.

Someone picked up on the third ring. "Hello?"

"Good evening. I need to speak to Anthony Williams. Is he there?"

"No, sorry, he is out of town," came the short reply.

"This is Tomoko Sazama in California. Do you know how I can reach him? Do you have his cell number?"

"Ah, Ms. Sazama. He has mentioned you to me in the past. My older brother, Anthony, and you were both at that camp in California, right?"

"Yes. I apologize for such a late call, but this is rather important."

"Well, you are in luck, he is there in California. There is some kind of 75th memorial tomorrow at that camp. Can you get there?"

* * *

The weather on that early spring Tuesday was beautiful and spared the gathering of grandparents, parents, and grandchildren any hint of the weather hardships their relatives had endured in the camp from 1942 until 1945. The morning was comfortable and bright with a slight breeze. The speeches were many, and the messages and stories were very similar in content. One speaker commented that in the darkest and worst of times, we must strive to stay grounded in our core values and let those core values lead us. Another speaker said we need a blend of drive, from the mind, balanced by matters of the heart. Another commented on a Japanese American who had refused to be locked up in the camp and took his case all the way to the United States Supreme Court. Some called this a dark chapter in the history of the United States, and others talked about how this was an "unfortunate" reaction to the Japanese bombing of Pearl Harbor. In some ways, the Anglo-American speakers danced around the real subject at hand, but some touched on it.

But no one really apologized.

The Americans of Japanese ancestry spoke of hardships, with bittersweet language: loss of freedom, loss of businesses, loss of dignity, and questions about self-respect. The memories might be fading, but not the pain of those memories.

The speeches were over, but the crowds still lingered; the 75 years had not dulled much of the agony and loss. People pointed to what was left of some old barracks, an old latrine now open on three sides, piles of rotted lumber which had been different things, important now as only memories. Many stopped to stare at guard towers, still standing as if the soldiers had just climbed down from them moments before to get coffee.

"I cut seed potatoes on tables right there every year," commented a man struggling with a walker.

"Did you know this was the largest town in Northern California by 1944?" asked a grandmother of her grandkids, as she waved her cane around pointing at the size of the camp.

One man showed his grown children a gate in what was left of a section of fence by the old railroad tracks. "I think this is where your grandfather and men like him were loaded into trucks every morning before dawn and driven out to the farms to work."

Bobby pushed Tomoko's wheelchair when the soft dirt did not give Yuni the traction needed for the chair to propel itself as they searched for the man with the answers. "He must be here," pleaded Tomoko. "He has to be here!"

"If we find him, how do we tell him who I am?"

"Play it by ear."

I think I once said that to you, Ichiro.

Bobby was suddenly struck by the realization that very few Anglo-Americans were to be seen. Sure, they were around when the speeches were being made and when photographers from the newspapers were conducting interviews. But now, most of the people Bobby could see were probably of Japanese ancestry. Tomoko and Bobby were at the old corner of West Street and American Way when they saw a man sitting in a wheelchair with his back to them as he stared at what was left of the northwest fence. As they got closer to him, they could see his hands gripping the wheel rims so tightly that his old, gnarled knuckles had turned white from a lack of blood. The old man was lost in a memory, reliving a horror that he knew all too well. He heard them approaching, released his hands, and slowly looked down and behind to his left. He recognized Tomoko and softly smiled. "Wanna race?"

All three chuckled, though the laughter seemed forced, but it was still needed. Tomoko extended her hand and with difficulty, it was accepted by a hand stricken with severe arthritis. Tomoko admitted, "It has been too many years. Where have they gone?"

"I should have written you, or called," he offered. He looked up at Bobby and said, "I'm Anthony Williams, and you are ..."

"Bobby King. I live and go to high school here in Tulelake, sir." He extended his hand.

"Sorry, I have not been able to shake a hand in years," he said as he slowly raised his arms. "It's hell to get old. I am 95 now and starting to push a headstone. Not sure I will be around much longer.”

Tomoko quickly said, “Then it is even more important that we talk now about a subject very close to me, and to you, Anthony.”

“Oh? What?”

“Where is Ichiro Hisakawa?”

Chapter 31
6:25 p.m., March 7, 2017
The Tulelake Diner

The waitress recognized Tomoko and Bobby by the wheelchair. "Welcome back! The table y'all had yesterday is open if that will work for you." Tommy replied that it would be fine. The waitress led them to the table, gave them menus, and said, "I'll be back with some water for you in a minute, and then I can take your orders if you're ready. But there's no hurry."

Bobby said, That's very kind of you."

"Not a problem." She pointed at Williams' lapel and said, "I see his WW2 pin. Nothing is too good for our veterans."

She left and Williams immediately said, "I'm not comfortable talking about Ichiro."

"But why?" pleaded Tomoko.

"I just don't want to, and that's it." He started to push away from the table.

Bobby had had enough of the pleasantries. "How long did it

take to heal that oozing wound in your side? That was from shrapnel, wasn't it?"

Williams' hand shook as he reached into his pocket for a box and withdrew a pill that he popped under his tongue. After a few minutes, he felt better so he asked, "Who the hell are you?"

Bobby looked at Tomoko and said, "I think those may have been your exact words yesterday." He turned to Williams and said, "I guess you should have been here yesterday at this very table when I explained it to Tommy, but I don't mind explaining it again. Especially to you, Corporal Williams."

"Anthony, just call me Anthony. Start talking, young man."

Again, Bobby explained everything. Williams had more questions than Tomoko so the conversation lasted two hours. Their three dinners were barely touched. Bobby ended the last question and answer with, "Now it is your turn. What happened to Ichiro?"

"He saved my life!"

* * *

Williams explained the aftermath of the explosion at the northwest fence, how the two young Japanese boys were tending to Tomoko, how Juan Tu was holding his dead friend and screaming at the top of his lungs, and how Weston had run away – running, stumbling, falling, and running again. Williams was on his side facing the fence, and when he regained consciousness, his blurred vision saw Ichiro walking toward the fence. Williams started to order Ichiro to halt but did not have the power to yell. He felt a strange sensation in his side as he rose to his knees and then to his feet. He realized he had a wound, so he cinched up his belt almost to the point of slipping back into unconsciousness and staggered after Ichiro.

"I lost him for a few minutes, so I took to the higher ground to spot him. He was in a ditch."

"And so was Weston."

"Yes. Things got a bit woozy, but then I remember hearing Weston and Ichiro talking, something about avoiding a hanging and bullets and escape plans and ... and to this day I'm not sure about all of that."

"Please go on." Tomoko could see that Williams was reliving this in his mind like a slow-motion video.

"I called out to Ichiro to come to me. Somewhere in all this, Ichiro threw a knife at Weston, and as he did, Weston fired."

Bobby said, "You were shot."

Silence hung heavily as a tear trickled down Williams' face. "No. He saved my life."

"What?"

The words came slowly and quietly, "The bullet caught Ichiro in the heart. He must have died almost instantly."

A moan came from Tomoko as she clutched her chest. Bobby now knew what he had only sensed for two days. He hung his head in grief as he asked, "And then?"

"I heard an awful gurgling sound. I looked, and Weston's eyes were bulging, and he was grabbing at his throat. Ichiro's knife had found its target from six feet away. I tried to revive Ichiro, but I couldn't. I walked over to Weston and his eyes were begging me to help him. Part of me wanted to help, but another part wanted me to spit in his face and laugh as he died a horrible death."

"What did you do?"

Red eyes looked deeply into theirs and asked, "Does it really matter?"

They sat silent for a while until Williams started again. "I noticed that Weston had no identification on his uniform or in his pockets, so I left the body there. And before you ask, I made sure no one would be able to identify the body. My anger took over."

"What became of Ichiro's body?"

"The camp was in total chaos. By the time I returned, there was still gunfire, explosions, burning buildings, dead bodies, wounded internees, wounded soldiers, wounded civilians, and screaming people running everywhere. People were searching for family and friends. Pockets of gunfire still sounded here and there. Captain Shackleford was desperately trying to restore some sort of order to the disorder. No one noticed a dirty, bloody soldier carrying a body across the camp. I buried him myself. There were no mourners, no flowers, no funeral procession, no graveside service. Just me, the man he saved, the man he gave his life for."

Chapter 32
6:45 p.m., March 8, 2017
The Old Camp

Bobby somehow got permission to borrow his dad's truck so he could drive seven miles southeast of Tulelake to what was left of the Tule Lake War Relocation Center. The tourists and speakers from the memorial were long gone. Part of the old camp was being slowly restored as a memorial of sorts, but funding was tight. Most people apparently just wanted to forget the tragedy and for the place to simply disappear. It was deserted when Bobby passed by just before sunset. If he stopped and listened intently, he could probably hear the ghosts that everyone claimed haunted this place at night. He might hear Saburo or Etsuko. It wouldn't take much to hear Sergeant Weston's loud voice in the wind, but he would have to listen harder to hear Private Lawson or Corporal Williams.

The ruins of the camp were scattered everywhere. Cheap materials, wind, sand, rain, snow, fortune hunters, and scavengers had taken their toll on the buildings and terrain. Much of the 6-foot tall chain link fencing and barbed wire were gone, salvaged by farmers and ranchers, and some of the fence was buried under years of dirt, trod over by the curious or by wild animals passing through. Parts of the stockade jail were there, but the 250-foot by 350-foot fencing around it was gone. Parts of the motor pool, watchtowers, and military police offices still stood. The back wall of Sergeant Weston's old office had been torched. Many barracks had collapsed, burned down, or were in a state of absolute neglect.

He passed the southeast side of the camp and headed for a grove of scrub trees that marked the unmarked Camp Cemetery, overgrown in weeds and scrub trees. He stopped the truck and surveyed through the windshield the whole area near the railroad tracks for a few moments.

Tomoko had ridden shotgun in the truck, trying to explain what had happened. "My wheelchair was almost turned over in the explosion, and I was knocked unconscious by flying debris or by the concussion wave. As I came to, I remember screaming and more screaming, until I passed out again. It was so still, yet so noisy at the same time when I woke up groggy. Does that make sense? It was as if I had had a fitful, restless sleep. I was still groggy when I felt something heavy across my legs. It was Ichiro, face down and trying to protect me. I started to reach for him when I realized he had clasped my hand and still held it tightly. That was the last time I saw him. I don't remember much after that. Maybe I passed out again. I must have passed out again because when I next opened my eyes, Ichiro was gone."

"I do remember that Kenji and Gordo were acting as interpreters the next day for teams of soldiers searching for people, and a bandaged Corporal Williams, who clearly was in a lot of pain and should have been in a hospital bed, led a team right to where we had been. He turned over three bodies where we had been standing before the explosion. He identified one as Private Escobar, one as Isao Hun, and one that might have been Kaede Matsumuro, though that body and the face were very messed up.

Captain Shackleford later identified another body as a former preacher from Tulelake, a man named Jared Hodges, who had been the head of a local militia and probably the man who instigated the attack on the camp. Another body was found 200 yards away in the woods near the dry gulch. It took time to identify that body as Sergeant Weston because it had so many bullet holes in the head and chest and a knife wound in the neck. I later talked to people that saw that body and they told me it was horribly damaged and unrecognizable." Tomoko visibly shivered and bit her lip.

As Bobby slowly drove further in silence, Tommy continued after regaining some composure, "The bodies of the Japanese Americans were brought back to the camp. Many did try to escape but were gunned down. And sadly, I know a lot of those people were simply trying to get away from the fighting in the camp. With so many of the barracks being blown up and on fire, and with so many people shooting, there was nowhere to hide. Getting out of the camp seemed like the safest place to go. Probably most of them would have come back of their own free will once the fighting stopped – if they'd had the chance. But instead, they were shot like escaping criminals, killed for just trying to stay alive.'

Their bodies were buried here in the camp with no ceremony, but thankfully not in a mass grave. The burial spots were recorded, but not marked until after the war. I'm sure there are people buried here who have never been identified, so nobody has ever visited or mourned them."

Tommy took a deep breath, then continued, "Militia men were wrapped in burlap and driven into Tulelake to an old, abandoned church called the Temple of Hope so they could be claimed. The soldiers were wrapped in burlap with their dog tags strapped to the outside of the wrap. Some Army group came with trucks and picked them up in a few days. The smell of death was in everything – and was everywhere – in our clothes, our noses, and deep within ourselves for weeks. For some, it's still there. They did not know what to call it then, but today it's called Post Traumatic Stress Disorder, PTSD. Everyone in the camp and around the camp existed in a stupor for quite some time."

"I spent four months in the hospital. My left leg was broken in two places, but I could feel nothing. My recovery was slow, I was extremely sad. With Ichiro gone, I didn't care if I got better or not. Masako came to see me after a couple of weeks. Part of her face was still bandaged, and she looked as if she had not slept since that horrible day. She had probably lost twenty pounds and looked like a skeleton. She tried to talk but could not. She sobbed, the tears rolling down her cheeks, and she left without ever saying anything. One day I woke up to find her father, Saburo Hisakawa, with his chest wrapped in bandages and standing stiffly by my bed. He said nothing but gave me a formal bow and walked away. I never saw him, or his wife, Mrs. Hisakawa again."

The tarnished truck pulled up next to the old cemetery with its rusted gate, which hung askew on the fence hinges. The quiet and the stillness was a marked contrast to the rough dirt road, with its years of unrepaired potholes, they had just driven. Bobby turned the engine off but gripped the wheel harder than when he was driving. After staring out the windshield at something that all started 75 years before, he turned to face Tomoko. "You barely know me, but please believe me, I know you."

"As impossible – and as crazy as it sounds – I was here with you. I was inside Ichiro's body, inside his mind. I saw what he saw, heard all that he heard, and I knew what he felt. We talked to each other, a lot actually; I grew to think of him like a brother. He was a good person, and he taught me a lot. I loved him. And as alone as you may feel here today, in your sadness, you are not alone. I feel terrible sadness too. But my sadness is new. While you have been dealing with this for 75 years, to me this all happened a week ago. So, this is just really, really hard for me. Like you, I didn't get the chance to say goodbye." He paused and caught his breath. "Who knows… had Ichiro lived, I might still be in him now, and you and I might have spent the last 75 years together. I know he was thinking of your future together. Wow … this is so crazy! I don't know how any of this is real, but it is real. It did happen. God, I guess, can do whatever he wants to with people, and this was definitely a God thing. Why? Who knows? Maybe I needed to be taught a lesson. Yep, I did learn some lessons, that's for sure. I will never be the person I used to be."

Tommy listened with sympathy, and she put her hand on Bobby's arm. Her heart ached at witnessing his raw pain, and in imagining what her life might have been like had Ichiro lived.

She would never have met Bobby, though he might have always been with her, a silent partner. She had no words. He got out and retrieved the wheelchair from the bed of the truck. It was a rough, stony terrain getting to and through the cemetery gate, and he had to work to push and sometimes pull backward on the chair, which threatened to topple over a couple of times on the uneven ground.

Tomoko gave him directions to find one specific grave in the old camp cemetery that Williams had written down in shaky handwriting. After a few minutes of searching and pushing the wheelchair, he found it. A small headstone announced just the name 'Ichiro Hisakawa' twice – once in English and once in Japanese. There was no mention of his birthdate, his death, his family, or what the young hero did.

Tomoko reached as far as she could to place her quivering hand on the headstone. "Williams had this headstone replace a rock that had his name on it. That was in 1959. I do not even know if his parents or his sister ever saw the headstone or returned to this place. I do not know what became of them or any other internee I knew from the camp. It's as if so many of them never existed."

Bobby wiped the headstone off as Tomoko patted its top. She said, "I told you about the 50th anniversary reunion in 1972. Those two reunions and today are the only times I have ever come back. Too much pain. Too many horrible memories."

Bobby thought a moment before he said, "But there was one wonderful thing that came out of it. Ichiro loved you. He may never have said it, but he thought it. Often."

"And I loved him."

The setting sun reflected purple and red tones on the scattered clouds overhead, and the gentle winds carried the night songs of a Northern Mockingbird.

"Please, take me away from here now," she whispered as she fought back tears.

Epilogue

Bobby returned to the cemetery the following day without Tomoko. This was something he had to do by himself and for himself. Was this an obligation? A responsibility? A requirement? He was not sure what to call it, but he just had to do it.

Skies were overcast, threatening either rain or late spring snow. It was just after 2:00 p.m. when he arrived and soon found the lonely, almost lost, resting place of his friend … his brother … his better half. He noticed in brighter light that the headstone was leaning and made a mental note, *I must fix that. I'll bring some tools and clean up the grave. Then I can fan out from here and work on the other graves. The world may have forgotten this event and these people, but I remember, and I can do something about it. Maybe I can find the resting place of Miguel Takemura. He only wanted to be remembered, and I promise I will. Ichiro, we can talk each time I come to work. I'll work, and you can listen.*

He knelt and placed some flowers he had brought, plus a Lone Ranger comic book that fluttered in the breeze. He put a stone on the comic book so it would stay. He wiped some tears from his face, which had not happened since his mother left. He said something not recorded here.

He stood, bowed his head in silence, then quietly said, "Adios, Kemo Sabe." He started to walk away but turned back and said, "Rest now. I love you, my brother."

The end.
Owari.
終わり。

About the Author

WM Gunn is a native Texan who spent many years in the pharmaceutical industry in sales, sales management, and training and development. He is active in writing groups and volunteering with non-profit groups. He lives in his hometown in Texas with his high school sweetheart bride of many years. To date, he has written many short stories, novellas, and novels. **Holmes, Moriarty, and the Monkeys** and **Chasing the Sun** are two novellas released earlier in 2024. Visit his website wm-gunn.com.